I0571415

The Voyage of Maeldun

John Conlee

Pale Horse Books

Although this work of fiction takes its inspiration from an ancient Irish text, its characters and dialogue are the product of the author's imagination. Any resemblance to actual persons is entirely coincidental.

Coypright © 2014 by Pale Horse Books

All rights reserved. This book, or parts thereof, may not be reproduced in any form without expressed written permission. Published in the United States by Pale Horse Books.

Library of Congress Control Number: 2013911570

ISBN: 978-1-939917-07-2

Cover Design: Sally Stiles

www.PaleHorseBooks.com

Also by John Conlee:

THE DRAGON STONE
A CUP OF KINDNESS
THE KING OF MUD & GRASS
IN THE SUMMER COUNTRY
THE HEATER
ROUNDING THIRD

"A boat floats upon sea waves.
Will their voyage be long or short?
Seventeen men are in the boat;
seventeen men; or do I see more?
A rhymer is one, and one is not of us.
Will their voyage be long or short?
I see vengeance, bloody vengeance, crimson and red.
Will their voyage be long or short?
I see a lad of coal-black hair, a lad of red-gold hair,
a lad like a toad.
I see a rhymer and a warrior not of us.
Will their voyage be long or short?
Seventeen men sail upon the sea waves;
or do I see more?
Bringers of justice, crimson and red,
Seventeen bringers of justice.
Will their voyage be long or will it be short?"

— The Vision of Crimthain

PROLOGUE

The sound of the bell tolling softly awakened only a few of the sleeping men. The others, glutted with food and drink, slept like satiated dogs — for several, like loudly snoring satiated dogs.

Hearing the bell, Ailill of the Sharp Edge sat up, rubbed his eyes, then rose to his feet for a better look. Conn and Luga, who'd awakened also, glanced up at their leader; then Luga lay back down, pulling his heavy cloak closer about his ears. Conn, however, remained fully alert. Ailill rarely acted foolishly, and yet Conn sensed that something out of the ordinary, foolish or not, was about to occur.

The bell was calling the small group of nuns to their late-night service. Earlier in the evening, after Ailill and his band had beached their curragh on this tiny, sandy island and discovered the monastery, Ailill had given his men strict orders to leave the nuns alone. Now, it appeared, he was the one who couldn't restrain himself.

Conn watched through slitted eyes as Ailill snatched up his cloak and sword and moved quietly away from their small encampment on the beach. Conn crept up to the crest of the large, sandy dune and watched as Ailill strode across the intervening dunes toward the small abbey church, a squat gray structure surrounded by a dry-stone wall.

A young nun, perhaps just a novice, stood beside the entryway to the austere monastic enclosure, softly sounding the small brass bell.

Conn watched as Ailill stopped for a moment and stood still, drinking in the sight of the young woman alone in the moonlight. Ailill seemed entranced. Normally a man of rock-solid self-control, he appeared to be overcome, his senses befuddled. Could it be the drink? No, Conn knew it was simply the sheer loveliness of this slender young woman standing alone in the moonlight.

Before she was aware of his presence, Ailill was beside her. Conn was too far away to hear what words passed between them, but he saw Ailill reach out and catch her by the arm.

What Ailill said to the girl was, "Come. Do not call out. I will be gentle with you. But you must come."

Curiously, she didn't appear to be frightened. She tried to pull her arm free of his grasp but must have quickly realized that resisting could make matters worse and that calling out to her sister nuns might bring disaster down upon all of them. She seemed resigned to what lay ahead.

Ailill led her back through the dunes toward the encampment. "Lie down here," he said softly, spreading his cloak in a small hollow between two dunes. "I will be gentle with you."

No voyeur, Conn crept back to his own sleeping hollow and curled up again in his thick warm cloak. He couldn't help wondering at this unusual behavior in his closest friend, a man whom he'd known since childhood, a man who rarely joined with the others in their frequent debouches. Conn couldn't help smiling at the thought that Ailill wasn't so different from the rest of them after all.

*   *   *

When Ailill awoke in the dawning, the girl lay quietly in his arms. He knew he had responsibilities to his men, but for the moment all he wanted to do was to luxuriate in the warmth of her young body and the scent of her dark hair.

When he realized she was awake and looking at him, he whispered, "What is your name?"

"Maire," she replied softly. "Soon, I shall be Sister Maire."

"No," Ailill said to her. "You will never be Sister Maire. You must not take the vows of your religion. You must wait for me. I shall come back for you and bring you away with me. You shall be my wife, my queen. Together, Maire, we shall have many sons and many daughters. And in times to come, our children's children will tell tales of us and sing songs of our great love."

"I do not even know you," she replied sternly. "How can you come and do what you have done and then speak of our great love? No!" she said. "I have only one great love — and He is the one to whom I shall dedicate my life."

"You will come to know me, Maire. In time, you will come to know me. And after I am gone, then you can dedicate your life to your god. But until that day, you must dedicate your life to me as I shall dedicate mine to you."

She looked at him with an unblinking stare. She could tell he believed what he was saying, and she couldn't help being impressed by his passion — a passion that was entirely for her. No one in her short life had ever expressed such a passion.

"What are you called?" she asked him at last.

"I am Ailill MacEoin," he replied, wondering if the name held any meaning for her. "I am from Inis Mor in the Aran Isles, the eldest son of Eoin MacEoin. Maire, you must not take your vows. You must wait for me to come back. That may not be for a month or even for three months. But come I shall. You must wait for me, Maire. Will you promise to do that?"

The young woman was not quick to reply. She stared deeply into his eyes, trying to fathom the mind of this strangely insistent man, this man who was so passionate yet so gentle. She doubted his sincerity, though he gave every appearance of believing what he was saying. Surely, she thought, in a day or two he will have forgotten me. Yet at the same time she realized that he had awoken in her strange feelings, ones she'd never experienced before.

Finally she said, "I cannot promise that I will wait for you. But if you truly mean to come back for me, it cannot be in a month. If you truly intend to come back for me, it must be within a week. On the eighth day from this day I shall enter the abbey and give my life to God. Ailill MacEoin, I cannot promise that I will go with you. But if you want my answer, you must return within seven days. I will give you my answer then."

"Are you testing me?" Ailill said, his gray eyes still brimming with fierce desire. "Do you doubt my sincerity? Well then, Maire, if I must come back for you within seven days, that is what I shall do. But when I come, you must give me your answer. And your answer must be yes."

"When you come — if you do come — I will give you an answer. I cannot promise that it will be yes. If you do not come, Ailill MacEoin, I shall give my life to God."

The days of the following week went slowly by. Maire did not expect the man to return, despite his fervent protestations that he would. As she waited, she found herself torn by conflicting desires, hoping by turns that he would come and then that he wouldn't. What answer she might give him if he did return she did not know.

When the sun rose on the seventh day, Aillil MacEoin still hadn't arrived. Nor had he arrived by the time the sun set.

On the following day, Maire entered the abbey and took her vows. She gave her life to God.

*   *   *

Conn Iron-fist set down his heavy burden and stared at the grisly sight before him. The grassy hillside sloping down toward the sea was bestrewn with bloody corpses. Eight of the roughly two dozen bodies, Conn quickly noticed, had been neatly decapitated. Among them were Conn Iron-fist's two most beloved friends, the brothers Ailill MacEoin and Luga MacEoin. Conn's arduous journey up the valley to fill the leathern pouches at the fresh-water spring had saved his life. But without his beloved companions, what value was there in still having his life?

Conn tried to rein in his reeling, swirling emotions. But the shocking sight was too much, even for him. For several moments all he could do was stand there and stare in stunned horror. Eight of his closest friends. Dead, mutilated, decapitated. Conn could tell that they had put up a brave fight. They had killed more than their own number, even though they had to have been greatly outnumbered. But Ailill MacEoin? How could he be dead? Dead in the very prime of his life. The finest man Conn had ever known. Conn mourned them all, but none more than Ailill.

Sounds from down on the beach intruded upon Conn's despairing thoughts. The raiders were just now climbing into their boats. Yes, there were far fewer of them than when they had arrived, as attested by the bodies remaining on the hillside. Indeed, the two departing curraghs were now only lightly manned. In those boats, Conn knew, would be the cherished possessions of his now-dead companions. But far more important to Conn were the severed heads of his friends, heads taken by the raiders as battle trophies.

Conn's eyes remained fixed on the boats as they crawled slowly over the wrinkled sea. Conn Iron-fist knew who the raiders were. They were the Reavers of Roonah — the scourge of the western clans.

As he watched the two boats disappearing from sight, Conn knew that henceforth his life had but one purpose — avenging his friends. And he knew that above all else he must retrieve their severed heads — or die in the attempt. Without their heads, the spirits of his friends could never embark upon their final journey. When he brought them back to the Aran Isles, Conn would place them beneath a huge cairn so that for generations to come Clan MacEoin could venerate their slain companions.

Conn heard footsteps behind him. He swung around to see Derga, the red-haired lad who'd gone with him for the fresh water, just now arriving with his heavy pouches. Conn heard Derga's gasp and watched his terror-stricken face as the lad took in the horrific sight. He watched as Derga slumped to his knees and wept.

Eventually the lad looked up at Conn, his face streaked by tears. "What . . . what . . . do we do . . . now?" he stammered.

"I will scrape out a hollow while you begin the gathering of stones. It will only be a temporary cairn, just enough to protect their bodies from birds and beasts. The day will come, I hope, when we can take them back home and build a cairn to last for all time." A cairn, Conn hoped, in which their heads and bodies would lie together as they ought to lie.

It took the two of them the rest of the day to complete their work. Perched three-quarters of the way up the hillside, the small cairn looked out over the sea. Perhaps their spirits will be watching for me, Conn thought, watching for my promised return. Inside the cairn, on the chest of Ailill's headless body, he had placed his own amulet, a small, leaf-shaped, silver brooch, his pledge to his friend that he would not fail him.

"Where shall we go now?" the red-haired lad queried.

"In the morning we will build a small curragh. Then I shall see you safely home. It will be a long and arduous journey with just the two of us to steer it on the open sea. But we can manage it."

"And then what will we do?"

"Then?" Conn replied. "Derga . . . I do not know."

*   *   *

Nearly four months later, Sister Maire stood silently before the abbess, her hands clasped in front of her coarse gray habit. She did not know why her Mother Superior should have summoned her. She had committed no offense that she was aware of. In the short time since she had taken her vows, she had done all she could to abide by the rules of her order. And though she knew there were a few occasions on which she had erred, she had been assiduous in revealing them during her regular confessions.

"Sister," the abbess said, her eyes staring frankly into those of the youngest member of the convent, "today I wish to speak with you not just as your spiritual advisor but as one woman speaking to another."

Seeing the younger woman's agitation, the abbess quickly continued. "My child, my concerns have nothing to do with your progress here in the abbey. That, Sister, has been exemplary. No, my child, it is your health that concerns me. You are pale and thin and you eat almost nothing. I see from the dark rings about your eyes that you have hardly slept in a good long while. Sister Maire, I have to tell you that I have come to a decision about you. A reluctant decision, but a firm one."

"Oh, Holy Mother!" the younger woman sobbed — "please do not send me from the abbey. Please, Holy Mother. I must never leave the abbey."

"My dear child," the abbess said softly, tears beginning to glisten in her own eyes, "indeed you must. But only for a time, only for a very short time. We need you here as much as you need to be here. But for now, Sister Maire, you must return to your father's rath. The healing women there will be able to care and provide for you far better than we can. And there, child, you will be safe from prying eyes."

"From prying eyes?" the young woman said, not quite understanding the older woman's meaning. And then suddenly she did. "Oh," Maire gasped, placing her hand on her stomach.

With her eyes directed toward the rough flagstone floor, she finally said, "Holy Mother, I do not wish to return to my earthly father's rath. But I have sworn a vow of obedience and I shall do as you tell me to do. But please, tell me that will you take me back. With all my heart, I pray you to take me back. Rath Murtagh is no longer my home, no longer where I belong. Here is where I belong, Holy Mother, here in my Father's House."

"That is so, Sister Maire. This is where you belong. And it is my secret hope that one day you yourself may rise to the spiritual leadership of this convent."

At the old abbess's kindly words, the younger woman looked up at her face. "Holy Mother," she said, "my humility forbids me to say that I hope so too."

"Humility, my child, is an essential virtue in those who aspire to spiritual purity. The leader of a convent, my child, must possess abundant humility." The hint of a smile on the old abbess's face helped sustain Maire through the tribulations of the following months.

*   *   *

Conn Iron-fist stood alone on the highest point at the center of the island, his thoughts and emotions as stormy as the weather about him. More than two months had passed since his and Derga's return to Inis Mor and Clan MacEoin. He had known it would be a bitter return. How could it not be, considering the terrible news he and Derga had brought — that the king's eldest two sons were dead and buried on a far shore, along with six of the clan's finest young warriors, all fallen victim to the Reavers of Roonah.

But Conn hadn't anticipated the antagonism the clan would feel toward the bringer of that message. Perhaps their resentment was natural toward the bearer of such tragic news, but Conn couldn't help sensing that the clan elders felt an animus toward him simply for being alive. Why should he still be alive when the others had fallen? Why hadn't he fallen alongside them? Had he done everything in his power to aid them? Conn, in his heart, couldn't help sharing some of those feelings.

How had the attack even come about? Could his friends really have been taken so completely unawares? And why hadn't he heard the sounds of battle? He had been less than two miles away. One thought that kept intruding into his mind was that it was all some kind of divine retribution, a vengeance brought about because of what Ailill had done that night to the young nun on the sandy island. Ailill, Conn feared, had angered her god. He wondered if there was any way to propitiate such a powerful god.

Conn's thoughts also turned to the Reavers of Roonah. He had sworn to seek vengeance against them, a promise he desired more than anything to keep. But it could not be a swift vengeance. He couldn't do it alone, and now, with the cream of the clan's young warriors destroyed, it would be a long time before he could train a cadre of warriors who would have any chance of doing what needed to be done. He hated the idea of postponing his much desired revenge, but he knew that for now it must wait.

Conn noticed the dark shape slowly approaching and knew that it was Derga, who was having as hard a time as he was fitting back into the life of the clan. Derga seemed to take comfort in Conn's presence, and oddly, Conn did in Derga's. With his other friends dead, Derga was all he had left.

Derga was a quiet lad, neither especially intelligent nor physically gifted. Conn had worked with him on his sword skills, and while Derga was not a quick study, he had made some progress. He was on the verge of becoming an adequate warrior, though he would never be anything more than that. Still, Derga was a lad who spoke very little and undertook his menial chores without complaint, traits that Conn valued.

"Derga," Conn said at last, "I am thinking of setting off again. You need not come, but if you wish to, I would be pleased to have you with me."

Derga's face lit up. There was no concealing his delight at such a prospect.

"I have only the vaguest of plans, Derga. For one thing, I wish to go back and improve the cairn we made over the bodies of our friends. I'd wanted the cairn to be here, but perhaps it is better it be where they fell. I also wish to visit once again the little island with the monastery. Do you remember it? Beyond those two things, I do not know. Perhaps we will merely tread whatever path the fates assign us."

They took their leave with little ceremony. It was almost as if the elders of the clan were glad to see the last of them. The king was now grooming his third and fourth sons to fill the roles that Ailill and Luga had previously filled, and he had asked another man to train them in weapon-play, a slight Conn knew was intentional. No one shed a single tear at their departure. It was as if the clan had turned its back on them.

It took them two days to reach the hillside where, nearly three months earlier, they had made the small cairn. Now, aside from the modest pile of stones, there remained no signs of the terrible carnage that had occurred there. Nature had erased them entirely.

They remained there for five days, improving the cairn, practicing their weapon-play, trying to commune with the spirits of their dead friends, renewing their pledges of retribution upon their slayers. They also trekked up to the fresh water spring and filled their water pouches. As they were coming back down, Conn had a sudden premonition that what he would see upon their return was a hillside bestrewn with bloody corpses.

But the sight that greeted Conn and Derga was peaceful and serene — just a gentle grassy slope upon which rested the impressive memorial they had erected to their fallen companions. For a moment, Conn wished that he too was now lying within that cairn. Maybe after his death, he thought, such a thing might be possible. He must remember to tell Derga of that desire.

*   *   *

It was a few more weeks before they reached the little sandy island, a few more weeks because Conn kept finding excuses not to go there. What was he afraid of? He didn't know himself, though deep down he wondered if it could be fear of a god who could bring swift and terrible vengeance down upon the heads of those who offended him.

The little island was just as Conn remembered it, and he and Derga beached their small craft at the place where they'd done it before. They established their camp in the dunes and settled down for the night. At one point Conn was awakened by the soft tolling of a bell. He pulled his cloak tightly about him and tried to shut out the sound.

In the morning he crept up to the top of the tallest dune, a spot from which he had a good vantage point. The drab little monastery looked just as he remembered it, a squat gray structure surrounded by a dry-stone wall. He remained atop the dune for the entire day. From time to time he saw signs of activity, and at regular intervals he heard the singing of the nuns. None of them left the enclosure.

In the evening as Derga was preparing their meal, Conn was surprised by an unexpected visitor. She was an elderly woman, dressed in the coarse gray habit of the nuns. She stood quietly and gazed down at them from atop the large sand dune.

"You are welcome to our island," she said. "I was about to ask you to join us in a simple meal, but I see you have already prepared your own. Still, I would like to invite you to join us for the service of Vespers. You are welcome to worship with us."

Conn wondered at the confidence of this woman, who didn't seem frightened of them at all. Was her god really so powerful that she feared no harm? And was she actually inviting them to come with her back to the monastery? Hospitality to strangers was always of the greatest importance to the western clans, but he hadn't expected to receive it from these religious women.

"We do not belong to your religion," Conn replied. "Indeed, we know nothing of it."

"You are welcome nevertheless," she replied. "Perhaps you will find that our religions are not so very different after all."

Derga looked nervous at the prospect of going with this woman and entering the gray stone building. Conn shared his anxiety.

"When should we come?" Conn replied at last.

"Come when the sun has dipped into the sea. We will wait for you."

Conn and Derga were content to remain on the island, at least for the time being. They dutifully attended a few of the nuns' religious services, but not being comfortable there, they soon stopped going. The nuns remained friendly and hospitable, and before long the two men had begun to perform various small chores at the nuns' request. Within a few days they'd formed a tentative friendship and alliance, and Conn couldn't help noticing with amusement how often shy Derga now eschewed his company in favor of that of the younger nuns.

It was perhaps two weeks later that the chief nun came to ask Conn's help in a much more serious endeavor.

"Conn, your recent assistance to us has been most kind and generous. Please know how grateful we are to you. But now I wish to ask your help in a much more difficult and much more important matter." She went on, in her matter of fact way, to tell him what it was she hoped he would do for them. Conn heard her out in silence, then told her he would need a little time to reflect on the matter.

"Of course, my son. But this is a matter of some urgency, so we will need an answer soon." Conn nodded his understanding.

The task she'd described was one that would take him and Derga away from the little island. But Conn had already realized the time was approaching when they should be going anyway. This serene little place was not where the fates meant him to be. And as he reflected on the chore she'd proposed, it crossed his mind that perhaps carrying it out might help to placate and appease the powerful god of these Christian women, a god that Conn still feared had exacted retribution upon his friend Ailill.

In the morning Conn sought out the old abbess and told her yes, he would attempt to do her bidding.

With a loving smile she reached out and grasped his huge and powerful hand. "Conn," she said, "may God bestow all of his blessings upon you."

"Holy mother," Conn thought privately, "I hope you have some serious influence with this god of yours!"

When Conn returned to their little camp on the beach, Derga was in the process of mending a small hole in one of the nuns' pots.

"Derga," Conn said, "when you have finished that chore, start preparing for our departure. We will be leaving in the morning."

"Leaving?"

"Aye. Our time here is over."

Red-haired Derga looked more crestfallen than Conn had seen him look since they'd left Inis Mor, six weeks earlier.

"Must I come with you?" Derga asked.

"Yes, you must. I will need your help. But once we are finished with this heavy chore, then you may return here, if that is what you wish. I doubt that I will ever be coming back. But if that is what you wish, Derga, the choice is yours to make."

Derga's look of relief told Conn that his days of being in the company of Derga were about to end. The fates, it appeared, had different plans for the two of them.

CHAPTER 1
Rath Murtagh

Conn Iron-fist and Diuran the Rhymer stood side by side on the wall, watching the lads contesting on the field below them. The two men were a mismatched pair, the first hints of gray in their full beards their only shared feature. Conn, who stood nearly a head taller than Diuran, was a man of few words, whereas Diuran's whole reason for being was words. He was the chief bard of Clan Murtagh. Following in his father's and his father's father's footsteps, he'd become the clan's most revered poet and teller of tales.

Conn Iron-fist was an outsider, a man who'd arrived at the rath more than fifteen years ago, come on a special mission involving one of the king's daughters. After discharging his obligation, he'd asked permission to stay on and serve the clan in whatever way they might allow him to serve. In a short time he'd proved his worth in clashes with the clan's enemies; and within just a few years he'd risen to the position of the clan's chief Weapons Master, the man responsible for shaping and honing the skills of its young warriors.

Diuran was no outsider. His entire life — from birth, childhood, and first youth — he had lived in the rath. From the very beginning he had avidly pursued the poetic arts — music, song, the composition and recitation of verse. For several of his teenage years he had also studied with the Druids, becoming proficient in the lesser Druidic arts. But that was never where his heart lay. Diuran's heart was consumed by a different kind of magic, the magic of words, the magic of poetry.

As often happens, these two quite different men had forged a close bond of friendship. And now they stood silently together, watching the weapon-play of the youths on the practice field. It was Diuran who broke their silence.

"They cause my heart to leap up, these beautiful lads with their quickness and agility, their energy and eagerness. I stand in awe of all of them. But Conn, it is hard for me to recognize which among them is the most able. Which of them, to your professional eye, stands out as the most promising of the lot? Perhaps it is Dris? Or perhaps it is Ronan?"

"Dris? Or Ronan? Or maybe the powerful Celtchar? They are all impressive in their own ways. But yes, you were right first guess. Most people, at any rate, would say that Dris is the most promising."

"But you, on the other hand, would not?"

"I'm not making any judgments just yet — though Dris is well ahead of the others in most respects."

"And yet you find yourself disliking him. And that is because Dris, you are thinking, is vain and smug and arrogant. That, Conn, is what you especially dislike about him. Am I right?" Conn merely grunted.

"Dris, you are thinking, is much too cocky. He struts and preens and you hate that. He needs to be brought down a peg or two, and you long for that to happen. Am I right?" Again Conn merely grunted.

For another five minutes the two men continued their watching in silence.

"We will know more about Dris," Conn finally said,

"when he gets his first taste of defeat. That's when we shall come to know a good bit more about the lad."

"Dris has never tasted defeat?"

"Not yet. But it will happen. No one, no matter how good, ever escapes defeat for long. How a man responds to that first defeat often says more about him than all the victories he's piled up beforehand."

Out on the field Dris was now competing with Garluan, a slender lad with lightning-quick reflexes. Garluan was generally considered one of the lesser of the youths because he lacked the powerful arm-strength of the others, though his deftness and agility often stood him in good stead. But now Dris had cornered him in an angle of the wall, and even with his quickness Garluan couldn't escape. Dris, frustrated by the merry chase Garluan had led him, began raining blows down upon him with his wooden sword, blows that Garluan could only partially block.

"Enough!" shouted another lad. It was Maeldun, Garluan's closest friend. "Dris! These are only practice bouts!"

Dris spun around and swung a tremendous blow at Maeldun, but Maeldun expected it and blocked it with his wooden sword. Then at nearly the same time Maeldun threw his left fist with full force into Dris's exposed midsection. Yet Dris's taut stomach muscles withstood the powerful blow, and before Maeldun could regain his balance, Dris brought a mighty, two-handed blow down upon Maeldun's helmet. Maeldun's knees buckled and he dropped to the ground, momentarily stunned.

Dris laughed gleefully, as did his brother Ronan. Garluan and Maeldun kept their eyes upon them as the two walked jauntily off the field. It will not always be this way, Maeldun told himself. There will be a time when things will turn out differently.

While this incident between the lads was playing out, Diuran closely observed Conn's reactions. Conn, he knew, was a man who never played favorites and a man who preferred letting the lads settle their squabbles amongst themselves. And yet Diuran suspected that, deep down, Conn had a soft spot for Maeldun. Conn had never revealed that soft spot to anyone, neither through word nor deed. Yet Diuran felt sure it was there.

"So Dris, Ronan, and Celtchar are the most advanced of the lads. And how has young Maeldun been progressing? Was it a good thing just now when he came to the aid of his friend, or was he out of line to do that?"

Conn breathed out a big sigh. "It was typical," he said. "He knows he's not yet up to tackling Dris, but he couldn't help himself when he saw Dris venting his frustrations on Garluan."

"So you might say he acted foolishly yet also nobly?"

"Yes, I suppose you might," Conn replied.

"Just the way you yourself might have acted?"

"No," Conn replied with a straight face, "you are certainly wrong about that. For the one thing I never, ever do is act nobly." Diuran smiled, knowing how far from the truth that was.

Maeldun and Garluan were sitting cross-legged on the rushes near the far end of the long, low table, a table heavy with meats and breads and vats of a dark and potent drink. The two young men, both foundlings who'd been raised in fosterage by two of the king's daughters, had been close friends since they were squalling babies. Now as youths verging on first manhood, they had earned their places among Conn Iron-fist's fifteen or twenty most promising warriors in training.

It was the Eve of Lughnasa, the harvest festival near the

end of summer, Maeldun's favorite of the four great festivals marking the quarters of the year. At Lughnasa the weather was usually perfect, and the dancing, singing, and tale-telling created for Maeldun a very satisfying sense of ripeness and completion.

Garluan was tall and slender, and though not the most powerful of the youths being trained by Conn, his sinewy arms and legs possessed unexpected strength. He was the fastest runner in the entire rath and the greatest leaper, as he proved repeatedly during festival games. Maeldun, as a result of a recent growth spurt, was now only a little shorter than Garluan, though he was thicker in chest and thigh and broader in shoulder. Maeldun's unruly mane of coal black hair contrasted starkly with the ripe field of barley that sprouted atop Garluan's long, narrow head.

"Ah, Maeldun," Garluan sighed lustily, "don't ya see her there a-leanin' down over the table? Don't ya see that sweet pair of apples that I be seein'?" Again he sighed lustily.

"You lecherous old swine's head," Maeldun said with a laugh of his own, "you randy old pig's pizzle"; and he dug his elbow deeply into his friend's boney side, causing him to grunt. "She doesn't even know you exist, my pitiful friend. But when I have finished with her, if you're lucky, I just might pass her along to you."

"When you have finished with her? Hah! When I have finished with her, well then, I may just have to go back to the beginning and do it all over again. And then maybe I'll do it once more, just for good measure."

The two youths laughed at each other's ribald witticisms; and in the moments that followed, their attentions shifted swiftly from girl to girl to girl, including in their youthful imaginings every attractive woman in the building, regardless of their ages.

Tonight everything pleased Maeldun — the food, the company, the singing and the dancing — and soon, he eagerly anticipated, there would be the story telling. Now the joyous sounds of the harp filled the rath; now this child or that would stand up and sing, or a small group of them would improvise a spritely dance step. Between the courses of the feast the younger men and women would rush forth to dance, the women flirting outrageously and the men taking every opportunity to touch the young women in places they shouldn't. Even the old king joined in the singing and dancing, and he, too, joined in the not-so-subtle touching of the young women, bringing a grin to his craggy old face.

The old king was in his fourth decade of reigning over Clan Murtagh, and while he seemed as healthy as ever, concern regarding his successor now hovered over the rath. Despite his efforts with numerous women, the old king had produced only daughters. His eldest daughter, Niamh, was Maeldun's own foster mother. Becfola, his third daughter, was Garluan's foster mother. It was her misfortune to have borne no children of her own, making her an object of pity in the rath.

The king's other two daughters were estranged from the life of the clan. The youngest, who had been half-witted since birth, was rarely seen in the rath. She dwelt on the hillsides in the company of the cattle herders, men who doted upon her as they doted upon their precious beasts. Even farther removed was the king's second daughter, who had left Rath Murtagh to live amongst a group of women who followed the new religion. These were women who had renounced the old pagan ways; women who called themselves Christians.

So the king's hopes rested largely on Niamh's three sons — Dris, Ronan, and March — Maeldun's own foster brothers. Because of his great affection for his foster mother, Maeldun tried hard not to bear his foster brothers malice, though he'd realized long ago how spoiled and willful they were, and he knew at first-hand how vicious and devious they could be. Perhaps in time one of them would prove a suitable successor to his grandfather. That, at least, was the hope in the rath. Maeldun had his doubts.

Throughout the evening Conn Iron-fist kept a watchful eye on the antics of all his young charges, but especially on Maeldun and Garluan. Their exuberance and high-spirits reminded him of another pair of young men who'd once behaved in a similar fashion. The youths he was recalling were Luga MacEoin and Conn himself. Ailill MacEoin, Luga's older brother, had always remained a little apart, a little aloof from the light-hearted doings of the others. Whereas Conn thought of himself and Luga as equals, Ailill, he felt, had always been his superior. In his more than three decades of life, Conn had never known another man like him. Conn had worshipped Ailill MacEoin; he would have followed him anywhere.

Now as Conn studied Maeldun, he couldn't help thinking of Ailill, whose face and sturdy build were mirrored in the lad. Only his dark hair and pale blue eyes were different, traits he shared with his mother. Sister Maire's eyes, Conn supposed, was just one of the many things that had so entranced his friend. Ailill had been mad for the girl. In all the years Conn had known him, that was the only time he'd ever seen Ailill succumb to the frailties of the flesh. Why it had happened that one time, Conn couldn't begin to understand. But it had certainly happened. "I shall marry her," Ailill had declared to Conn and Luga. "I shall make her my queen, and she will be a queen like none other."

At Ailill's words Conn and Luga had exchanged knowing glances. In a day or two, they believed, she would be completely forgotten, just as the two of them had always forgotten their own fleeting dalliances.

But they had been wrong. Ailill had had every intention of returning for her and taking her away with him to Aran. And if it hadn't been for the Reavers of Roonah, he would have.

Now Conn's thoughts drifted to the Reavers of Roonah, against whom he had sworn his vengeance, a vengeance still not forgotten, not even after all these years. Indeed, in his heart Conn fervently believed the day was finally coming when those killers would receive their just desserts. The vengeance he envisioned would come, he hoped, at the hands of this troop of young men whose training was nearly completed. And he hoped it would come particularly at the hands of Conn and Maeldun, Ailill's own son. Together they would re-pay the long-standing debt. That was very much Conn's hope — it was the hope that had motivated his actions for the past sixteen or so years.

At the end of the room opposite to Maeldun and Garluan sat most of the clan's high-born men. Those at the top of the social hierarchy were the king's hand-picked companions and advisors, men who enjoyed great privilege and prestige. Sitting close to them and ranking just below them were the clan's warrior elite, the men who guarded the rath and its herds and fought the clan's battles. About a dozen in all, these warriors were idolized by the young boys and lusted after by the young women. Conn Iron-fist, as Weapons Master, was a member of this group, despite his origins as an outsider. He was one of them but he was not of them. He had formed no close bonds of friendship with any of them, at least not like the bond he had formed with Diuran or with his young charges.

The clan's finest artisans and craftsmen also enjoyed special status, as did its ablest bards and musicians. Diuran the Rhymer, though himself the son and grandson of famous bards, had earned his esteemed position through merit, not birth.

Among all the men of special status and privilege in the clan there was only one who stood completely apart from all the others. He was the old druid named Crimthain, the clan's chief spiritual leader and the king's personal advisor. Among all the influential voices in the rath, his was the most revered, the most potent. He was a strange and enigmatic man, as Diuran knew well from the time he had studied with Crimthain. He was a scholar, a priest, a prophet, and a visionary. He knew more of the druidic arts than any man Diuran had ever encountered. And he was the only man in Rath Murtagh whom Diuran feared.

Now as it grew late on the Eve of Lughnasa, now as the eating and dancing and singing were winding down, the time finally came for the crowning event of the festival's first night — the telling of tales. Diuran the Rhymer, the clan's chief bard, was only called upon to perform on special occasions, and the Eve of Lughnasa was one of them. So when he rose and moved out in front of the tables, a hush quickly fell upon the room.

The older men, mellowed by drink, leaned back against the walls with their eyes closed, ready to envision the dangerous events and adventures Diuran would be describing. But the eyes of the younger men remained open, shining with anticipation. What story would the Bard tell them this night? No doubt it would be one of the most celebrated of the ancient tales, but which one would it be? It would probably be one they all knew quite well, but even so, tonight the singer might embellish it in some new and surprising way. Diuran was a teller famous for his surprises.

As always at such festivals, Conn's eyes remained fixed

on Maeldun. He watched as the lad, enthralled, drank in the performer's words. Maeldun loved the old tales, and on this night the Rhymer was in top form. On this night the tale Diuran told was an ancient tale of crime and punishment. It was the tale of Brian and his brothers and the vengeance Lugh took upon them for the murder of his father.

For most of an hour the Rhymer captivated his audience, spinning out his complex tale of the brothers' dangerous journey and their bold enterprises in an attempt to atone for their terrible crime. As he brought the long tale to its poignant conclusion — the point at which Lugh must decide whether or not to heal Brian and his brothers with the magical pigskin they'd suffered so much pain to bring him — Diuran paused dramatically. He was allowing his audience the momentary hope that for once Lugh's heart might be softened by all the brothers' sufferings and noble deeds. This time, everyone hoped, Lugh would spare their lives.

But then, as always, the stony-hearted Lugh Lamfada, Lugh of the Long Arm, scornfully denounced Brian and his brothers, telling them he wouldn't forgive them for killing his father if they'd brought him "the breadth of the earth in gold." Then, all hope being lost, Brian and his brothers died from their wounds. Their aged father, broken-hearted, fell down upon their bodies and died as well.

"They were buried at once," Diuran declared, "all four in a single grave. But good can come from evil. For all the magical gifts they'd achieved through their many adventures in their hope of forgiveness were put to good use in the great battle with the Fomori. In the end, Brian and his brothers did not die in vain."

At the conclusion of Diuran's tale, there was only one pair of dry eyes in the entire rath. They were the eyes of Conn Iron-fist.

CHAPTER 2
Dris, Ronan, and March

In the weeks leading up to Lughnasa, Diuran had been puzzled by Conn Iron-fist, who'd seemed unusually preoccupied. Always a sober and serious man, Conn's mood had seemed even darker, tinged with a genuine grimness. Something was consuming his friend, though Diuran couldn't begin to guess what it might be.

Since Conn tended to keep his own counsel, he wasn't an easy man to read. Over the years Diuran had ferreted out a few things about the mysterious Conn. He knew that Conn had grown up in the Aran isles where he'd been a man of high social rank within Clan MacEoin. He knew that Conn hoped one day to return to his boyhood home and live out his final years there in peace. But it remained a source of frustration to Diuran that his friend was so tight-lipped about his earlier life. It seemed to Diuran that Conn had taken upon himself some form of self-imposed exile or perhaps even penance. Had he committed some terrible crime for which he was trying to make amends? That hardly seemed likely, for Conn was a man of true virtue, one of the foremost reasons why Diuran had taken to him so quickly. But what was going on in Conn's mind now? Diuran didn't know. And it worried him.

Throughout the long afternoon and evening of Lughnasa the young men of the rath competed in the festival games — horse racing, foot racing, leaping and jumping, javelin tossing, the slinging competition. Maeldun's three foster brothers, who had grown up on athletic contests, greatly excelled in them. And on this day each of them had been the victor in one or more of the events, always accompanied by much boasting and chest-thumping. Garluan, predictably, had won the sprint races and the leaping contests; and Maeldun, for the first time, had taken the honors in both of the javelin events, the long toss and the accuracy toss.

Finally they had reached the culminating event in the festival games, the one most anticipated — the individual combats. Only the top eight lads, selected by Conn Iron-fist, advanced to this final set of competitions, competitions every man, woman, and child in the rath was eager to see.

For the first time, Garluan and Maeldun were among the final eight. Dris, Maeldun's eldest foster brother, was last year's victor, and it seemed likely that he would win again this year. This year Maeldun's other two foster brothers, Ronan and March, were also among the eight finalists. Since this was the first time all three of the king's grandsons had earned places in the personal combats — and since it was widely known that there was no great love between the brothers — this year's matches possessed greater allure than ever.

Maeldun and Garluan stood nervously at the end of the line of the eight young participants, knowing that the king's herald would soon announce the pairings for the initial round of combats.

"What do we do if it comes down to just you and me in the final match?" Maeldun whispered to Garluan.

"What do you mean *if?*" his friend whispered back. "Mael, you don't think any of these effeminate louts can best us, do you?"

"Well, it's more likely one of these effeminate louts will best you than me," Maeldun teased.

"If it comes down to just the two of us," Garluan whispered back, "I promise to go easy on you. But I'll try not to make it look too obvious."

"Oh, my friend," Maeldun said with a laugh, "please do go easy on me. And please don't make it look too obvious."

Everyone listened eagerly as the herald announced the matchups. Maeldun had the good fortune to be paired against March, the youngest of his three foster brothers. Though a year younger than Maeldun, March was by no means a pushover. In some respects he was already more skilled than his older brothers, but he had a chief weakness, as Maeldun knew well. For in his vanity and overconfidence March always tried to do more than he was truly capable of doing. So Maeldun planned to be patient and wait for the moment when March overreached himself.

Garluan hadn't been so fortunate. His opponent would be a squat toad of a lad named Celtchar, a squat toad of a lad with arms as thick and solid as a pair of standing stones. Earlier in the day Celtchar had easily won the stone toss, heaving the great stone well beyond the next best mark. As a fighter, Celtchar wasn't quick or agile or subtle. But unless his opponent *was* quick and agile and subtle, Celtchar's powerful blows would pound him to sawdust.

The excited spectators who lined the circular walls of the rath shouted out encouragement to their particular favorites. Although there were a few shouts of good-natured abuse, everyone took pride in these fine young men. They were their sons or their brothers or their cousins; or they were their lovers or their would-be lovers. Most of the spectators favored one lad or another, but the general feeling was one of good will toward all, for these eight young men were Clan Murtagh's finest youths, men who would soon take their places among the warrior elite.

Once more Diuran and Conn Iron-fist watched together from atop the walls. Conn knew that he too, in a sense, was on trial today, for these young lads were the products of his tutelage. He was more responsible for their abilities than anyone else. And thus he was also more familiar with their strengths and weaknesses than anyone else.

Diuran the Rhymer, who was far from an expert in such things, couldn't help wondering what his friend might be thinking as the combats were about to commence.

"Do you fancy anyone in particular today, if I may be so bold as to ask?" he said.

"Of course you may ask. But need I answer?"

"Only if you wish to, Weapons Master."

"You mean you haven't already made all the bets you plan to make? It's a bit late to be seeking inside information," Conn said with a grin. "But if you really must know, I would say that Dris is most likely to win. Ronan is probably next most likely, and if Dris or Ronan get careless, Celtchar has a chance to prevail. Young March is rather a long shot, though the sly young fox, to his credit, has come up with some deceptive moves recently entirely on his own. Still, I wouldn't be placing any bets on March today."

"What of Maeldun?"

Conn turned to look at his friend. "Maeldun? And why should you mention young Maeldun? Do you find the lad to your liking, Rhymer?"

"Actually, I rather do. It's largely based on the fact that I like his general demeanor, I suppose. I like his quiet confidence and his lack of swagger. Or is a lack of swagger not such a good thing?"

"You can't fool me, Rhymer. Why, you're almost as sly a fox as young March is. You are a man who knows more than he lets on. But since you ask about Maeldun, I will answer. With his recent growth spurt, he may now have the extra strength he's needed to complement his quickness and intelligence. It's still early days for Maeldun, though his foes had better not take him too lightly."

"What of his companion, the lanky lad with the bristly head of hair?"

"Ah, Garluan — a lad with a sense of humor. A valuable trait. It helps keep things in perspective. The lad has real skills, too, though I doubt he'll be able to withstand Celtchar's withering blows. But he's a cunning fellow who should lead Celtchar a merry chase."

Though a self-proclaimed novice, Diuran really did know more than he let on. He knew, for example, the three main ways in which a fighter could be defeated in these combats: by being disarmed; by being knocked off his feet; and by being forced outside the circle of white quartz stones in which the bouts took place. In past bouts Diuran had also seen instances in which bloodied fighters had simply had enough. Dropping down to their knees, they'd laid their weapon on the ground before them, signifying their capitulation. Diuran hoped that wouldn't happen today. Capitulation was considered shameful.

As the four pairs of fighters faced off in the four small circles of stone, a great roar went up from the spectators. But it soon subsided to be replaced by the sound of stout wooden weapons thwacking against each other and against the small wooden shields that each warrior carried.

Maeldun and Garluan, Diuran could see, were following defensive strategies in their bouts, allowing their opponents to carry the fight to them — Maeldun because he knew March would want to display all his fancy new moves, and Garluan because he had little choice against the relentless pursuit of the toad-like Celtchar.

Dris faced one of the older lads, a slow-witted opponent named Ferben, who managed to hold his own for the first five minutes before falling prey to one of Dris's subtle, disarming maneuvers. Before Ferben quite knew what had happened, his weapon was knocked free of his hand and landed with its blunt point in the sandy soil. Ferben dipped his head respectfully, acknowledging defeat.

Maeldun's match also concluded quickly. March had spun about in a lightning fast move designed to bewilder his opponent and followed it with a sudden lunge toward Maeldun's apparently unguarded chest. Maeldun slipped deftly beneath the threatening weapon, then seized March about the middle and threw him mightily to the earth. Though not the most sophisticated maneuver, it was entirely effective. March's flash and dash had fallen victim to Maeldun's quickness and strength.

Conn Iron-fist couldn't help grinning at Maeldun's simple stratagem. It wasn't a trick he'd taught the lad; but in a one-on-one combat, what matters is success, not style.

"Was that legal?" Diuran asked. "Are you allowed to do that?"

"Almost anything goes in these matches, other than bashing someone in their private parts."

"Thank goodness for that," Diuran replied.

Ronan and his opponent, a lad named Dolb, were engaged in a tactical battle of thrust, parry, and counter-thrust.

Both youths displayed excellent footwork and both had the quick reflexes required for such a classic encounter. In the end, Ronan's skills were just superior enough. When Dolb attempted to surprise him with an underarm thrust, Ronan was ready for it and brought his stout wooden sword crashing down on his opponent's wrist. The weapon fell from the lad's hand marking his elimination.

The remaining bout involved Celtchar and Maeldun's good friend Garluan — a bout in which Garluan danced and dodged and flitted, and Celtchar plodded ever onward in relentless pursuit. The combat ended when the judges announced that time had expired.

"What's happened?" Diuran asked. "Why didn't they finish?"

"They have finished. Because time is up."

"But no one won. The match was inconclusive."

"The judges will declare one of them the winner, the one they think was getting the better of the other."

"But that's not fair. The match was perfectly even."

"Actually, Rhymer, what you say is true. The match *was* even. But they will make their decision. And the winner will be Celtchar."

"Because Garluan spent most of the match evading him?"

"Yes, even though Garluan landed three times as many blows."

In the second round, Dris faced Celtchar and Maeldun faced Ronan. If the two brothers each won their bouts, then the king's eldest two grandsons would go against each other in the final bout, precisely what most of the spectators wanted and expected.

The match between Maeldun and Ronan started off much

like Ronan's first match, as a tactical battle between two able swordsmen. But whereas in the earlier match Ronan had the advantage in quickness and subtlety, this time it was Maeldun who held that edge. When Ronan tried his trick of luring his foe into making the fatal underarm thrust, Maeldun appeared to fall for it. Ronan, taken in by Maeldun's feint, brought his weapon hurling down where he expected Maeldun's wrist to be. And suddenly he found his own wrist gripped by Maeldun's powerful left hand. Now with his sword arm immobilized, Ronan tried a desperation maneuver. Slipping his foot behind Maeldun's ankle, he threw the full force of his body against his foe, hoping to cause the two of them to topple backward. If Maeldun hit the ground first, Ronan would be the winner.

Maeldun's young torso, now bearing the full weight of his opponent, was just strong enough to support both young men for the split second he needed to drop his free leg backward for additional support. Then, with a powerful twist of chest and shoulders, Maeldun threw Ronan tumbling to the earth.

"Ha, ha," laughed Conn Iron-fist. "Yes indeed, the lad has now found the physical strength he'd lacked. A year ago Ronan's move would have worked. Not now. Not any longer."

"Maeldun does seem rather good at tossing folks around," said Diuran.

"Listen, Rhymer, he doesn't just toss folks around. Did you not notice his skillful sword play? Did you not notice the speed of his reflexes? Did you not notice how he anticipated his foe's every move? Oh, Rhymer, Maeldun didn't just win by brute strength alone."

"Weapons Master, I stand humbly corrected. Please pardon my ignorance."

Conn looked suspiciously at Diuran. "Rhymer, are you

making fun of me?"

"Making fun of you? Weapons Master, far be it for me to ever make fun of you," Diuran said with a grin. Conn gave Diuran an affectionate whack on the shoulder, nearly knocking him off the high wall.

The remaining bout, between the strutting Dris and toad-like Celtchar, was totally one-sided. Whereas Garluan had led Celtchar a merry chase, Dris had the strength and quickness to stand up to him. Celtchar's mighty blows bounced off Dris's shield and sword, and every time Dris checked one of Celtchar's blows, he followed it up with a scoring blow of his own.

Blood flowed from Celtchar's nose and lips, bathing his massive torso in red ooze. Celtchar's stolid advance slowed, his blows now fewer and less harmful. Frustrated, he made a desperate overhand swing at Dris's head. Dris dodged it easily. In the next moment the squat toad went crashing to the ground, his legs neatly kicked out from beneath him.

Rath Murtagh rang with victorious shouts.

In the short pause before the final confrontation, Garluan carried an earthen jug of water to Maeldun, who sat upon the ground leaning back against the stone wall of the rath. His two previous fights had taken a lot out of him. And the bout before him, he knew, would be far more arduous than those he'd already fought.

"Beat this cocky bastard, Maeldun!" Garluan growled softly, as he knelt close beside his friend. "Beat this cocky bastard, and all the riches of the world will be yours. Look up at those walls, my friend. Look at all those women! Mael, you will have the pick of all those women." He gestured up at the high walls lined with spectators. Maeldun smiled at his friend's well-intentioned remarks. At the moment, though, women were not uppermost on his mind.

"Garluan, did Celtchar's blows take much of a toll on Dris?" he asked hopefully.

Garluan, reluctant to tell Maeldun the truth, said, "Yes, they definitely did. They took quite a goodly toll. I wish they'd taken more, but still, they took quite a goodly toll."

"Thank goodness for that. The more worn down he is, the better for me. Garluan, I'm feeling pretty worn down myself."

"You look as fresh and fragrant as a soft and steamy cow pat," Garluan said with a grin. "Dris had better watch what he steps in around you!" Maeldun couldn't help grinning also.

Despite the fact that this final bout wouldn't be between two of the king's grandsons, its fascination for the spectators hadn't diminished. If Maeldun and Dris weren't true brothers, they were still foster brothers; and though the two of them had never been the closest of companions, they shared a closer bond than Dris shared with either of his brothers.

"Wouldn't it be something," Diuran said to Conn, "if Maeldun made it a clean sweep of all three brothers? Wouldn't that truly be something?" Conn made no reply to Diuran's remark, though he had a broader smile than Diuran had seen for some time.

"How do you suppose it will sit with folks if Maeldun ends up besting all three?" Diuran went on.

It was a good question. Surely there wasn't a single person in Rath Murtagh who bore Maeldun any particular malice. Still and all, he was only a foster son and a youth of dubious lineage. With the whole question of succession being so vexed, if Maeldun defeated the three most likely heirs it could complicate things seriously. Indeed, it was difficult to predict just what strange developments it might precipitate.

"Perhaps it would be better if he didn't win," Diuran

whispered to his friend. "Have you thought of the difficulties his winning might cause?"

Conn didn't answer for a moment, though he looked at his friend with a steely-eyed grimace. "Nothing I can't handle," he finally said, his hand dropping down to his sword. "Will you stand with me, Rhymer, if push comes to shove?"

"*What?* Oh, my friend," Diuran stammered. "Let us not let push come to shove."

"If it does, will you stand with me?" the huge man repeated sternly, glaring fiercely at his friend.

Diuran looked up into the dark eyes of his towering companion, a man he respected and admired but a man he wished he understood a little better.

"If push comes to shove," Diuran said at last, "then yes. You have my solemn pledge that there is at least one man in Rath Murtagh who will stand with you."

CHAPTER 3
Crimthain's Vision

The factions and divisions amongst the inhabitants of Rath Murtagh ran deep. Each of the king's grandsons had tight-knit groups of loyal supporters. Dris's, curiously, was probably the smallest. He and his circle of friends hadn't achieved the broader popularity of Ronan, perhaps because they hadn't bothered to try. If push came to shove, Ronan would lay claim to far more backers than Dris. There were also quite a few who secretly favored Maeldun, sensible folks who saw in Maeldun greater potential than in any of the king's grandsons. So although Conn and Diuran weren't fully aware of it, they were far from alone in their admiration for the young lad.

Now the arrogant Dris, with his typical insouciance, stood within the circle of white stones, a haughty look on his face, as he waited impatiently for Maeldun to present himself.

"Oh, there you are, foundling," he said scornfully, as Maeldun finally entered the circle. "I was beginning to think you mightn't come. Perhaps it would have been better for you if you hadn't."

"Brother," Maeldun said, "the thought of opposing you has me shaking like a rowan berry in the autumn wind. Perhaps I should just capitulate now."

"It would be less painful for you if you did, little foundling. And yet I find myself hoping that you won't. To give you your due, Maeldun, you've never been half bad at all of this, and lately you've gotten a whole lot better. Why, there's even a chance you could get lucky today and win. Besides, if you were to capitulate now, it would spoil all my fun."

"I wouldn't want to do that," Maeldun replied. "I wouldn't ever want to spoil your fun, dear brother."

"I didn't think you would. That would have saddened me. But what really saddens me, Maeldun, is that you have no family here today to watch you suffer your humiliating defeat. It must be a terrible thing, being a fatherless boy. My own father may not be much of a man. But at least I know who he is."

Stung by Dris's nasty remark, Maeldun couldn't help reacting. Impulsively he grabbed at his sword and sent a vicious, slashing blow straight at Dris's head. Fully expecting it, the smirking Dris blocked it neatly.

"Ah, foundling," he sneered, "I expected you to do better than that."

The back and forth exchange between the two lads couldn't be heard up on the walls, but Conn, knowing them well, had a good idea of the prattle between them.

"Dris has been goading the lad," Conn whispered angrily. "He wants to destroy his concentration."

"Apparently he's succeeding," Diuran replied.

"Calm down, lad," Conn muttered to himself. "Don't let the villain unnerve you."

After fending off Maeldun's opening attack, Dris immediately went on the offensive, his rapid-fire blows forcing Maeldun to backpedal around the inner edge of the stone circle, parrying for all he was worth. Having his hands full with an aggressive opponent was probably a good thing for

Maeldun, for it took his mind off of Dris's vile insults.

When this initial flurry of action subsided, the bout settled down to being another tactical match-up, a game of chess between two skillful and well-matched foes. Maeldun, though less experienced than his opponent, displayed his strength and quickness and an uncanny ability to anticipate Dris's subtle ploys. Still, using his considerable wiles, Dris began taking control of the bout.

Then, in the midst of a flurry of lightning quick blows, Dris made a completely unexpected upward thrust, smashing his weapon against Maeldun's unprotected wrist. Before Maeldun knew what had happened, his wooden sword shot free from his hand and twisted through the air. With cat-like agility, Maeldun dropped his shield and shot out his left hand, just managing to grasp the sword's hilt before the weapon hit the ground. He'd come within an eyelash of defeat.

Dris was on him in a flash. And Maeldun, his right hand hanging uselessly, now checked his foe's attack with his weapon gripped firmly in his left hand. Infuriated by his near defeat and by the pain shooting through his wrist, Maeldun blocked Dris's blows and delivered a fresh flurry of his own.

Disconcerted by Maeldun's recovery and his left-handed attack, Dris rocked back on his heels. A left-handed swordsman was a rarity, and Dris seemed confused, unsure of what tactics to use. Maeldun now fought as effectively with his left hand as he'd done with his right, and for a moment it appeared that his slashing left-handed attack might bring him victory.

But what happened next was even more astonishing than Maeldun's left-handed attack. For just as victory appeared to be within Maeldun's grasp, a terrible and piercing shriek rang out over Rath Murtagh. It was an earth-shattering cry of such agony that everyone, including the two fighters, froze right where they stood. For a long moment the horrendous shriek echoed and reverberated through the rath.

Only a few people in Rath Murtagh had ever heard such a horrifying shriek before. But those who had knew that it portended some momentous event. And in all likelihood, it foretold a coming event of catastrophic proportions.

All eyes stared toward the highest structure in the rath, a looming tower of gray stone known as the Druid's Needle. There, with arms outstretched, pain-wracked face tilted up-ward, loomed the red-robed figure of Crimthain the Druid. While the echoes of his first shriek still reverberated, the Druid cried out a second time and then a third. And before the echoes of his final cry subsided, the old druid collapsed in a tangled heap of scarlet. Crimthain had entered the Druid's trance.

The final combat in the Lughnasa games was abandoned, the two combatants as stunned and mesmerized by this far more significant occurrence as everyone else. Neither Maeldun nor Dris had had any experience of the Druid's trance, though they had both heard many tales. And they knew that it always presaged an event of great magnitude, an event most often involving some impending disaster.

Eventually the Druid, his eyes still shut tight, seemed to partially emerge from his trance. Rising back to his feet, he lifted his druid rod, his long thin oaken staff, high above his head. Crimthain the Druid began to chant. What he chanted was this:

> "A boat floats upon sea waves.
> Will their voyage be long or short?
> Seventeen men are in the boat;
> seventeen men; or do I see more?
> A Rhymer is one, and one is not of us.
> Will their voyage be long or short?

I see vengeance, bloody vengeance, crimson and red.
Will their voyage be long or short?
I see a lad of coal-black hair, a lad of red-gold hair,
a lad like a toad.
I see a Rhymer and a warrior not of us.
Will their voyage be long or short?
Seventeen men sail upon the sea waves;
or do I see more?
Bringers of justice, crimson and red, seventeen bringers of justice.
Will their voyage be long, or will it be short?"

Three times Crimthain repeated his enigmatic chant. Then he opened his eyes and looked about him, seeming to cast his gaze upon all the denizens of Rath Murtagh. Finally his eyes settled on the solitary figure of Maeldun, who stood far beneath him in the center of the combat ground.

"Maeldun!" came Crimthain's screech. "Too long have you tarried! Too long has your father's body lain unrevenged in its cold stone cairn! Too long has his spirit been captive! Maeldun, his slayers still roam the face of the earth in safety. Go now, oh bringer of justice! Go now, Maeldun, son of Ailill of the Hard Edge! Bloody justice awaits your father's slayers! Bloody justice, which you must administer. Go now, Maeldun, and release his captive spirit."

"*Maeldun?*" cried Dris, from far below. "Avenge his father? How can a fatherless boy avenge a father he never had?"

"Hush, fool!" Conn Iron-fist shouted down at Dris. "When the Druid speaks, be silent and listen."

"Go now, Maeldun!" Crimthain continued. "Find the slayers. Bring them crimson justice. Take with you sixteen men, seventeen in all. *Not one man more.* You must take a rhymer, a warrior not of us, a lad like a toad, a lad with red-gold hair, twelve others, and you. Maeldun, you must not take

45

one man more. Seventeen men, *not one man more.* Avenge your father, Maeldun. Release his spirit! Restore honor to Clan Murtagh!"

"Aye," Conn Iron-fist said softly to Diuran, "restore honor to Clan Murtagh, and more importantly, to Clan MacEoin. But Rhymer, if I understand the druid correctly, it appears that you and I will be having a hand in the restoration of that honor. Are you prepared to do that?"

"Well," Diuran said, with a wan smile, "perhaps I am. Perhaps the time has come for me to broaden my horizons a bit."

"Yes," the grinning Conn replied, "perhaps it has."

CHAPTER 4

Conversations

Bewildered by these sudden events, Maeldun's thoughts were all a-swirl. He was excited, anxious, fearful. At the same time, he felt seriously betrayed. Why had those he'd trusted kept things from him? Why hadn't they told him the truth about his parents? Why let him grow up bearing the stigma of the foundling? Why let him suffer abuse at the hands of his foster brothers? Maeldun felt anger and disillusionment.

Since he'd been old enough to be aware of his status as a foundling, Maeldun had pondered the matter of his parentage. He'd convinced himself his parents had been people of real consequence. Why else would the king's eldest daughter take him into fosterage? Now he knew that what he'd imagined to be true, hoped to be true, really was true. And yet confronted by the prospect of learning his parents' true identities, Maeldun felt trepidatious. What would he discover and what would he be called upon to do? According to Crimthain the Druid, the answer to that question was clear. Maeldun did not believe that Crimthain was wrong.

His father — whoever he had been — no longer lived. But what of his mother? Who was she? Did she still live? And if so, where was she? If she lived, Maeldun knew that his first goal would be to find her and speak with her.

It was dawning on Maeldun that for the foreseeable future — for months, perhaps even years — his life would hardly be his own. Henceforth his actions would be dictated by one purpose only, discovering his father's slayers. But before he could set about doing that he had to know more. His quest for information would start with his foster mother; then it would move on to Conn Iron-fist. Then, assuming she still lived, he must find and confront his real mother. Deep down, Maeldun believed she did still live.

Finding his father's killers would be difficult and hazardous. In doing that Maeldun and his companions would face great dangers. Once they had, then they would face even greater perils as they meted out justice. Some of his companions, perhaps all of them, would die. Maeldun himself might die. But there was no choice.

For a fleeting moment the adventures of Brian and his brothers from Diuran's tale of the night before entered his mind. Like Brian and his brothers, Maeldun and his companions had to go. They had to do all they could to avenge the death of Maeldun's father, even if it ended with their own deaths. They had no choice. The deed must be attempted.

So on the final night of the feast of Lughnasa, with all these thoughts and feelings rubbing up against each other, Maeldun sat nervously beside Garluan. Since Crimthain's great public proclamation, the two lads had become figures of keen interest to the denizens of Rath Murtagh. Maeldun didn't like folks staring at him, wondering about him, sizing him up. Even the light-hearted Garluan seemed discomfited by the sudden attention.

It was midway through the meal that Dris strolled over

to where they were sitting. Squatting down next to them, he grinned and clapped each of them on the shoulder. Dris was acting like the pair of them were two of his closest pals.

"Maeldun," he said brightly, "that was some match we had today. You were really fighting your arse off out there! All along I'd been thinking I could handle you no problem. And then, shite, there you go, showing me how wrong I was. Today, lad, you were every bit my equal; by the Dagda, maybe *more* than my equal."

Dris reached out and touched Maeldun's arm gently. "How is it? Has Miach the Healer taken a good look at it? Is this his work? I really hope your arm's going to be okay."

Maeldun held up his right arm to let Dris have a better look. It was swathed in thick cloth wrappings dipped in lime, wrappings that had hardened about Maeldun's wrist.

"Miach's put this herbal wrap on it," Maeldun said. "He's given me a few other herbs for the pain. Doesn't hurt so much, really. He says it should heal up pretty good in three or four weeks. I hope so."

"So do I, Maeldun, so do I. But damn it, lad, I couldn't believe it when you started fighting with your left hand. By the Dagda, you were fighting just as well with your left as with your right! I've never seen anything like it! Where in blazes did that come from? Shite, Mael, I'm really in Crimthain's debt. If that old geezer hadn't started in on all his babbling, there's no telling what might have happened. Maeldun, you had me in pretty deep shite! But I guess you know that."

For Maeldun, Dris's show of magnanimity wasn't anything new. He'd seen it often enough before — though never directed at him. No, whenever he'd seen it before it had always been directed at someone of real importance — the king, or his mother, or Conn Iron-fist. Maeldun knew that whenever Dris went into that particular mode of behavior, he was trying to get something from someone. Now, apparently, that someone was Maeldun. Though for the life of him he couldn't imagine what Dris could want.

"I won't lie to you, Dris, that was a terribly stinging blow you gave me. Hurt like anything. Good thing for me you weren't using a real sword! If you had, I'd be a left-hander permanently."

"But he'll be okay in a few weeks," Garluan joined in. "You gotta admit that our Maeldun is made of pretty tough stuff."

"And that's no joke, either," Dris replied. "Your friend here earned my respect today." Then, reaching out and touching Maeldun familiarly once more, Dris said, "Well, lad, I just wanted to check on you. I'm glad your arm's going to be okay. Mael, I hope there's no hard feelings."

"I entered that contest with you willingly, Dris, fully expecting to take my lumps. And take 'em I did. But my arm's going to be fine. Thanks for your concern. I appreciate it."

As Dris strolled back down toward the other end of the table where he'd been sitting, Maeldun said, "Gar, what in the name of the Dagda did you make of that? Dris is up to something, but I have no idea what it is."

"Seriously? Oh, Maeldun, come on, lad, you aren't as dense as all that, are you?"

"Umm . . . I guess I am. What do you mean?"

"Isn't it obvious what he wants?"

"Not to me it isn't."

"Mael, he wants to *come*!"

"Come?"

"He wants to be one of the seventeen, you dense-head. He knows you'll have a lot of say about who's selected to go. He really wants to be one of them."

"Why would he want that? He's got to know there's a good

chance none of us will even return. By staying here he'd have a clear path to succeeding his grandfather as king."

"Oh, Maeldun. I've always given you credit for being so much brighter than pitiful me. More fool, me. He wants to come, dense-head, because he doesn't want you to hog all the glory. He wants a big share of that glory himself. If he stays here all safe and snug, he'll miss out for sure. And if you do return to Rath Murtagh trailing streams of glory, Dris will definitely be the big loser. He can't risk it. He simply can't risk it. "

"It would probably cost him the kingship."

"Gosh, Mael, I'm utterly astonished at your sudden intellectual acuity. I stand in awe of the lightning quickness of your ever-so-keen mind."

"Gar, why don't you just go and . . . "

"Go and what?"

"Uh . . . why don't you just go and find yourself a furry little sheep. I saw a very pretty young ewe earlier today. She looked just your type, all fresh and ready to go. I've no doubt she would be just to your taste."

"Trust you, Mael, to be the real expert on judging fresh and sexy ewes. There's no one better in all Rath Murtagh at that than you — my oh-so-brilliant friend."

The feast had reached its highest point, the great ritual bonding of all the king's highest ranking men. In this ritual the king's daughters, Niamh and Becfola — Maeldun's and Garluan's foster mothers — served all the nobles and highest ranked men with Clan Murtagh's two great ceremonial cups, one of gold and one of silver.

Now holding the bejeweled golden cup between her two hands, Niamh worked her way down one side of the long table toward where the two youths sat. Knowing that Maeldun was staring at her grimly, she didn't allow their eyes to meet. When she came to where her foster son was sitting, she extended the cup to him. Maeldun grasped the large vessel primarily with his left hand, using the hand of his tightly wrapped right arm only for support.

"Maeldun," she said softly to him, fearing that their relationship had been seriously altered by recent events, "dearest of sons, drink from Lugh's Cup. Drink to his glory and the glory of Clan Murtagh."

Holding the cup firmly in his left hand, Maeldun raised it to his lips and drank. "Mother," he said softly as he handed the cup back to her, "it appears there is much you have never told me."

"Not so very much," she said, her eyes now meeting his. "I never believed there was anything so important that you needed to know it. Perhaps I was wrong, though perhaps not. Anyway, I will certainly tell you what I know. I suspect that Conn should be able to tell you more, especially in regard to your father."

The lad held her eyes with his. "I wish I had known, mother, I wish you had told me," he finally said.

"I didn't think there was any need," she replied, her eyes looking away from his.

"Oh yes, mother, there was need. Of course I will forgive you. But I am very upset with you."

"I understand," she said. "Come to my chamber in the morning. I will tell you what I can."

Maeldun gave her a tight-lipped nod. At the moment, he didn't trust himself to utter any further words. Niamh proceeded to hand the cup of Lugh to Garluan. Then she continued on down to the end of the table, with Maeldun's eyes upon her the entire time.

*   *   *

Maeldun sought out Niamh's chamber within the royal quarters, a small room built into the thickest section of the stone wall a safe distance from the rath's main entrance. He hadn't been there since he was three years old, and it brought back memories. Pleasant ones, memories of before he'd been turned over to the rough and tumble of the royal nursery — a place where he'd learned harsh truths and where he'd formed his bond of friendship with Garluan, the two foundlings often being objects of the other boys' scorn.

Niamh sat on a low stool beside the glowing turf fire, its smell pervading the small room.

"Come, Maeldun," she said softly. "Come and sit by me."

"Hello, mother," he replied, lowering himself onto the rushes near her feet. She reached out to tousle his hair but Maeldun brushed her hand away.

Without any further preliminaries Maeldun said, "Who was she, mother? Or should I say, who is she?"

"She was my sister. I haven't seen her since your birth."

"Nor have I," Maeldun asserted grimly.

"She was my sister, Maeldun, whom I loved very much. After you were born she went away, planning never to return. She hasn't."

"So she didn't want me?" Maeldun looked up at his foster mother's face. He saw the tears forming in her eyes.

"It wasn't that she didn't want you. She'd never intended to have you. In the life she was living, it wasn't possible for her to keep you."

"I don't understand."

"She had chosen a different kind of life for herself, a life quite unlike the one we live here. In the life she'd chosen it wasn't possible to keep children." Maeldun reflected on his foster mother's words.

"Can you tell me her name?"

"Her name is Maire. Where she is, I believe she is called Sister Maire."

"Sister Maire? So she is a Christian?"

"You know of the Christians?"

"Only a little."

"They are a gentle people, Maeldun."

"A gentle people with a fierce and vengeful god."

Niamh looked down at him. "Is that what you think?"

"It is what Conn thinks. He has seen the power of their vengeful god. There are few things that Conn Iron-fist fears. The god of the Christians is one of them. But mother, do you know where I can find this woman named Sister Maire? — this woman who is my mother but who has never *been* my mother? I want to see her. I want to hear from her myself how she could bear a child and then just walk away. I need her to tell me how she could do that. And even more, I need her to tell me of my father. I need to know who he was and what happened to him."

"Maeldun, I cannot tell you where she is, for I do not know. And if I did know, I'm not certain that I would. I do not believe she would want to meet you. Nor do I think she could tell you what you wish to know about your father. You would do better speaking with Conn. Although he doesn't know Maire as well as I do — or at least as well as I once did — he is the one to tell you about your father."

Maeldun studied his mother for some time without speaking. Finally he said, "So protecting your sister, who turned her back on Rath Murtagh and adopted another faith, is more important to you than being honest with me and telling me who I really am."

"Oh Maeldun. You are a beautiful young man — intelligent, handsome, strong, gifted in so many ways. Who you are,

Maeldun, is who *you* are. It doesn't matter who your mother was, or who your father was. What matters is who you are."

"It matters to me, mother. It matters a very great deal to me."

"What matters to me, my dear son, is your well-being, but also my sister's. If you must, go and avenge your father's death. Maeldun, please do not torment my sister. She's been tormented enough."

"I will try not to torment her, mother. But I must find her and speak with her. I am sorry to go against your wishes. But surely you can understand why I must find her."

Niamh reached out again to tousle Maeldun's hair. "My dear son," she said, "my dear, dear son." This time Maeldun didn't brush her hand away.

In the early evening of that same day, Diuran the Rhymer looked out from atop the walls of the rath, his eyes following a pair of dark figures who were walking together toward the high hills above the rath. They were not the figures of herdsmen but rather of Conn Iron-fist and young Maeldun. Diuran suspected they wished to keep as far away as possible from the eager ears of those within the rath. The conversation they would be having was meant for their ears only. Diuran was as eager as anyone to hear this conversation, but as the two figures receded into the distance, all he could do was imagine what the two men might be saying.

Conn and Maeldun, mentor and pupil, climbed the hills in silence for the better part of an hour, passing beyond the clan's herds of cattle and their herdsmen, eventually climbing the steeper slopes of the Paps of Anu. When they reached the top, they halted and turned to stare off into the dimness. Beneath them they could now see the fires of the rath; and far off beyond it, the glimmer of the great western sea, the water reflecting the rays of the setting sun.

It was Maeldun who broke their silence.

"Why didn't you tell me?" the young man said, biting off each word. "You knew more than anyone else, and I trusted you more than anyone else. You knew my father, and yet you could not tell me about him? You are the one who brought my mother here — here where I could be born and raised as a fatherless foundling — and yet you could not tell me about her? Weapons Master, how could you have been a party to such a cruel scheme? Why did you do that to me?"

The lips of Conn Iron-fist were firmly compressed. His narrowed eyes looked fierce as a hawk's. If Maeldun was angry, then Conn was equally angry. Was his anger directed at himself? Or at the youth? Or maybe at both of them? Perhaps it was just that he was a man who hated to have accusations hurled at him, even if those accusations contained a degree of truth.

"Maeldun," he said at last, "I did what I thought was best. Best for you, best for your father, and also best for me. It may have been best for your mother, too, though I'll admit I wasn't especially concerned about her. You may view things differently, but that was what I thought. I thought it then, and it is what I still think now.

"There were many reasons why I chose not to tell you those things. I wanted you to grow up living a normal life and having a carefree, joyful childhood. I didn't want you to be known as the king's grandson because I didn't want you to turn into a pampered and spoiled youth like your foster brothers. But the most important reason, Maeldun, was that I didn't want you to grow up with hatred in your heart. It would have poisoned you. Had you grown up that way, you wouldn't have become the man you are. Believe me, I know what it is to have hatred in your heart.

"Maeldun, I've been eager to tell you those things. I've wanted to since you were small, but I knew I must wait till you'd become a man. I knew that time was drawing near. I was planning to wait one more year. That's when I felt you would be ready. Now Crimthain's vision has altered things."

"That's when you felt I would be ready? Ready for what, Weapons Master?"

"Ready to comprehend and cope with the things you are now discovering. Ready to begin the process of doing what honor requires you to do. Ready to undertake the tasks that lie before you."

"So what you are saying is that you do not think I am yet ready to undertake those tasks."

"Maeldun, I had to be certain. If you weren't ready, we would have little chance of success. I planned to be patient. I didn't want to rush things. Now it appears that, ready or not, the time has come."

"Yes," Maeldun said, "ready or not, the time has come. I will tell you here and now, Weapons Master, that when my arm is fully healed I will be ready. So you tell me now, Weapons Master, are you prepared to help me undertake the deeds that I must undertake?"

"There is nothing in the world I want more. It is what I have been living for for the last sixteen years."

"So," Maeldun said, supporting his right arm with his left and staring off at the far horizon, "perhaps it is time that you spoke of my father. Who was he, Weapons Master? How well did you know him? What kind of a man was he? What did he mean to you?"

"Everything," Conn whispered, more to himself than to Maeldun, "he meant everything."

As the darkness descended about them, Conn Iron-fist began speaking to the youth about the man named Ailill of

the Hard Edge, Ailill MacEoin of Clan MacEoin. Conn spoke
from the heart, and Maeldun listened avidly. As the darkness
deepened, the words of Conn Iron-fist penetrated deeply
into the heart of the young man named Maeldun — Maeldun
MacEoin of Clan MacEoin.

CHAPTER 5
Alim the Wanderer

In the days that followed, Maeldun slowly began to come to terms with his new feelings and knowledge. The sense of betrayal and the anger he'd felt toward his foster mother and his trusted mentor began to ebb away, as strong emotions do in time. Indeed, he understood their reasons for acting as they had acted, even if he still harbored some resentment in regard to the price he'd had to pay for their choices.

But now his thoughts turned away from the past and toward the future, a future in which he would play the principal role. Conn hadn't been certain that Maeldun was ready, but Maeldun believed he was. He realized he would need much guidance and support from others, that he would be just one of seventeen who would undertake the momentous task of achieving vengeance; yet he felt certain he was the one who would make all the difference. By nature, Maeldun was a modest lad. But this was going to be *his* adventure, come what may. Whether he made a glorious name for himself or proved an abysmal failure, this would be his adventure.

*   *   *

"It should take us about a month to complete our preparations, I think, possibly a bit longer," Conn said.

It was two days later and he was speaking with Diuran the Rhymer and Maeldun MacEoin, the three of them perched on the highest of the three stone ledges inside the wall of the rath. The sun had burned off the morning's mist, and its warmth felt pleasant. At that moment, sitting there in the sunshine, the dangers of their voyage seemed far away.

"We must choose our companions carefully and begin their training," Conn went on. "We must give careful thought to how we will provision the boat. But far and away the most important and immediate task is the boat itself. We will need a vessel larger and sturdier than any the clan now possesses, and we will have to build it from scratch. We must set the craftsmen to work as soon as we've determined how to design a craft to serve our needs."

"I know little of boats," Maeldun said. "Other than the small coracles we use for fishing the streams and lakes, I have had no experience with them. I have never been out on the sea in a boat."

"Nor have I," Diuran said. "Oh yes, I've told many a tale of sea adventures — tales of Manannan's wondrous boat 'The Wave Sweeper.' But my tales, alas, are no substitute for real experience."

"I have spent much time on the sea," Conn said, "and I do have some knowledge of boats, though I am far from being a true expert. Before we do anything further, we must find ourselves someone who is, someone far more knowledgeable than I, a master mariner. We must seek his advice in designing the boat; we must persuade him, if we can, to become one of our voyagers. In our group of seventeen, no one will be more important than our master mariner."

"Master mariner?" Maeldun said. "I know of no such person here. I doubt if we will find such a person in Rath Murtagh. Perhaps we should look elsewhere."

"I think there may be one," Diuran said.

"Yes," Conn agreed, "perhaps there is one. Diuran, are we thinking of the same man? The man I have in mind is called Alim." Smiling, Diuran nodded.

"Oh, Weapons Master, surely you can't be right," Maeldun said. "Alim? That drunken old sot? Weapons Master, when he's drunk — which is most of the time — Alim's naught but a wind bag and a jackpudding. When he's sober, he's so morose he darkens the mood of everyone within a hundred miles. As for his strange tales of sea-wanderings, they cannot be anything but the idle ramblings of an addle-brained idiot. Weapons Master, surely you do not credit Alim's fantastic tales? Those tales were born in a vat of coal-black ale!"

It was Diuran who replied first. "Maeldun, you are correct in thinking that Alim is a drunk and a windbag. And yes, he can be a killjoy like none other. But do not underestimate him. He is not quite the senile old fool he often seems. Indeed, Alim is probably the only man in Clan Murtagh who has had any extensive experience in sailing the western sea."

"Seriously?"

"Yes," Conn said, joining in, "seriously. He may embellish his wild tales in order to entertain and impress young lads like you. But the man has truly spent much of his life in boats, and he knows the sea like no one else." Maeldun couldn't help shaking his head in disbelief.

As they were discussing the pros and cons of Alim, they noticed the old king now moving slowly across the open yard in their direction. They hadn't yet discussed their plans with him, and they knew he would have the final say in whatever they did. As the king drew near they lapsed into silence, waiting for him to address them first.

The king stopped and stood before them, running his eyes over the three of them.

"I suspect I know what you've been discussing," he said, "Crimthain's vision. I've questioned him on it, challenged him on it, disputed it with him, but he stands firmly by it. He refuses to believe there is any alternative. If you do not go, he is convinced that great harm will be visited upon us.

"So . . . it seems you must go. That is not my wish, but I dare not defy the druid. He says, as you know, that you must take precisely seventeen in your party. I suspect you have given some thought to who those seventeen might be. Perhaps that is what you are now discussing? Clearly, you are three of the seventeen, along with the lads named Garluan and Celtchar. So that makes five. Who else are you considering?"

It was Conn who spoke first. "We wish to ask Alim to go as our master mariner."

The old king smiled at that. "Alim? Alim the Wanderer? Yes, I can see why you might want that. Well, if you want him, I have no objection to that. If you can somehow keep him sober, he might even serve you well."

"We haven't discussed who else might go," Conn said. "My preference would be to mostly take the young lads I've been training, maybe six or eight of them, along with maybe three or four of your more seasoned warriors, if you were willing to relinquish them to us. I know you can't spare many, but I was hoping you might be willing to give me a few. It would be well to have a few veteran warriors mixed in amongst our inexperienced youths."

"Yes, I see the wisdom of that," the old king said. "I will allow you to take three, three that I will select myself. I promise you they will be among my better men. So Conn, which ones from among the younger lads do you have a mind to take?"

Conn named off the names of half a dozen lads, including those of Ferben and Dolb, two of the lads who'd made it to the final bouts at the festival games. But he was careful to avoid mentioning any of the king's three grandsons.

"So, what of Dris, Ronan, and March? What of them, Conn? Do you not consider them good enough to go with you?"

"Sire, it is not a question of whether they are good enough," Conn replied guardedly. "They are easily good enough. It is a question of your wishes. We would happily include any of them within the party. We could take all of them or none of them, just as you might wish."

Maeldun and Diuran knew that Conn's words did not reflect his true feelings. They didn't believe for a second that Conn wanted Maeldun's foster brothers to be among the seventeen voyagers. Maeldun himself remained unsure about the matter. He knew how badly Dris wanted to go, and he also knew that his foster brothers possessed skills and abilities that might help them complete their task. They were, after all, three of the clan's most capable youths. But he knew, too, that taking any of them posed a variety of risks.

"So it is up to me to make that decision?" the king said. "Hmm. No, Conn, I think I shall leave it to you. You are the one who has been training our youths. You know them best — their strengths, their weaknesses, their virtues, their shortcomings. You choose. Take from amongst them whomever you wish to take. Take Dris or Ronan or March. If you wish, take all three. But if you do, I will be counting on you to bring them back safely."

"Thank you for your confidence in me, sire. Since you are leaving the choice to me, I must consider the matter carefully."

"I am sure you will," the old king said. He nodded his

farewells to Maeldun and Diuran, and slowly retreated back across the open space toward his royal chambers.

Later that morning Conn sought out Alim. He found the man lying on his back on a sunny patch of grassy ground outside the rath's walls. He was lying in a semi-stupor, his eyes closed. Conn suspected he was nursing a hangover.

"Alim, wake up and listen to me," Conn said sternly.

The old man raised himself halfway up, cocked his head sideways, and shaded his eyes with one hand. "Who's there?" he said. "Whatta ya want with me?"

"It's Conn, Alim. I've come to speak with you about a most urgent matter."

"Conn Iron-fist, you worthless piece o' excrement," Alim grunted, his eyes still closed, "I've told you before you can't have my recipe for bragget. So go on with ya now and leave me be."

"Alim, have you heard the druid's prophecy?"

"What's that you say?"

"The druid's prophecy. Of the voyage we must make. Of the revenge we must seek. Have you not heard these things?"

Alim's eyes slowly began to focus more sharply. Perhaps the clouds in his brain had begun to disperse just a little. "The prophecy? The voyage? Yes . . . I believe I have heard something about those things."

"Alim, we want you to help us. We need your advice on the building of a new boat. And if you are willing, we want you to consider coming with us — as our master mariner, Alim." The look that came over Alim's face was one of shocked surprise.

"Me?" he finally said. "Conn Iron-fist, are you telling me you want me to come with you? You want me to be your master mariner?"

"Yes, Alim," Conn replied. "You are the man we want."

"A drunken old sot whose tales of strange isles and stranger beasts are believed by no one?"

"An experienced seaman who knows the ways of the sea and knows more about boats than any of us ever will. Alim, we must begin building a new sea craft, one larger and stronger than any we now have. We need to set about it immediately. Will you help us? Will you give us your advice?"

Alim rubbed his hand slowly back and forth through his scraggily gray beard, his lips now bearing the faintest hint of a smile, his eyes taking on a strange new glow.

"A new sea craft?" he said, "one larger and stronger than any we now have?" He seemed to ponder the matter for a lengthy moment before finally saying, "Yes, Conn, I believe that I could do that. Yes . . . I believe that I shall help you." And as he slowly nodded his agreement, his eyes gleamed and glittered even more and his smile became broader than before.

"Yes, Conn," he said again, "I believe I shall."

Of the group of seventeen, five of the voyagers were predetermined by the druid's pronouncement — Maeldun, Conn, Diuran, Garluan, and Celtchar — and now Alim made the sixth member. Of the remaining eleven, three would be drawn from the king's personal guard and eight from Conn's youthful charges. Maeldun and Conn decided not to choose those final eight until it was nearly time for them to embark, though they were nearly of one mind about which of the lads they believed should be selected. The really tricky question remained what to do with Maeldun's foster brothers. On that matter the two of them were not of one mind.

*   *   *

The next morning, the boat building began. A sullen but sober Alim, with Conn and Maeldun close by his side, set about directing the craftsmen in their activities. But although Alim looked much the worse for wear, his eyes retained their gleam from the day before. Observing that gleam, Maeldun wondered if perhaps Alim's thoughts were of distant isles and the strange creatures inhabiting them.

As the sun warmed the morning air and as beads of sweat began appearing on the necks of the workers, Alim also warmed to his task, barking out his orders briskly. On occasion, those closest to him could hear the man singing a strange and eerie-sounding song beneath his breath. Perhaps it was a song he'd once sung to himself years ago when Alim the Wanderer had been a solitary seaman plying the waves.

Throughout the morning, Conn and Maeldun stood nearby observing all the activity. Conn had had his own notions of the kind of craft they needed, but it didn't take long for him to realize that Alim's ideas were far superior to his own; so for the most part he kept his thoughts to himself.

Maeldun watched as stout poles were driven into the ground forming the outline of the boat-to-be; as piles of withes accumulated nearby, materials which would be interwoven to form the pliable wicker sides of the craft; as in the nearby field cowhides were gathered to be cured in vats containing a pungent solution of oak bark. Higher up in the pasture, other large vats were being readied for the making of pitch to tar the outer skin of the craft and make it watertight.

Curiosity ran high through the rath, and soon many of its inhabitants came out to observe these activities. Among them were Garluan and Celtchar, two of the youths already chosen, thanks to the druid's proclamation, to be members of the boat's crew.

Garluan and Cheltchar were about as different as any two

lads could be — Garluan tall and slender and quick, light-hearted and voluble; Celtchar thick and powerful, stolid, plodding, and virtually wordless. Celtchar was the "lad like a toad" in the druid's pronouncement, Garluan the "lad of red-gold hair." The two of them walked together to where the boat was being constructed and stood close beside Maeldun, Conn, and Alim.

"Dunderheads!" Alim shouted at the workers. "Stinking pieces o' excrement! Not like that, ya shaggers! Here's how ya do it! By the Dagda, what worthless pieces o' shite!"

Impatiently, he showed them for the third or fourth time the precise manner in which the withes should be woven in and out around the several tall poles standing upright in the ground, poles around which the wicker framework for the boat was just beginning to take shape.

Alim was stone-cold sober. As a consequence, his mood was about as dark as Maeldun's raven-black locks. At Alim's words, Garluan and Celtchar exchanged amused looks. But if there had been any doubt in anyone's mind that Alim knew what he was about, there wasn't any longer. That was a relief to Maeldun, who'd been one of the skeptics and doubters.

"You!" he shouted at Celtchar. "Grab on to this end and hold it tight — you massive piece o' crap!" The massive lad meekly obliged.

"You!" Alim suddenly shouted at Garluan — "you skinny piece o' crap. Pack that withy down tight against the one beneath it. Pack it tight, I tell you, *tight!* You don't want to drown, do you? — you scrawny, worthless bugger!"

Garluan pushed down upon it until he turned red in the face. "That okay?" he offered.

"It'll have to do," Alim replied sourly. "Scrawny bugger."

In the hours that followed, the outline of the craft began to take shape. It would be roughly fifty feet in length and about eight feet across the beam at its central section, though narrower and sharply pointed toward its ends. It would be a keel-less craft of light construction, with only a few wooden ribs inserted at intervals to stabilize the wicker framework. The prow and stern would be curved slightly upward to make it easier to crest the waves on rough seas, though its bottom would be flattish in the middle to make it easier to drag beyond the tideline on sandy beaches where there would be no moorings.

Eventually the curragh would have a pair of short masts for sails, three stout thwarts across the middle, sets of six oars on each side amidship, and a large steering oar attached to the left side near the stern. The craft would be heavier than was usually the case for a curragh, though light enough for its crew of seventeen to drag it high up on beaches, or even to carry for short distances, if need be.

In the afternoon Conn sent all of his young charges, along with the three older veterans, off to the nearby lough to spend several hours rowing the few crafts the clan already had. He aimed to toughen up their hands and get the muscles of their shoulders and chests accustomed to the arduous task of rowing for long periods of time. The new boat's small sails might prove a boon when winds were favorable, but rowers would supply its primary source of locomotion. Out on the sea, they would ply as many as a dozen long oars. For maneuvering in streams, rivers, and narrow coves, they would use a set of short, stout oaken paddles.

In less than two weeks the vessel was essentially ready, the cured cowhides sewn to each other and to the wicker frame with strong linen twine, the seams thoroughly covered with pitch. Alim said he needed another week to make final adjustments, so the youths carried the boat over to the lough where they began practicing anew with the craft itself. The next-to-last things Alim added were two pairs of curved "hoops" over the boat's prow and stern, hoops to support protective coverings for when they faced heavy seas and harsh weather. Finally he added the oculi, the pair of eyes he painted on each side near the front end of the boat.

"Now you can see where you're going, my beauty," he said softly to the boat, patting her with a gentle, loving hand.

So the craft was finished, the provisions gathered, the crew's training completed. The time had come for Maeldun and his companions to depart.

With the sole exception of the seventeenth man, the crew was now set. Maeldun argued vigorously in favor of making Dris the seventeenth man. Not because he knew how much his foster brother wished to go, and certainly not out of any great love for Dris. But Maeldun didn't feel right about completely excluding his foster brothers. And if they did take one of them, he much preferred Dris, the most able of the three and the one least likely to cause problems. Ronan and March, as he'd known since early boyhood, were far more devious than Dris and far more likely to defy his and Conn's authority.

Conn wasn't having any of it. He wanted nothing to do with the king's three grandsons.

He tried to veil his reluctance within a cloak of reasons — that the king would resent the absence of his favorites; that the king's most likely successors should not be put at risk; that the king had told Conn that if he took any of his grandsons, he must guarantee to bring them back safely, a guarantee no one could possibly make.

But Conn's real reasons, Maeldun knew, were much simpler. Conn didn't like them, didn't trust them, and didn't want any of the glory the expedition might achieve to accrue to them.

John Conlee

So, in the end, the seventeenth member selected for the crew was a very young lad named Taman. Given his youth, he was an unlikely choice. But Taman, besides being a lad of true promise, happened to be the finest young harpist in the rath. His music, Conn argued, would cheer the others as they labored and might even come in handy in dealing with hostile clans, since bards and minstrels enjoyed special privileges of hospitality.

When Dris realized he'd been excluded, he angrily grabbed up his cloak and scrip and departed from the rath. He disappeared off in the direction of the high hills and didn't return. Not having to confront Dris's anger and disappointment was a great relief to Maeldun. But at the same time, Dris's absence worried him. What was Dris up to? It seemed certain he was up to something.

The other brothers had seemed to pay little attention. Neither of them had ever expressed a keen desire to go anyway. And yet on the evening before the seventeen were to depart, Ronan and March mysteriously disappeared also. It wasn't clear where they'd gone. What could his three foster brothers be about? Maeldun wondered. They weren't simply sulking, he felt certain of that. Those fellows had a plan.

CHAPTER 6
Departure

In the morning, the boat and their essential supplies were borne to the river estuary, to the place where they would embark on their journey. A great many people accompanied them to say their farewells and to pray for a safe journey. The king did not come, though he'd bestowed his royal blessing upon them before they departed from the rath. There was still no sign of Maeldun's foster brothers. They had not returned to the rath, nor did they come to the river to watch the voyagers' departure.

Crimthain the Druid, however, did come, and when the crew was finally settled within the craft, standing on the river bank he raised his druid rod high above his head and loudly intoned a supplication to the gods. When he finished, a hush descended upon the entire gathering.

"Push off!" Conn cried out, shattering the silence. "Push off. Now row!"

Using just their short paddles, the crewmen began propelling the vessel out into the deeper channel of the river estuary. And as they did, a great keening arose from the women assembled there — the mothers and grandmothers, the sisters, the lovers, the secret admirers. In their hearts they feared they would never see their men again.

They stood on the shore and watched as the long narrow craft began to snake its way down the wide estuary. They watched as fourteen men plied their paddles, with Alim standing alone in the stern handling the steering oar and with Conn, Maeldun, and Diuran standing close together in the prow. They watched until the boat became a tiny floating speck. They watched until it could be seen no more.

As the smoother waters of the estuary gave way to the rough chop of the western sea, Alim kept a watchful eye on how the craft handled when cresting the waves. He seemed generally satisfied, though he remarked to Maeldun that when they beached the boat at the end of the day, he would seek out more ballast. Even fully loaded with their fresh provisions, the boat rode higher in the water than he preferred.

Once the craft was out on the sea, the crew shifted to the long oars. Under normal conditions six men rowed at a time, three on each side, the others spelling them at regular intervals. Maeldun's injured right arm, though now nearly healed, as yet kept him from doing any of the rowing. Diuran and Alim were exempted as well, though Conn and the three veteran warriors took their turns along with the others.

When they were well clear of the land, Conn ordered the rowers to ship their oars and the craft hove to. Then Alim, leaving the completely inexperienced Maeldun in charge of the steering oar, made his way to the front of the boat. In his hands he carried a large earthen jug. He moved forward to the tip end of the prow where he stood with extended arms, the jug held firmly between his hands.

Alim stood in silence for several seconds, the jug held out in front of him over the sea. He began speaking words, words that no one else was able to make out, and if they had, they probably wouldn't have been able to decipher them anyway. But those words were not meant for their ears. When he finished, he began to tilt the jug slowly, slowly — pouring its golden contents into the sea. It was a libation, a libation intended for the great god of the sea, the great sea god named Manannan MacLir.

Alim poured out the entire contents of the jug, holding it steady until the final few drops fell free of its rim. He bowed his head for another long moment; then, using both hands, he suddenly flung the jug out into the water as far as he could throw it. When it hit the surface of the water with a small splash, the entire crew uttered a great cry of exaltation.

Alim stood there a moment longer, then turned about and made his way slowly back to the boat's stern where Maeldun stood still gripping the steering oar uncertainly.

"So, Mael," Alim said to the lad with uncharacteristic cheerfulness, "why don't I show you exactly how this thing works, eh?"

"Yes," Maeldun replied, "that might be quite a good idea."

When they finally beached their craft toward the end of a long day on the sea, the oarsmen were tired and sore and in need of food and drink. They soon heaped up a roaring fire to dry their damp garments and warm their chilled bodies. It wasn't long before the strong drink was having its effects on many of them.

"Alim," Diuran said, walking over and extending a cup to the master mariner, "I suspect you have much need for this."

"Truer words were never spoken, Rhymer. I certainly have much need of it. But regretfully, I must decline. I have sworn my oath to Manannan. No strong drink shall touch these lips until this voyage is concluded. I dare not offend the great sea god, Rhymer. I will, however, gladly accept that joint of meat in your other hand, if it's not too much trouble."

"Oh, well, of course." Diuran hadn't intended the meat for Alim, just the cup of drink, and he'd already taken a few bites from it himself. But that made little matter to the famished Alim, who was quickly gnawing away.

"Thank you, Rhymer," he said, his mouth already chock-full, his lips greasy from the roasted meat. "Most hospitable of you."

As the voyagers ate and drank, the youth named Taman removed the covering from his harp and began to play. For the first half hour or so he played the dancing tunes, which fitted the mood of revelry the drink had inspired amongst the jolly crew. Then he moved on to playing the sad tunes, and before long their mood became far more thoughtful and sober, some of the voyagers no doubt reflecting on the seriousness of their undertaking, some no doubt thinking about the loved ones they'd left behind.

Finally Taman began to play the sleepy tunes. By the time he'd played only a few of them, his gentle chords were accompanied by a steady chorus of snores.

Maeldun and Conn, however, remained awake. In hushed voices they discussed what the days ahead would bring. Conn, knowing that Maeldun wished first of all to find his mother and speak with her, explained to Mael the route they would follow up the western coast of Ireland. They would stop first, he said, at the cairn where Maeldun's father and seven others were buried. It was about two days' travel away. Conn had not been there for many years, though his thoughts traveled there often.

Next they would go to the small island with the monastery, the monastery where Maeldun's mother had chosen to become a Christian nun. They would discover if Sister Maire still lived, and if she did, Maeldun would insist upon speaking with her. Once the lad was satisfied, they would continue sailing northward, not stopping at Inis Mor in the Aran Islands, the home of Clan MacEoin. While the time to do that would eventually come, Conn said, that time was not now. They would not go there until after Maeldun's father had been fully avenged.

It would take several more days of northward travel to reach the area where the Reavers of Roonah were known to live. As they neared their destination, they would camp well short of it in order to reconnoiter and to plan. They must move slowly and carefully, not giving any hint of their intentions. Their action when it came, though, must be swift and decisive. It must come as a total surprise to those upon whom their vengeance would be visited.

In the dawning, Alim roused out Garluan and Celtchar, the two members of the crew who, much to their chagrin, had emerged as his particular favorites. Whenever he was in need of help, they were the ones he called on.

"Come on now, you lazy pieces o' excrement," he growled at them, all the while grinning an evil grin. "Time ta rise 'n' shine, my sweetings, rise and shine." The sleepy-eyed lads grudgingly obliged, Celtchar with stoic resignation, Garluan all the while muttering vile imprecations beneath his breath.

Alim had found two large stones he believed would suit his purpose, his purpose being to improvise what he called killicks. These were objects that would do double duty, providing the craft with sea anchors and also with the ballast Alim believed it still needed. So Alim set the lads to the lifting and carrying while he was fashioning wooden frames to fit about them. "Now I'll show ya just how to be attaching the cables, lads," he said, when the stones had been snugged into the frames.

He looked on with an approving grin as the lads completed the work, and when they were finished he congratulated them on their efforts. "Good on ya, then, my sweetings. Well done, lads, ya lovely pieces o' shite."

"Okay if we eat now?" Garluan hazarded. As they'd worked, he'd watched gloomily as the rest of the crew were already tucking in to their early morning meal.

"Eat? A skinny lad like you? Now Celtchar here, with the build and bulk of a stone jakes, he's a lad who certainly needs ta eat. But you, Garluan? Why, you look more like a wraith than a rake. You look like a fool who's been fasting three months for Imbolg."

"Master Mariner, modesty forbids me to say what you look like. I wouldn't want you to think I was being disrespectful."

"Disrespectful? Why, Gar, I'd never think that of you, lad. Not of you, Gar. So lad, why doncha just go and fetch yourself some food, eh? Whatta ya standing there for, my lovely laddy, with your thumb still up your bum?"

The sloping green hill hove into view. From half a mile away, Conn could see the cairn he and Derga had erected high up on the hillside. He wondered if Ailill's spirit was there watching, wondered if it had been comforted by the amulet he had left with Ailill when he first buried him, the silver, leaf-shaped brooch, his pledge to never forget his friend; his pledge to come back someday and release his spirit.

"Is that it?" Maeldun asked, pointing.

"Yes," Conn replied. All the mariners gazed up at the hillside and the imposing cairn, beneath which lay the bodies of Maeldun's father and his seven companions. Their spirits, they believed, remained there also.

They pulled the craft high up on the shore above the tideline. Six men, including Alim, remained with the boat while the others trooped up the hill. Led by Conn, they climbed the grassy slope to where the cairn serenely lay. Without being asked, they silently formed a wide circle around the site and stood there reverently, out of respect for Maeldun and respect for the spirits of those who had died here and were buried here.

After a few moments, Conn sent four of the men on up the hill on the lengthy trek to the fresh water springs, a trek this time he wouldn't make himself. It would take the small party the better part of an hour to reach the springs, fill the pouches, and make their return. An image of that return was burned deeply into Conn's mind, an image of the carnage he'd found many years ago, when he and Derga had come back from the springs.

Taman the Harper sat down near the cairn and began to play gentle tunes on his instrument. Maeldun stood all alone, thinking of the father he'd never met, the father he only knew from what Conn had told him. As he stood there, he sensed the presence of his father's spirit. "I have come, father," Maeldun said within his mind, "and I hope to achieve that which will make you proud."

Conn wandered off by himself, lost in his own thoughts. He had known all of these men who were buried here. They had been his friends and his kinsmen. Because he had survived, he had a great debt to pay to all of them. It was a debt he hoped would soon be repaid. He hoped that once it was, all their spirits would be at peace.

Eventually all the others drifted back down to the boat, leaving only Conn and Maeldun on the hillside. Conn walked over and stood beside the lad. He placed his hand on the younger man's shoulder, the two of them bound by their powerful feelings for the men who lay within the cairn, and especially for one of them.

"We shall stay as long as you wish," Conn said softly.

"Just a little longer," Maeldun replied.

As Conn looked out from the hillside, his eyes sensed a small movement out on the sea. He shielded his eyes with his hand and stared intently. Yes, it was really there. It was a boat — he couldn't tell how large — and it was coming this way. Could it actually be the Reavers of Roonah? Could history be about to repeat itself?

"I'm ready now," Maeldun said, his words intruding upon Conn's thoughts.

"Let's go down, then," Conn said.

Late in the afternoon, the green hill far behind them, their curragh once more plied the sea in a northward direction. Conn believed they were now no more than two days away from the small island with the monastery, possibly less. It had been more than sixteen years since he had been there. For a moment he thought of the old abbess at whose request he had undertaken the task involving Maeldun's mother, a task that had led him inexorably to the present moment. He wondered if Derga was still there, red-haired Derga who'd preferred to remain in the company of the nuns rather than stay with his long-time friend. Conn bore Derga no ill-will for his choice, and he smiled at the prospect of seeing him once more after all the intervening years.

"I think I see a boat, Weapons Master," Diuran said. He extended his arm, pointing in a southerly direction.

"Rhymer," Conn said, "your eyes do not deceive you."

"A boat?" asked Maeldun. Now he too was staring in the direction in which Diuran had pointed.

"By the Dagda, I hope it isn't the Reavers of Roonah!" Diuran said. "Could they have gotten wind of our plans somehow?"

"The Reavers of Roonah, hah!" scoffed Alim. "It certainly ain't them. If it were, yes, we'd surely be in a bit of a jam. But it ain't them shaggers for sure, no, it surely ain't them. It's just those foolish young lordlings — no-good pieces o' excrement!"

"The young lordlings?" Maeldun said.

"Your no-good foster brothers, lad — worthless pieces o' shite!"

"So they've decided to come along anyway, it seems," Conn said. "I'm impressed, actually, at their sailing skills, especially in such a puny little boat. It's a wonder they haven't foundered yet. Very good thing for them the weather's been so favorable."

"Yes," Alim said, "though that's about to change." He pointed off to the west toward where a tall, thick bank of gray-black clouds loomed ominously. "We'd best find ourselves a safe haven soon. 'Twill be a bitter night for certain. Be a right good idea ta have a solid roof over our heads this e'ven, methinks."

"Yes," Conn said, "and I believe I know just where we may find such a place."

"Aye, I believe I do as well," Alim said. He'd already shifted their course by means of the great steering oar he'd been holding all the while.

CHAPTER 7
Fintan's Cave

The high, dark opening to Fintan's Cave loomed up before them, maybe fifty yards above the tideline. The mariners, lifting the curragh up onto their shoulders, bore it well beyond the shingly beach before laying it down again and tipping it on its side.

"Leave the boat here," Conn said. "The cavern is large, but not large enough for the boat and us too in comfort. The rain won't hurt it." The men snatched up their possessions and carried them into the gloom beyond the gaping mouth of the cave.

They'd reached their safe haven before the storm broke, but not by much. The wind was already whipping up, and now the first sheets of rain were sweeping in from the sea.

"Make the fire there," Conn said, pointing to a low ring of stones well back from the mouth of the cave, a small fire-circle that had probably been used by sea-travelers for years beyond measure. "Look around you. There's plenty of dry driftwood for the fire."

"If it ain't completely dry, lads, we surely don't want it!" Alim exclaimed. "No sense in smokin' ourselves out. Gar, you check every single piece o' that wood before you allow it to be used, right lad?"

Once more Garluan performed Alim's bidding with his usual willingness. Without being asked, Maeldun came over and joined his childhood friend in selecting the wood and arranging the fire. Once the two lads got the initial flames going, they began to build it up slowly, piece by piece.

"Not a fit night out there for man nor beast," Diuran muttered, looking toward the cave's entrance.

"And which one are you, Master Rhymer?" Alim said with a grin.

"Right now, perhaps more beast than man," Diuran replied, holding his shirt up to his nose and taking a good whiff. "Whew, beast is right."

"You could go out 'n' give your stinkin' self quite a good bathe, you know," Alim said, pointing out toward the storm. "Don't believe there's no shortage of fresh bath water out there on this night, Master Rhymer."

"No, on this night I think I'll be perfectly content to remain more beast than man."

As the fire blazed up inside the cave, the rain poured down outside, creating a thick, smoky veil over the great opening to the cave. The warmth from the crackling fire and the smell of the wood smoke soon created a sense of comfort. It didn't take long for the air in the large cavern known as Fintan's Cave to become pungent with the smell of roasting meat and the fragrance of many unwashed bodies.

As their meal was winding down, Diuran the Rhymer borrowed Taman's small harp and began fingering a sequence of delicate chords. He looked about him at all his companions who were sprawled out in a variety of postures about the fire.

"Fintan's Cave," he said loudly to the group at large, while still playing chords on the instrument, "the place to which Fintan fled from all those pursuing women. Yes, here we all are in this hallowed and legendary place. I never expected to find myself here. Did you?"

"We won't be turned into salmon, will we Rhymer?" Celtchar said, his remark producing a handful of guffaws, the loudest coming from Alim the Wanderer. "Good one, lad," he muttered beneath his breath, "ya lovely piece o' excrement."

Garluan nudged Maeldun gleefully. "Did you hear that, Mael? Celtchar just made a joke! First one I ever heard from the guy."

"Gar, I think he might've been serious," Maeldun replied.

"By the Dagda, Mael, you could be right!"

"Yes, Celtchar," Diuran continued, though he was really speaking to the entire troupe of marineers, "this is indeed the place where Fintan was turned into a salmon. Would you like to hear the tale?"

His question was rhetorical. Of course they would like to hear the tale, even though most of them had heard it many times before. And so Diuran, his eyes now closed, began to sing a short version of the legend as he strummed his gentle chords:

"I am Fintan the White, I will not conceal it,
I was here before the Flood and here after the Flood –
From Cessair to Nemed to Amergin.
Yes! the tuneful Takings of Ireland I have seen every one.

We came from the East with Cessair on her boat,
The daughter of Bith, granddaughter to Old Noah.
Yes, we came with Cessair – fifty women and three men.
They were Bith and Ladra and the third was me.

The Voyage of Maeldun

We sailed first to Egypt, sailed onward to Spain,
We sailed through tempest and storm for nine days,
Were driven to Eire to The Meeting of Three Waters –
To where there's the mingling of the three mighty rivers.

Then Cessair divided her women in thirds,
Seventeen, seventeen, and sixteen in each.
Ladra went with sixteen, old Bith with seventeen,
But I was for Cessair and her choicest maidens.

When Ladra died, his women came to us,
Twenty-five to each; when Bith died on his mountain,
They all came to me – oh yes, they all came to me.
They were too many, too much, for one single man,
Even for me, I will not conceal it.

I fled from them all, sought refuge from their longings,
Fled here to my cave where they couldn't find me.
Then the Flood found us all, swept us all away.
But the Dagda took pity – I lived on as a fish.

As a salmon I survived beneath the deep waters,
No sustenance nor sleep for the full of a year,
Till the waters receded, the dry land reappeared,
And the green hills of Ireland belonged solely to me.

In time came the others, the Partholonians first,
Cursed and ill-fated, they soon passed away;
Then came Nemed the valiant, the Fomorians' bane,
Though the Sons of Nemed were not long for Eire.

The Fir Bolg came next, a wondrous people,
Though more wondrous yet were the Tuatha de Danaan.
But it was the Sons of Mil who won out in the end,
Stronger in battle, they vanquished the Men of De.

Yes, a long life befell me, from the start to the finish.
I have seen all the Takings, I will not conceal it,
A marvelous thing – from Cessair to Amergin.
I was here before the Flood and here after the Flood.
I am Fintan the White, a great noble sage.

Diuran, his eyes still closed, strummed a few more chords, then paused to look up at the assembled voyagers.

"Fifty women for one man?" Garluan said with a laugh. "I can think of worse ways to die!"

"Gar," scoffed Alim, "it'd take far less than fifty to finish you off, lad."

"That's what you think!" Garluan shot back. "I'll match my prowess with that of any man here."

"Who knows, Gar," the Master Mariner replied, "before this adventure is over, you just might get your chance to demonstrate that great wondrous prowess of yours." Alim's remark produced a lot of surprised looks.

"You aren't thinking of the Island of Women, by any chance, are you?" Conn Iron-fist asked.

"Ah, the Isle of Fair Women," Alim replied dreamily. "Of all the Western Isles, there's no place more wondrous. Happiest year of my life, that was. Exhausting, yes, but it were paradise on Earth."

"There's not *really* any such place, is there?" Diuran said.

"Was it all then just a dream?" Alim replied. "Well, perhaps it was. But if it were, it were a dream like none other I've ever experienced."

"It was a dream born in a vat of coal-black ale," Maeldun said harshly.

"Oh, lad," Alim replied, "and there I thought I'd made a believer out o' ya. 'Tis a pity, Maeldun, to see you still a-doubtin' me. It aggrieves this old heart of mine, it surely does."

"Some of those fifty women that chased after Fintan musta been pretty darn ugly," a lad named Dolb remarked. "Couldn't all o' them been beauties."

"That's as may be, Dolb," Alim said, "though it sure ain't that way on the Isle of Fair Women. Not a single one there that ain't absolutely a keeper."

"Master Mariner," said Garluan, "maybe we should just forget about this voyage we're making for Maeldun and head straight for that Isle of yours. Think you could get us there?"

"All right, then, that's enough of this idle chatter," Maeldun said with some heat. "Everyone of you, get yourselves some sleep. We'll have plenty to do tomorrow once the storm subsides. Marineer, the first thing we'll have to do is search for my brothers. We can go no further in this quest until we do. Is that clear to everyone? Is it? I hope to the Dagda that it is."

"With all due respect, Mael," Alim replied in a more deferential fashion, "I don't believe there's a shred o' hope for them lordlings. If they were out on the sea when the storm caught 'em, then them lads' chances are just about nil. Less'n the Dagda turned 'em into salmon."

"We shall go no further in this quest," Maeldun repeated sternly, "until we know their fates."

Conn Iron-fist was watching Maeldun intently. Up until this moment it hadn't been entirely clear who was fully in charge during the voyage — Alim, who knew the waters and the sailing of the craft? Conn himself, who knew weapons and planning and the waging of warfare? or Maeldun, the youth for whom this voyage had been undertaken? Now Conn knew it would be Maeldun. And that answer pleased him mightily. Maeldun had begun acting just as his father would have acted. And that pleased Conn mightily.

CHAPTER 8
The Rescue

The morning broke clear and fresh. The storm had scoured the skies and the azure-blue sea sparkled. Small whitecaps topped the waves. Alone, Maeldun climbed the high cliff above the cave and then stared off into the west. As far as the eye could see the sea was empty. Where were his brothers? Maeldun refused to believe they were dead.

A few moments later Garluan clambered up to join his friend. Maeldun's silence answered Garluan's unasked question. Garluan had no great love for Dris, Ronan, and March, but he felt his friend's sorrow nonetheless.

"Perhaps we could make a careful search along the shore," Garluan finally offered. "They probably sought shelter just as we did."

"Yes, we should do that. You, Celtchar, and Ferben go south. I'll send Dolb and some others north, though I doubt if they could be north of us. If you don't find them between here and Cenn Bera Point, get back here as quickly as you can."

While the search parties scoured the shoreline in both directions, other mariners readied the vessel and re-stowed their provisions and equipment. Maeldun sent a group of four to refill their water pouches and look for fresh game. They returned with the pouches brimming with a brace of freshly killed hares.

At mid-day a disconsolate Garluan returned. When Maeldun looked at him hopefully, he just shook his head. The other searchers had had no better luck.

Before setting off again in the curragh, Maeldun gathered the entire party in a wide circle about the long, slender craft. They all stood there together offering up their silent prayers for the spirits of Maeldun's foster-brothers. Despite the fact that few of them had liked the brothers, the ties of clansman to clansman ran deep.

"So today is the day, Weapons Master, that you think we should reach the place where we may find my mother?" Maeldun said to Conn. The two stood apart from the others at the boat's prow.

"Almost certainly. The little island lies in a wide shallow bay just beyond that headland." Conn pointed toward a dark finger of land extending into the sea well to the north of them. "We're leaving Munster now and entering the coastal waters of Connachta, roughly halfway up Eire's western shores. My own home and clan lie two more days to the north, the place where your father and his brother and I came of age together."

"Why have you never gone back?" Maeldun asked. Conn remained silent for a while before answering the youth's question.

"Pride, I suppose. Or maybe just sheer stubbornness. They didn't want to forgive me, Maeldun, for not dying alongside the others. And I didn't want to forgive them for not forgiving me. They turned their backs on me, so I turned mine on them. I, who had been your father's closest, most loyal friend

— would never have failed him, not if anything else had been humanly possible.

"No, Maeldun, some larger force conspired against me. I've always suspected, always feared, that it was the god of the Christians. I greatly fear that god, Maeldun. Your father made only one mistake in his entire life, but he paid for it dearly, thanks to that god. I will confess to you that I wish we were not going to seek your mother. I do not know what will come of it."

"Conn," Maeldun said — no longer referring to his mentor as Weapons Master — "I think I understand what you are saying, I truly do. But I must speak with her. I must hear from her lips exactly what happened and hear from her lips why she did to me what she did. I mean her no harm, Conn. I do not believe that her god, however powerful and vengeful he may be, would deprive me of that solace."

"Maeldun, do not underestimate her god." Conn turned away from the youth and began moving toward the rear of the boat, where Alim stood gripping the great steering oar.

The day was drawing on when Celtchar suddenly let out a huge, indecipherable bellow that startled the entire crew.

"Lad, lad!" Alim cried out, "what's a-ailin' ya now, lad?"

"There!" Celtchar finally managed to articulate. He pointed off toward the southwest. All eyes followed his gesture.

"What is it?" Diuran asked. "I don't see anything at all."

"Oh, it's something all right," Alim replied. "Like as not it's one o' them dratted whales. If so, we surely do need to be steerin' clear of the dratted thing — the stinkin' piece o' shite!"

"No," Maeldun said in a loud and commanding voice. "Sure as anything it's my brothers. Alim, I want you to steer a course straight for them. Do it now, Alim."

"No, Alim!" Conn exclaimed. "You must steer away from them. Master Mariner, we cannot place the craft in jeopardy at this point. Whether it's a whale or just some flotsam, either way it poses a grave danger. We must not take any chances with the boat."

"Alim!" Maeldun shouted out, countermanding Conn, "I *order* you to steer for them!"

Many a man began to cast glances back and forth between Conn and Maeldun. They hadn't expected the situation to turn into a showdown.

"Yes, Alim," Garluan said so loudly that all could hear. "Do as Maeldun says. And if you don't, then I certainly will." Garluan had already slipped quickly to the back of the boat. Now he stood tall and unyielding beside Alim, prepared to wrest the great oar from the mariner's hands if necessary.

"Mael," Alim said with resignation, "it be your funeral, lad. Though the Dagda knows, it may prove to be ours as well."

So Alim chose to obey Maeldun and ignore Conn. Conn Iron-fist, standing alone in the prow, his arms crossed upon his muscular chest, stared blankly out at the tossing sea.

For more than an hour the rowers bent to their oars, the rough seas working powerfully against them. They substituted oarsmen regularly now, and even Conn took a turn at an oar, venting his anger at Maeldun through physical exertion.

As they drew nearer, it became increasingly clear that what Celtchar had spotted was not a whale. Nor was it a clump of dangerous flotsam, as Conn had proposed. It was a small, upturned vessel. It was a coracle. And there was only one boat it could be, the one in which Maeldun's foster brothers had vainly pursued the larger curragh.

"I don't see anyone," Diuran said.

"No hope in the world for them lads now," Alim ventured, "not in these cold, rough seas. Them lads is goners."

But Alim was wrong. As they got closer, they could see that three figures still clung to the capsized boat. Somehow, the young men had managed to secure themselves to the boat with ropes. Now, though, they showed no signs of life. Their inert forms rose and fell with the movement of the boat.

"Come on, Gar," Maeldun said. And without saying anything further, he was over the side of the curragh and swimming toward the small boat. Garluan was right behind him.

"We need the rope!" Maeldun cried, "toss us the rope!" As he worked frantically to free Dris, Garluan was doing the same for Ronan.

"Hurry up, you pieces of shite!" Garluan cried out. "I'm freezing my arse off out here!"

One by one the three apparently lifeless forms were hauled into the larger boat. Their sodden clothes were stripped off and their pale and blue-ish bodies wrapped snuggly in the mariners' own cloaks. Maeldun and Garluan shed their own cold, wet garments also, their teeth chattering, their bodies shivering.

"Here's somethin'll perk ya up in no time, lad," Alim said. He held out a small clay vial to Garluan. "But take only a few drops lad, only a very few."

Ignoring Alim's advice, Garluan took a stiff pull at the small vial, then coughed and sputtered. "Alim, what in the name of the Dagda! You trying to kill me or something?"

"Always works wonders, that stuff does."

"What in the name of the Dagda is that stuff, Alim?"

"Oh, that's for me ta be knowin' and for you not ta be knowin'. Besides, ya might not like findin' out what it really is."

"Alim, my head's all a-swirl," Garlaun said. "What have you done to me, Wanderer?"

Alim just grinned and shrugged his shoulders. "I told ya ta only take a very few drops, did I not?"

All the while Maeldun and Ferben and Dolb had been attending to the brothers, each one trying to rub some life back into their semi-frozen bodies. Eventually Alim came over and poured a few drops of his magic elixir into the mouths of each one, causing them to make a visible start, which everyone took as a good sign. In Dris's case, he even flickered his eyes for a few moments.

"Wonder of wonders," Alim finally declared. "I do believe them lads is going ta make it after all. I never woulda believed it. The gods musta been lookin' out for them pieces o' shite."

"Perhaps so," Maeldun said. "But now it's us who need to look out for them. We all of us need to do that" — and he cast a look in Conn's direction — "just as we all of us need to look out for each other. We must work together for the good of everyone."

As the dark of evening settled about them, Conn Iron-fist and Diuran the Rhymer stood together at the boat's prow, out of the hearing of the others.

"You don't seem so happy, Weapons Master," Diuran said. "You're not pleased that we rescued the young princes?"

"Diuran," Conn said, "do you remember the druid's prophecy? Do you remember what Crimthain warned us against doing?"

"I'm not sure what you're referring to, Conn."

"So you don't remember, hmm? Then let me remind you. He told us we had to take seventeen in our company. He warned us against having any other number. He said seventeen, Rhymer, no more, no less. And now with our rescue of the young princes, how many do you think we have now?"

"I'm no mathematician, Conn," Diuran said, his right hand slowly massaging his chin, "but I see what you mean. Yes, now you mention it, I recall that Crimthain was rather insistent on that point. So Conn, what do you suppose will be the result of our having taken in the young princes? Do you think there will be dire consequences?"

"I'd been afraid of provoking the god of the Christians, Rhymer. Now, I fear, we have provoked our own gods as well."

"Hmm. I very much hope you are wrong, Weapons Master."

"Not nearly as much as I do, Rhymer."

CHAPTER 9
At Sea

For most of them it was not a pleasant night. Rocked by the motion of the sea, a few slept fitfully but most not at all. In the wee hours, Maeldun stepped carefully through the men as he made his way from stern to stem. He glanced at each of them as he passed, these men for whom he cared so deeply. The one sound sleeper amongst them was Celtchar, whose basso profundo snores threatened to awaken spirits from the vast and briny deep. Maeldun grinned down at Celtchar, a lad so quiet by day and so noisy by night.

Conn Iron-fist, as had become his habit, stood alone in the prow staring out at the night.

"Weapons Master," Maeldun said, "do you mind if I join you?"

"Why should I not?" Conn replied guardedly. "This craft, I believe, is entirely yours to command."

"Conn, I am sorry you are angry with me. I wish you weren't, though I understand why you are. Indeed, I may understand your anger even better than you do. Still, sir, if there is one person here who knows why I had to try and save my brothers, it should be you."

Before replying, Conn reflected for a moment on Maeldun's words. "There is no comparison between the man your father was and the men your foster brothers are. None, Maeldun, none."

"I'm sure you are right, sir — but they are still my brothers. Despite their faults, I love them as a brother should love his brothers. Conn, I know how much my father meant to you — far more, I suspect, than my brothers mean to me. But Weapons Master, although I didn't know him, I love my father also. And I, too, wish more than anything to avenge his death.

"Anyway, sir," Maeldun continued, "my desire to rescue my brothers was as much your fault as mine."

"How do you reach *that* conclusion?"

"You told me that you wanted me to grow up without hatred in my heart. In regard to that, sir, I am afraid that you succeeded. So in spite of their faults and in spite of all the shabby things they've done to me, I can only love my brothers."

"Then perhaps a little hatred hidden in the depths of one's heart may not be such a bad thing after all," Conn grumped.

"Weapons Master, you do not believe that. You taught me well, and for that I am deeply grateful. Your opinion of me matters, Conn, and I do not want you to think less of me because I did what I felt I had to do."

For the first time during this exchange, Conn looked directly into the younger man's face. Now, in the moon's dim light, the hint of a smile lurked on Conn's face.

"Maeldun MacEoin," the older man replied, "you have no right to be so much like your father, a man you didn't even know. I wonder how that can be."

"Perhaps it's because I once had a teacher who shaped and molded me in a certain way," Maeldun replied. "Perhaps he was trying to shape me in the mold of a man he'd once known and loved."

Conn said nothing more. But before turning away, for a brief moment he gripped the younger man's shoulder with his large, worn hand.

As Maeldun made his way back through the craft, he felt someone clutching at the hem of his cloak. It was Dris.

"Mael," he said in a harsh whisper. "Water? Please, could I have some water?"

Maeldun lifted a drinking pouch to Dris's lips and watched as his foster brother drank thirstily. "Not too much," Maeldun cautioned. "Go slowly, brother."

"I'm cold, Mael," Dris said, "cold."

Maeldun took off his own cloak and draped it about Dris's body. "Is that better?"

"Thank you, brother," Dris said. "Yes, that's a little better."

"Try to sleep, Dris. The sun will be up in a few hours. Then all of us will be warmer."

The morning found the curragh located much farther to the south than any of them had expected.

"Those sea anchors of yours, Alim, doesn't appear they did us a whole lot of good," Conn said to the master mariner. "We've moved a great distance during the night, and not at all in the right direction."

Alim was studying the distant shore to the east and the jagged outlines of a pair of islands off to the west. "Yeh, we have indeed. Not my fault, though, nor that o' the killicks. It's this dratted current. Been workin' against us from the start."

"What do you mean?"

"It weren't the boat that moved a far distance during the night, it were the sea that moved a far distance."

"Alim, you aren't making sense."

"We stayed right where we was, relative to the sea. But our

whole section of the sea went and moved south on us. There's this powerful current, don't ya see, flows all down the western side of Eire. Kinda warmish, too, which prob'ly 'splains how them lads survived for so long. The shaggin' thing pushed us back down to near where we started out. We'd best get ourselves out of it if we hope to make any headway."

"How can we do that?"

"We'd best be headin' off toward the west. Seems kinda illogical, I guess, headin' off ta the west before headin' north again. But once we get a bit farther off shore, maybe we can get ourselves outta this dratted current we be fightin' against."

"Maeldun, what do you think of what Alim is saying?" Conn asked.

"I have confidence in our master mariner," Maeldun replied. "And if he's wrong, we can always use him for fish bait."

Alim squinted his eyes at Maeldun. "Fish bait? That were meant ta be a joke, weren't it laddy? I really hope that were meant ta be a joke."

"A joke? Alim, I don't hear anyone laughing." Then from the back of the boat came Celtchar's massive bellow, which prompted the laughter of every other man.

"Okay," Maeldun admitted, "yes, it was mean to be a joke."

"Fish bait," Alim scoffed. "Har, har — ya scuzzy shagger!"

"Step the masts!" Alim shouted, and the men began preparing the two short masts and their sails. The boat's nose was pointed in a westerly direction.

Standing in the prow, Alim whispered down to the oculi, the pair of eyes he'd painted near the front of the craft. "You be seein' good, now, ya hear me? I be countin' on ya, my lovelies. You be keepin' a sharp watch out for us." He reached down and patted the side of the boat affectionately.

Conn stood at the steering oar, directing the boat toward two jagged islands that loomed up ahead. The off-shore breezes blew steadily and the craft gathered speed, even without any of the oarsmen, who were grateful for the respite.

Ahead to the left was an island of many rocky peaks that almost looked snow-covered. "That be the Island o' Birds," Alim said. "All that white ya do be seein', ain't nothin' but bird droppings. Can't land on the Island o' Birds. No place safe ta do it." As the boat drew nearer, it became clear that the island was encircled by a dark and swiftly moving cloud of birds. The noise of the birds came across the water to them in a great cacophony of sound. "Noisy buggers, them gannets," Alim said. "They surely do like that island, and I surely do not know why."

Ahead and to the right was an even larger island, this one looking like a single towering peak, though as the boat got nearer it became apparent that there were actually two high peaks, the higher one looming up directly behind the lower one.

"What's this island called, Mariner?" Garluan called out. "Have you ever set foot upon it?"

"That there's the Great Green Rock," he replied. "I been to it just the one time. And that were more'n enough. Went there searchin' for water. Didn't find a single blessed drop. Not one. No springs or streams on the worthless dratted thing. Had ta settle for eatin' raw birds' eggs. Them birds up there, they lay 'em in holes and hollows all over the island. Tasted pretty terrible too, but better'n starvin'. That was when that cursed devil wind came a-chargin' after me."

"Devil wind?"

"Aye. Howlin' and yowlin'. Chased me right off the island. Didn't want me there, I s'pose. Made that pretty clear. I think that island is one o' them places that's 'specially sacred to the ancient gods. I think I went to a place I weren't s'posed ta go. Chased me right outta there. But here's the thing. Once I was back out safely upon the water, all's a sudden a great double rainbow broke out ahead o' me in the western sea. I always believed those gods up there was biddin' me farewell and a safe journey. Nice of 'em, I suppose. After scarin' the shite out o' me."

"I think I see someone up there." The speaker, surprisingly, was Celtchar.

"What's that, lad?"

"Yes, Celtchar's right, up on the right-hand peak," Garluan said. "You can just make out a tiny figure. Looks like he's doing something. Hauling stones, I think. See beyond him? Looks like he's building a wall or some such thing."

"Might be one o' them old gods," Alim said. "That, or one o' them strange Christian folks they call hermits. I run inta a few o' them shaggers from time ta time also. Touched in the head, every one o' them."

"It must be a man," Conn said. "It surely isn't a god."

"Why mightn't it be a god?" Garluan asked.

"Do you think a god would actually spend his time moving rocks or building a wall? Seems unlikely to me."

"Well, not necessarily," Diuran said. "I know several stories in which the Dagda did quite a bit of rock moving."

"Rhymer, I do not wish to hear you say such things. Gods do not carry rocks. So why don't you just hush up about such things, eh?"

"Weapons Master, I have a feeling you are just a little bit touchy today on the subject of the gods. I hope there is no special reason for that."

"Diuran, I do not wish to hear you insult the gods. If you must speak of them, do it with reverence."

"Conn Iron-fist, I promise you I will tell no stories in which the gods carry rocks."

"If you do," Conn said, "you may find yourself becoming fish food."

"Weapons Master, I have a feeling that you are not making a joke."

It had been a day, a night, and most of a second day since the crew had set foot on dry land, and the prevailing mood grew gloomier by the hour.

"Alim," Maeldun said, "do you think we can find any place where we could disembark? We are all in need of it, and none more than my brothers. Attending to them on land would be far easier."

"There do be a few islands a-northwards of us, Mael, but actually findin' them tiny pieces o' crap is another matter altogether."

"Do your best, Alim. My brothers are suffering now. If we have to spend another night at sea, we'll all of us be suffering."

"Mael, lad, ya best get used ta the fact that the life of a sea-wanderer is a life full o' suffering. Ain't no two ways about that, sir."

"Well, do whatever you can. I know you aren't a miracle worker, but at this point pretty much any dry land would do."

"Not a miracle worker?" Alim muttered beneath his breath. "I'll have you know, Maeldun MacEoin, I've worked a few of 'em in my time, some o' them pretty impressive, too, if I say so meself."

With the craft now moving in a northerly direction, the oarsmen returned to their oars, their respite from toiling ended. They were fresh enough for the time being, but if they had to stay with it for many more hours, their reserves of strength would be dangerously depleted.

It was growing late in the day when the sea mists began rising about them. The mist, swirling and twirling in the soft breezes, soon enveloped the craft. Alim now manned the steering oar, appearing confident that he knew the direction in which they should be heading. Neither Conn nor Maeldun shared that confidence, both of them maintaining a grim silence as the oarsmen propelled the boat through the thick weather.

By turns the mist thickened and thinned; now and then glimmers of the late afternoon sun managed to poke through. Once again it was Celtchar who startled the crew with his excited bellow. "There! Look there!"

"What is it you see, Celtchar?" Diuran asked. "I don't see anything at all."

"See! See!" His finger pointed toward where there was a small break in the mist; everyone strained their eyes to see what it was that excited the lad.

"Aha!" sang out Alim. "Good on ya, laddy, the Dagda musta give ya one fine pair o' eyes. Well, lads," he cried out to the entire crew, "we do be in luck today, indeed we do. The gods are smiling upon us wayfarin' waifs."

Conn cast a doubtful look in Alim's direction but refrained from expressing his opinion about whether the gods were smiling upon them.

"Lads, that be one o' the most glorious islands of 'em all. Don't have the foggiest notion what it's a-doin' here. Sure shouldn't be here. But I ain't complainin' a-tall."

"So you recognize this little island?" Diuran asked.

"Aye, no doubt about it. It be The Fruitful Isle for sure. Ain't supposed ta be here. But I ain't complainin' one bit."

Half an hour later, as they were beaching the curragh on the soft, golden sands of The Fruitful Isle, the weary mariners felt their spirits soar. They'd reached a safe harbor and could look forward to a night on dry land. And according to Alim, this was a place where they could replenish their stocks of food and water.

"Master Mariner," Garluan asked, "is this some sort of an enchanted island?"

"Enchanted? Why o' course it is, Gar. It's the enchanted Isle o' Fruit. You see all them trees up there? They ain't nothin' but apple trees. And as for them apples, ya never did taste their like, neither."

"Who lives here, Alim?" Maeldun asked.

"Not nobody a-tall. Them trees just grows all by their selves. After supper, if ya wants, I can tell ya all about my experiences the one time I were here."

Maeldun, Garluan, and Ferben helped the three brothers disembark from the boat. Dris was able to walk on his own now, but Ronan and March still needed some serious assistance. The crew carved out comfortable hollows in the sand for the invalids, who before long were propped up there sipping on hot broth.

"Let me add just a little bit o' zest ta them bowls, lads," Alim said, squeezing a few drops of his precious elixir into each one. "There ya go, Dris. Now, that'll warm up your old bones for sure, laddy."

"Many thanks, Wanderer, many thanks," Dris said with a grin. He appeared to be well on his way to becoming his regular self again — for better or for worse.

"Why so glum, Weapons Master?" Diuran said to Conn. The two were sitting well apart from the others. The bond between the long-time friends remained as firm as ever, and the two of them took greater comfort in confiding with each other than in Maeldun or Alim. "Why so glum?" Diuran repeated. "All remains well, does it not?"

"Rhymer, do I need to remind you of the original purpose of our adventure? At this moment, sir, we are even further from achieving it than we were at the outset. What I greatly fear is that my misguided attempt to find Maeldun's mother has deeply offended the Christians' god. And now, by failing to abide by the druid's stipulations, we have offended our own gods as well.

"This quiet little haven we've found here may serve us well for tonight. But what then? Diuran, we have too many men for the craft and too few provisions. Alim says this strange island is not where it is supposed to be. And that can only mean one thing, Rhymer — we do not know where we are!"

"But at least we have a rough idea, don't we?"

"We had a rough idea when we passed the Great Green Rock. Now? Now, Diuran, it is anyone's guess."

"Perhaps I have more confidence in Alim than you have."

"Perhaps you do. You always have been a rather optimistic chap."

"I do believe, Conn, that it is always better to be hopeful. And at this point I am far from having lost hope."

Conn Iron-fist smiled grimly at his friend. Then, reaching out toward Diuran, he placed his huge hand on his shoulder and gave it a gentle squeeze.

"Remember when you said it might be time for you to broaden your horizons a bit?"

"Yes," Diuran replied, "I do remember saying those words."

"Rhymer, I have a strong feeling that you are just getting started."

CHAPTER 10
The Fruitful Isle

The mood of the mariners that evening was festive, their relief
at not having to spend another night at sea palpable. The air
on that late summer's evening was warm and pleasant, the fire
toasty, the drink they were sharing sharp and heady.

"So this island, Alim," Garluan said, "you say it's called
The Fruitful Isle? Is this really an enchanted island, Master
Mariner? How I hope that it is. I would love to experience a
truly enchanted island."

"Seemed that way to me, Gar, it surely did."

"I suppose it was quite a long time ago that you were you
here?"

"I was 'bout as young as you are now, Gar. About as green
and foolish as you are now. Early in my wanderings, it were.
Got blown here entirely by chance. I was surely in luck that
day, just as we are now."

"You were all alone?"

"Course I were. Not a big one for companions in them
days. It be nice ta have you fine young lads with me this time,
though. Nice ta have old Celtchar here ta do all 'o the heavy
liftin' for me, doncha know." The toad-like Celtchar beamed
at Alim with unconcealed affection.

"Anyways, on the night I got washed up here, I'll tell ya, my thirst was so great I coulda drained Gerg's Vat all by myself. Dry 'n' parched as a dragon's tongue, I were. Seven days, lads, seven whole days — that was how long I'd gone with nary a lonely drop ta drink."

"And for a sot like Alim, that's a really long time between drinks," Dris said with a chuckle. Ronan, who'd also been perking up, added his laughter to that of his brother.

Conn observed them warily. Their presence, he felt certain, boded ill for their entire endeavor. Alim also gave the princelings a bent-eyed look before continuing his tale.

"With nary a lonely drink 'o water's what I mean, o' course. It'd been all of seven long days since I'd escaped from that infernal Isle 'o the Giant Ants, and I'd long since run out o' anything ta eat or drink."

"Isle of the Giant Ants!" Ferben said. "What in the world is that?"

"I ain't a-talkin' 'bout that cursed place just now, Ferb. I be talkin' 'bout this here wonder-filled place. So's I'd 'preciate it if you could keep that mouth 'o yours shut tight for a bit, okay? — ya pitiful gobshite!"

"Sorry," Ferben said sheepishly. "Wanderer, please go on telling us about this island."

"This isle we be on, a wondrous fertile place is what it be. No people, no animals, but lots o' lovely springs and wells, and it be teemin' with the world's most glorious apple trees. Luscious ripe apples, shiny and golden. Sweet, juicy, inebriating apples."

"I was sure inebriating would come into it at some point," Dris remarked.

"Exhileratin's what I mean, young master Dris. Invigoratin'. Refreshin' and restorin'. Them words less objectionable to ya?" Dris just smirked in reply.

"What happened when you were here?" Garluan said.

"Had me the best dream ever," Alim said. "One o' them things they call a vision. I'll tell ya how it happened, if ya don't mind listenin' ta me without any more dratted interruptions." Alim paused and ran his eyes over the whole group.

"Master Mariner," Conn said, "you have our absolute attention. Isn't that right, Dris?" Dris, still smirking, nodded his agreement.

"Anyway, ya see, after I got myself all safely landed here, like we just done, a gentle misty rain began ta fall. Not no big storm or nothin', but enough ta send me in search of shelter. Trouble was, ain't no buildings on this island, ain't no caves, ain't a single cozy hideaway anywheres. Only thing there was was a little temple perched up there in the midst of the apple grove. When I found it, I wasn't so sure I should go inside o' it. Seemed like a holy place ta me. But I was gettin' thoroughly damp and chilled, so I decided ta go ahead and take a chance on it. Didn't want to offend nobody, but I was mighty tired and bedraggled, so I went in there anyways.

"I'll show it to ya tomorrow. As you'll see, it's got a dome-like roof all propped up by four stout columns, and inside of it a most beautiful mosaic floor laid out in a complex pattern, with blues and greens and cream-colored little pieces all a-makin' an intricate design. Right in the center of the floor, in shiny gold, is a shallow bowl 'bout six feet across. I hesitated only a moment before lying down inside that hollowed out place. That floor were hard for sure, but right then I weren't complainin'. And right there's where I fell into a most slumberous sleep. And that was when she come to me."

"Who did, Wanderer, who was it that come to you?" Celtchar couldn't help blurting out.

"Why lad, it were the Lady o' the Fruitful Isle, o' course.

No one else but she."

"What did she look like?" Celtchar asked, wide-eyed.

"The fairest skin you ever did see. The golden-est hair. The slimmest, most elegant bare arms. The most beauteous green eyes. The dasslin'-est smile. Her voice were soft and low. Her shimmering blue gown was a-clinging to her perfect, slender body."

"What'd she say?" said Celtchar, clearly entranced by Alim's description.

"Now here's the most strangest part of all," Alim said. "She told me she'd been waiting for me. She called me by name and said she was the one who'd drawn me here. She said she'd been waiting for me for a long time and was glad I'd finally come.

"So I asked her who she was and why she wanted me. She said she were Argante, the Lady of the Fruitful Isle, where she lived with her eight sisters. She told me they was the nine goddesses of fertility. They was the ones who planted all them apple trees. This was their sacred isle and their sacred grove, yet the apples were intended for the good of all. When you eat my apples, she said, you will be partaking of me. My spirit lives in every one o' them apples. If you take my apples along with you on your journey, you're takin' me right along with you.

"I told her I'd be delighted ta take her along with me. She laughed when I said that, and her laughter was like the tinkling of little silver bells. Then she told me to lie my head back down and to sleep the sleep o' the just. When I did, I fell into the deepest sleep o' me life. And when I awoke in the dawning, I never felt so refreshed in me whole life. First thing I did was pick me an apple and eat it. At the very first bite, I thought I heard the gentle tinkling of bells far off in the distance.

"The rest of the day I wandered all about this little island, but weren't nobody else here. I gathered me up a big bag o' them apples, and filled up all my water containers. The next day I headed on out ta sea, though when I got out a ways, I turned and stared back at the Fruitful Isle. My heart told me ta go back and ta never ever leave this blessed place again. But the great sea god Manannan had other plans for me that day. So, this is the very first time I ever did get back here."

"Did you ever see the lady again?" Celtchar asked.

"Only every time I bit inta one o' them apples, laddy. Every time I did that, that's when I seen her — in my mind's eye."

"That's a remarkable yarn, Wanderer," Dris said with a chuckle. "After hearing that yarn, I think I'll just excuse myself from the company of all of you fine folks and go and sleep inside that little temple, just like you did. I think that's definitely the right place for me." Dris began to raise himself up from his sandy hollow as if he really intended to do that.

"You can just set yourself right back down, young sir," came the commanding voice of Conn Iron-fist. "No one's going anywhere this night. In the morning, we'll all go together and have a look at Alim's temple."

"Yes," Dris replied, "I think I'll just set myself right back down again. Far be it for me to desert such fine companions on a lovely night like this one."

As the whole company settled down to sleep, Taman played gentle tunes on his harp, humming along softly as he did.

In the dawning, after the mariners had roused themselves from a much-needed night of sleep, Maeldun sent some of them off to gather apples, some to fill their water pouches, and others to scour the little island in search of fresh game. In the meantime Alim, with the help of Celtchar and Garluan, busied themselves preparing the boat for their departure.

In less than an hour all the mariners had returned, their tasks completed, though those who'd sought game came back empty-handed. Alim had been right. The apple trees were the island's only living things.

"So ya wants to see the temple, does ya?" Alim said to Conn and Maeldun. "If ya do, then you'd best come on with me now."

"Yes, we surely do," Maeldun replied. "And if there is a way for us to express our thanks to the Lady of the Isle, we certainly should. How can we do that, Alim?" Alim merely shrugged.

"We must do it with song," Diuran said. "We must offer the Lady a hymn of praise and thanksgiving."

When Diuran glanced over at Conn, he saw his old friend smiling and slowly nodding his agreement. Clearly, there was nothing Conn wanted more than to keep on the good side of the gods and goddesses.

This time, feeling it would be safe to leave the boat unguarded, the entire company tramped up the little hill behind Alim. It was only a mile or so to the structure that Alim called the Temple of Argante.

There, in a small clearing in the midst of the apple trees, stood the tiny building, its dome-like roof supported by four stout, stone pillars, just as Alim had said. The mosaic floor and the golden basin in the center of it were also as Alim had described them. But there was one thing there he hadn't told them about. Positioned just a little behind the basin was a low, black marble table. On top of it stood a small carven figure of a lady. In her hand she held a golden bough bearing three greenish-gold apples. The statuette seemed to be made of ivory, though the branch and apples appeared to be made of gold and other precious metals.

"No one is to go inside," Conn ordered sternly. "This is a sacred space. We must treat it with reverence and respect."

At Conn's words March, the youngest of Maeldun's foster brothers, snickered. When he did, his brother Ronan chuckled softly. Dris, the third brother, didn't join them; but his eyes moved first to Conn's face and then to Maeldun's, a smile lingering on his lips. Dris was gauging their reactions.

Maeldun shot March an angry look. "Hush, brother," he said firmly. "If you don't share our feelings, you may go back to the boat now."

March, with a little shrug, lowered his eyes, making a small show of contrition.

Diuran the Rhymer took charge of the little ceremony. Using Taman's harp, he played a slow and graceful set of harmonious chords, humming along as he played. Then, when he began to intone one of the clan's familiar prayers of exaltation, all of the mariners joined with him in singing the lilting melody.

When they'd finished, Diuran turned and looked at Alim. "Master Mariner? Do you wish to speak?"

Alim, looking flustered and embarrassed, shuffled his feet. But working up his courage, he haltingly began:

"Argante . . . most bounteous goddess. It's me, Argante, Alim . . . but I guess you know that. Anyways . . . you once told me I was welcome ta come back. Didn't expect it ta happen, but here I am again after all these years . . . . Sure do love this little isle of yours. Hated ta leave it before, and I'll be hatin' to leave it now. Guess I'll hafta . . . . Most bounteous Lady, I never did forget that wondrous vision you so kindly did give me . . . sure was a grand and glorious thing. Always be grateful for it. And for all these here wondrous apples o' yours. Best ones ever, dear lady. But I guess you know that. Anyways, I'll always be grateful to you and to your sisters. Thank you, most bounteous, most beauteous goddess . . . with all my heart, Argante, I thank you."

As Alim's words died away, the mariners stood there in silence, their heads bowed. Then, when Diuran began chanting one of the clan's traditional benedictions, once more all the mariners joined their voices with his in singing the plainsong.

Their orisons concluded, the mariners began trooping back down to the boat — all but one of them. March, the youngest of Maeldun's foster brothers, was the one bringing up the rear; but as the others disappeared from view beneath the apple trees, he gradually hung back, then halted. Believing himself alone, he quickly reversed course and headed back up the hill toward the little temple.

Pausing for a moment, March stood in silence on the threshold of the temple, his eyes fixed upon the little ivory statue of the goddess which sat upon the low black altar. Slowly, he began to advance straight across the mosaic floor, skirting the sunken golden bowl and approaching the altar. He stood there just for a brief moment before reaching out toward the object of wonder.

But before he'd grasped it, he felt a powerful hand suddenly grip the back of his neck. March froze where he stood.

"You need to go on down to the boat right now," came the firm deep voice of Conn Iron-fist. "You don't want to delay our departure unnecessarily."

"No, I don't," came March's hoarse reply. "Yes, I shall go back down right now."

As March's footfalls receded into the distance, Conn Iron-fist remained in the temple. He stood before the low altar with bowed head, his eyes closed. His low, murmured words were intended for no one but the goddess.

Then, when he'd concluded his personal observances, he pulled out the small pouch he always carried beneath his tunic, opened it, and removed an object. It was a small silver brooch in the shape of a leaf. It was the twin of the one he'd left in the cairn with the body of Ailill MacEoin. Conn Iron-fist placed it at the feet of the small statue.

Walking slowly, he exited the temple and moved off through the grove of trees.

CHAPTER 11
The White Island

Alim, manning the steering oar, pointed the nose of the curragh toward where a dull sun shone through the morning's haze. Eire surely lay to the east, though how far to the east was anyone's guess. Twelve rowers, six on each side, plied their oars in earnest, sending the craft skimming over the water. The optimists amongst them expected to have sight of Eire's western shores by day's end.

Maeldun, standing beside Alim, saw the wizened little man cast a wistful glance back toward the small island now receding in the distance behind them. What Maeldun hadn't noticed, though Diuran the Rhymer had, was that Conn Iron-fist had cast much the same glance back toward the Isle of Argante.

"Don't tell me you're feeling nostalgic for the Fruitful Isle already, Weapons Master?"

"That peaceful place was oddly comforting, Diuran, and I will confide something to you. While I didn't have quite the experience that Alim described to us last night, this morning I did have a rather strange experience of my own."

"You had a vision of the lady Alim calls Argante?"

"Not a vision, exactly . . . but I think I may have heard her voice . . . though perhaps I was only imagining it. I suppose I must have been."

"And what did she say to you?"

"I don't quite know. The voice wasn't exactly speaking in words. More in thoughts. I suppose that doesn't make a whole lot of sense. And yet it seemed to me a very reassuring voice . . . telling me that everything would be fine in the end. I don't even know what that means. And yet I found it very comforting."

"Conn Iron-fist, I believe you've had yourself a mystical experience. I never would have expected it of you. Perhaps there is more to you than meets the eye, my dear old friend."

"I wouldn't have expected it of me either. Nor am I certain that it really happened."

"I feel rather sure it did, and I am glad that it did. I take comfort in the fact that it did." Conn Iron-fist shrugged his shoulders, still not certain what to make of his experience.

An hour later, after Maeldun had taken Alim's place at the steering oar, Dris, having completed his turn at the oars, came and stood beside him. He stood there in silence, carefully studying his foster-brother's subtle maneuvers. "It looks easy," he finally said, "though I'm guessing it's not as easy as it looks."

"It took me maybe fifteen minutes to get the knack of it," Maeldun replied. "So it'll probably take you about twelve and a half. I can show you a few basic things, and then with a bit of practice you'll have it."

"Mael, I know that in my entire life I've never done anything to deserve your kindness. And yet I feel quite certain it was you who forced the others to come and rescue us." Maeldun just shrugged. "We were stupid fools to try and follow after you like that," Dris went on, "though it felt terrible to be the ones who were left out. That was Conn's doing, I suspect, not yours." Again Maeldun just shrugged.

"Mael, I know I've never been worthy to be called your brother. But from now on I intend to do everything I can to make up for that. I hope you'll give me a chance to do that. I can't make you any promises about Ronan and March. I'll do what I can to keep them under control."

"Yes," Maeldun replied, "it would be good if you would."

"Mael, will you give me a chance to earn your good opinion? I hope you will. That matters to me a great deal."

Maeldun looked hard into Dris's eyes. "I don't know, Dris. There's a lot to be made up for."

"Yes, there is. I guess you know, Mael, that I've often lied to you. And there's a good chance I'll lie to you again. But right at this moment, brother, I'm being as truthful as is humanly possible for me to be."

Maeldun couldn't help laughing at Dris's words. "Perhaps you'll find being truthful a life-changing experience."

"Mael, it feels good already. I hope it doesn't become too much of a habit."

"Do you know the old fable about the little gray goose who wanted to become a snowy white swan?"

"That's not me, brother, I'm more of a realist than that. No, I'll settle for being the little gray goose who wanted to give his feathers a very thorough cleansing."

"That would be a start, Dris, quite a good start."

Near mid-day the mariners saw before them a huge flock of raucous sea gulls — diving and squawking and frolicking joyfully.

"Are we nearing the coast?" someone asked.

"Nay, lad, but it be good news of a different sort," came Alim's reply. "It be a runnin' of the fishies, that it do. Mackerel, more'n likely. Grab one 'o them nets there, Celtchar. Garluan, you grab one 'o them nets, too. Would ya look at all o' them lovely little pieces o' crap, eh? Start a-scoopin' them up, Cel, start a-scoopin' them up, Gar!"

Before long, the two lads were empting their nets of the squirming little sea creatures, while the other mariners were busy grabbing them and knocking their heads against the thwarts. The smell of fish became more potent in the craft than ever.

"We'll spit 'em and toast 'em and broil 'em till their juices do run!" Alim cried out. "Lads, it'll be a fish feast for ya tonight, I can tell ya that for sure."

"Is that Eire?" Celtchar shouted out. "Look there! Is it Eire?"

The afternoon was now drawing on, and as the hours had begun to slip by, the mariners' earlier mood of hopefulness had been slowing seeping away. Now all eyes strained to see what it was that Celtchar was seeing.

"Nay, laddy, nay," came Alim's reply. "But at least it's a place where we can find safe harbor for the night. I know this place, laddy, indeed I do."

Lying not far ahead of them, hardly rising above the level of the sea at all, was a low flat island. As they approached it, the reflection of the late-afternoon sun gave it an eerie, gray-white glow.

"What is it, Alim?" Maeldun asked.

"It be the White Island, young sir, naught but the White Island."

"And what is that, Master Mariner?"

"A grim and desolate place, young sir, though not a dangerous one. Leastways, not when I were there before."

The small island they now neared was nothing but a small hump of limestone that barely rose above the sea; it was a part of a great formation of stone most of which lay submerged beneath the chilly Atlantic waters.

"Leap out now, lads, and ease the craft forward!" Alim shouted when they were still making their approach. "Whatever ya do, don't let 'er scrape bottom! Before she hits, you gotta lift 'er up on your shoulders and carry 'er in."

All twenty men leapt into the water which was still nearly waist high. Working in unison, they raised the craft up and carried it safely onto the rough and gravely beach.

"Take 'er up above the tideline, lads, then set 'er down gently. That's the stuff, now lads, that's the stuff."

As Alim said, the island was indeed desolate. It was composed of long, flat, rectangular slabs of limestone. Only a few scrubby bushes grew up in the cracks where the slabs fitted together. There seemed to be no other living things present, aside from some small crabs scurrying about and tiny shellfish clinging to the stones along the shore. Fortunately, there appeared to be ample drift wood for their cooking fires. There would be no soft, sandy beds for the mariners this night, but at least they would be high and dry.

"Weapons Master," Maeldun said, "while we still have a bit of light, do you think you might put us through our paces? We've had no practice since our departure." Conn grinned, for he had been thinking the very same thing.

"Alim," Maeldun said, "you, Diuran, and Taman will be our cooks tonight. When we've finished our weapons session, we'll be famished, so I'm expecting you to make good on that promise of a fish feast you were nattering about. Right?"

"Kitchen duty, eh?" Alim grumped. "Me, the master mariner, placed on kitchen duty!"

"And it had better be most delicious, too," Maeldun said, "unless you want to be fish food."

"Har, har, there you go again with that fish food crack o' yours. Well, you lovely piece o' shite, wait 'til you taste the supper me 'n' the Rhymer 'n' the Harper are a-gonna cook up for you laddies. I can tell ya right now, it'll be better'n anything ya ever tasted before!"

"Taman," Alim barked out, "you go 'n' snatch up some o' them little crabs ya see a-scurryin' about. We'll toss 'em into the pot 'long with all the little fishies. Diuran, you go gather up some wood and get them cook fires all a-blazin' hot. I'll be fillin' up the pots with seawater and then I'll take 'er from there."

The cache of weapons, wrapped in thick, tarred canvas, was unshipped and opened — swords, shields, throwing spears, slings and sling balls, and a few other individual weapons preferred by various members of the party. Each mariner collected his own cherished items, glad to have the familiar feel of them once more in his hands. Many of their swords and shields bore colorful names bestowed by their owners or by their owners' forbearers: Answerer, Yellow Death, Bone-biter, Bloody Revenge, The Basher's Bane.

Stretching, running, leaping. When Conn sent the entire group of warriors to run the entire circumference of the small island along the water's edge, it was slender, long-legged Garluan who quickly outdistanced the others, his long copper-colored locks flopping up and down as he ran. As Maeldun completed his long lap, the second man to finish, there was Garluan standing calmly at their starting point, barely breathing hard, grinning at his boyhood friend.

"What took ya so long?" Garluan said.

"Needed to stop for a bit and attend to a need," Maeldun replied, huff-puffing as he did.

"Oh, yeah, sure you did. If you ask me, you are still full o' crap.

The others straggled in, with Celtchar bringing up the

rear. The thick, squat lad had worked up quite a sweat. "I ain't fast," he grunted. "But I can run all day, if need be." He could, too.

As the men cooled down from their run, Conn started them in on practicing their javelin tosses. Maeldun was the one who was deadly accurate in the short throws, Celtchar the one who excelled in the high, arcing distance tosses.

Finally it was time for sword practice, and so Conn paired off the warriors in what he believed would be well matched competitions. He himself took up his arms against one of the men supplied by the king, a battle-scarred veteran named Cleanth, who was probably the finest swordsman in the entire group. Garluan, Celtchar, and Maeldun faced off in their bouts with the three young princelings. For them it almost had the feel of the Lughnasa festival games all over again — only this time the weapons they used were real swords, not practice ones.

"Try not to draw blood," Conn had ordered the men, "but do everything but."

His order notwithstanding, not long into their match March flicked the point of his sword right across Garluan's cheek, eliciting a small cry of alarm from the slender lad and causing a stream of blood to course down his face and neck. "You bastard!" Garluan shouted. Then, deftly checking March's sword with his own, he used his free hand to punch the young lord right in the jaw, knocking him flat on his back.

March's brother Ronan, abandoning his bout with Celtchar, swung a swift sword-blow at Garluan's head. Garluan's quick reflexes and agility just barely saved him. Ronan's sword, while clipping a few red-gold locks from Garluan's stringy hair, made no solid contact. Conn was about to intervene when Celtchar dropped his own sword and tackled Ronan, slamming him hard to the cold ground.

"No fair," he said to Ronan, "that weren't no fair. Don't ya go doin' nothin' like that again, you hear me?" Ronan, firmly pinned to the ground by the squat, muscular Celtchar, grunted his agreement.

Conn, quietly observing these events, offered no comment. Yes, the young princes were likely to cause them a lot of headaches. But it was a relief to see the lads taking control and reining them in without his interference.

Despite their rousing round of exercise, the mariners' mood during their evening meal was still somewhat subdued, since all of them had hoped they'd be eating this meal safely back on the shores of Eire, not on some rugged, remote little speck of rock stuck way off somewhere in the cold, dark sea.

"So Alim, what is this place?" Diuran asked, after all their wooden bowls had been filled with Alim's strange, fishy concoction and all the mariners had begun to slurp it up. "Did you say it's called The White Island?"

"Don't know what it's really called or even if it has name. That's just my name for it," he replied, " 'cause the time I were here, when I spotted it from out at sea, it were glowin' in the bright sun like it were robed in the white gown of Aenghus himself. Seems a bit grayer this time, don't it. Suppose it must be the time o' day."

"Do you have any idea where we are, Wanderer?" Conn asked. "Do you know where this island is located in relation to Eire?"

Alim rubbed his scruffy chin, appearing deep in thought. "Well, sir, I have ta admit that everything seems a bit confused ta me now. The Isle o' Fruit, it really weren't where it were supposed ta be, and nor is this one. I would swear that all day today we rowed ourselves in an easterly direction. And yet as

I remember things, this here little isle lies farther off to the west than does the Isle of Argante. It's all kinda confusin'. We seemed ta be headin' in the proper direction, yet here we are, havin' gone a goodly distance in the opposite direction. Don't make a whole lot o' sense ta me. No, it surely don't."

"Fill your bellies, everyone," Maeldun said, "and then maybe we'll all feel a little less grumpy about things. Mariner, while we're doing that, maybe you could tell us about that Island of the Giant Ants you mentioned a while back?"

"Ain't a pleasant tale, lad. Ya sure you wants ta hear it?"

"Tell it to us," Diuran said. "Perhaps I'll be able to take it and fashion it into a proper yarn sometime."

"You sayin' I can't tell no proper yarn?"

"Please tell us about the adventure you had there, Wanderer," said Garluan. "Don't worry about making it proper. Improper will suit me just fine."

"Har, har, Gar. Ya wants it improper, huh? Well, I hates ta disappoint ya, lad, but this here yarn ain't got a bit o' sex in it. Not like some others I could tell ya."

"Who cares anything about sex?" Garluan said with a grin.

"Well, maybe in time we'll get around ta that too," Alim said. Then, as the others continued filling their bellies as quietly as they could, Alim started in on his tale.

CHAPTER 12
The Island of the Ants

"Yes, well, okay then, the Island o' the Giant Ants. It lies somewheres way off in the western sea. Don't know where, exactly. My little boat and me, can't say how we ended up gettin' there. Must've been the doin' of Manannan. He must've been with me that day, 'cause I were totally unconscious when we landed. Washed right up safe 'n' sound on the shore.

"My little boat, she sure were a good 'un. Bore me in all by herself, she did. When I woke up it were mid-morning and I were parched and famished. And right there beside me was a little stream purlin' and gurglin', flowin' right down inta the sea. I flopped me weary self over the side and splash landed inta that little stream, lettin' its lovely cool water soothe me weary body. I drank up a goodly bit o' water, too. Fresh water it were, and most refreshin'.

"After a while I felt a bit restored, so I collected my wits and looked about me. Behind the little sandy beach lay a long low line o' cliffs, all a-pocked with caves and caverns. Spottin' a little trail up through them cliffs, I clambered up atop the cliffs and had a look at what was out beyond. It were a bleak-lookin' land o' bushes and scrubby trees, amongst which was all o' these large, heapin' mounds of soil. Off in the distance

I spotted a whole lot o' animals a-millin' about. I figured they was probably herds of sheep or some such. I sure were wrong.

"I were in sore need o' sustenance, so I set about findin' somethin' ta eat. Right then I weren't fussy, so I settled on some raw shellfish and a certain kind o' seaweed I'd become accustomed ta eatin'. Hunger often provides the best seasoning for a humble meal.

"As I was finishin' up, I heard a little scrabblin' noise behind me. Thought it might be some crabs or somethin'. That's when I got the fright of me life. Not more'n five feet away was this hideous lookin' ant, just a-standin' there a-lookin' at me. He were big as a wolfhound and ten times as ugly. I froze right where I was. Good thing, too, for I don't think he was a-seein' me so good. But he were definitely smellin' me. These long feeler-like things on his huge ugly head were a twitchin' ta high heaven.

"Without movin' me head, I ran me eyes all about ta see if there were any more of the blamed things. Didn't see none. That were a relief. But me knife were a few feet away, lying beside the dish I'd been eatin' from. So I decided me best course o' action was ta do nothin' at all. Maybe I'd get lucky and he'd leave me alone.

"As slowly and quietly as I could, I lay meself down flat to the ground, hopin' he wouldn't be able to see me there. But the ugly piece o' shite heard my movements. Slowly, he approached me and then he were standin' right beside me. He brought his huge, ugly head right down a couple o' inches away from me. He had a pair o' large, bulgin', shiny eyes, yet I sensed he couldn't see me so good with 'em. I lay there still as a stone. And then he begun ta run these long, jointed feeler things all over me. By the Dagda, what scared me most of all were his massive, powerful-looking jaws. Sure didn't relish the notion of his glommin' on ta me with them things!

"Then he brought one of his legs — the shagger had six o' the bloody things! — against me side and began ta probe. He had a couple o' sharp claw-like things on the tip end o' his foreleg, too, and he was a-pushing them inta me! Good thing I had a thick, wooly cloak wrapped about me, but even so, they pierced me right good in the side. He were tryin' ta lift me up, the shagger. He nearly managed it too. If I hadn't a-clung for dear life on to a large boulder, I believe he'd a-hauled me away. Me side hurt like anything, but I weren't about ta cry out. Finally — thank the merciful Dagda! — he gave up the effort. He stood there a moment, a-thinkin', I suppose, then he began ta shamble off.

"When he was a ways away, I stood up and watched him go. As I watched him move, it seemed ta me he were leavin' little drops o' some kind of wet stuff behind him as he went. It took me a second ta figure out just what the shagger were doin'. But then I knew what it were — he were leavin' a trail o' bread crumbs, so ta speak. That feller were a forager ant. He'd discovered a very tasty morsel, namely me, and now he were off ta tell his pals. He couldn't move me by hisself, so he were a-goin' ta get help.

"My knees were still a-knockin' from the fright the feller give me. But I figured I had a bit o' time ta collect meself and get meself ready to leave this cursed place, once and for all. Me little craft, she needed a bit o' attention, and I needed to fill my water pouches and the like. All o' that didn't take me so long, though. So when I were pretty much ready to leave this dratted place behind me, I walked up the little trail the ant had taken and from the top o' those cliffs I looked out at the scrubby waste land out there. And what do ya suppose I seen?" Alim paused in his telling and looked around at all his listeners.

"Ya saw 'em comin'," Celtchar said. "What ya saw were a whole army o' them shaggin' ants, and they was a-comin' for ya."

"Ah, laddy, your old mam didn't raise no fool, did she. Oh yeh, laddy, that were exactly what I seen. So I turned about and hied meself right back down that little trail. I were anxious ta leap inta me lovely little craft and make my escape from that feckin' Island o' the Giant Ants.

"And now a-standin' there right in front o' me boat were another shaggin' ant! And this one were even bigger than the last. And he looked even meaner and uglier. This time I did have my knife in its sheath at my side, but I sure weren't a-relishin' no fight with this most horrible-lookin' brute — it seemed, though, I had no other choice.

"He sensed my movements and readied himself for me. I rushed at him, then dodged to one side as he reared up in front o' me. I were gonna gouge 'im good in his big bulgin' abdomen when I slipped on a dratted patch o' seaweed and slithered down onta the ground. That's when he came at me, but I managed to lodge meself beneath another large rock, one with a lower part that a-jutted out from it. I snugged meyself under there far as I could. Maybe he wouldn't be able ta see me; maybe he wouldn't be able ta reach under there and get ta me.

"There came them blessed feelers of his, a-probing under that protruding ledge o' rock. My knife were still in my hand, so I sliced one o' them off. I hoped that would send the shagger packin'. All it did was make 'im madder'n a hornet. That was when his huge, ugly jaws tried to wedge under the ledge and snag me, but thank the Dagda, there weren't quite enough room for 'em. Then he thought ta use one o' his forelegs, and that were a much more successful approach ta things. He jabbed them two sharp claw-like things right inta me again, this time causin' me to yelp ta high heaven.

"I sliced at 'em with all the strength I had left. The pain of my wounds musta give me something extra, 'cause I actually did manage ta chop one of 'em off. Now *he* was the one who were feelin' the pain! When I peeked out, he'd limped a little ways away. And that were me chance. I wriggled meself out o' me hidey hole and made a mad dash for it.

"A moment later I was a-runnin' and a-splashing meself and me dear little craft out inta the surf. I never looked back 'til I was a hundred yards out. When I did, there on the beach were a ton o' them shaggin' ants, all a-wrigglin' and a-wavin' their feelers at me. I guess I got outta there just in the nick o' time.

"I headed out inta the open seas and never did look back. I were another seven days at sea, and within just a couple of 'em I was all outta food and water. But the great god Manannan musta been a-lookin' out for me — or maybe it were Argante. For after those long, lonely, hungry days at sea, that were when I got blown right onta the Fruitful Isle."

Alim stopped talking and looked up. He'd been as absorbed by his tale as everyone else.

"My word, Wanderer," Dris said, breaking the silence, "that's quite some yarn. Ants as big as wolfhounds, eh? Well, Wanderer, I must say, I'm very glad you made it out of there alive. Just got yourself a couple of small wounds, eh? Not so bad as it might have been."

"A couple of small wounds?" Alim said. "Oh, yeh, I surely did get those." He lifted up his thick, woolen jersey and there on his side, just a little above his hip, were two round red scars, each about the size of the ball of your thumb. Puncture wounds for sure.

"Sure, sure," Ronan said sarcastically, "Dris is right that that's quite some yarn. Ants as big as wolfhounds? Sure,

Wanderer, I really believe *that*. What a load of shite! So tell us the truth, Wanderer, none of that really happened, did it?"

Alim ran his gnarled old fingers through his scraggily beard and scrunched up his face. He tilted his head to one side as if deep in thought.

"Did it really happen, lad? Well, I don't rightly know. Sure did seem like it happened. O' course, maybe it were all just some kinda strange illusion, some kinda strange hallucination."

"Well, I don't doubt ya, Master Mariner," Celtchar said loyally. "Not for a second, I don't."

Alim grinned at Celtchar and then went on. "Yeah, I suppose it coulda been some kind of a strange hallucination after all. But if it were, then how did I get this?"

Again Alim lifted his thick woolen jersey, and this time he reached for his knife sheath and pulled out an ancient-looking blade. "Whoops, wrong one," he said. "This were the one I used ta slice the shagger."

On his left side Alim wore a second knife sheath. This time he extracted a very different looking dagger. It's haft was made of bone but its tang was formed by a slender curving "blade" that was black and shiny and slightly serrated. Its tip-end was needle sharp.

"Here ya go, Ronan," he said, "see what ya think o' this." He handed it to Celtchar, who looked at it with eyes as big as the full moon, then handed it on to the next man.

As they were passing the strange-looking knife around the circle to Ronan, each of the mariners studied it and felt it. Then it was Ronan's turn to gaze upon it.

"Ever seen the like, laddy?" Alim asked.

"What is it, Wanderer?" Ronan asked, appearing taken aback by this unique weapon.

It was Celtchar who answered. "Why, it can't be nothin'

but one o' them ant claws the Mariner chopped offa that
shaggin' ant," he said. "Can't be nothin' but that." Ronan
continued gazing at it, saying not a word.

"That's how it looks to me," said Diuran the Rhymer.

"To me, too," Garluan said.

"That's certainly how it looks to me," Maeldun said.

"It can't be anything but that," Conn Iron-fist said. "But
lads, I think that's enough yarns for one night. All of you
get what rest you can. There's another long day of rowing
awaiting us in the morning. If the gods are with us, perhaps
by tomorrow night we'll be back in Eire."

CHAPTER 13
The Island of the Little Cat

Choppy seas greeted the mariners. The wind was whipping up and the sky to the west looked forbidding. Once more the curragh's prow pointed eastward toward where the sun shone but dimly. "We'd best be prepared to batten down," Alim advised. "Could be a pretty rough 'un today." And it was.

By mid-morning, many a mariner was spewing last night's fish feast over the side. Only the most iron-cast bellies managed to hold it in — Alim, Conn, and Celtchar, most notably. The others weren't doing so well, especially Diuran the Rhymer, who was sicker than a mangy cur-dog, his face greener than bog slime.

But by early afternoon the heavy sea swells finally began to subside and the harsh winds blew themselves out. The sea grew calm and bright sunshine emerged. Twenty greatly relieved mariners floated in a small, slender sea-craft, somewhere to the west of Eire.

For once it wasn't Celtchar who first caught sight of land; it was March, Maeldun's youngest foster brother.

"I thought it was just part of a cloud," he called out, "but it's a tower." The mariners strained their eyes in the direction he was pointing.

"Glory be," Alim said, "it's the white chalk tower." It was indeed a soaring white tower that loomed straight upwards into the clouds. "I seen it once before, but I never did set foot on that there island. For some reason I can't explain, decided ta give it a wide berth. Maybe we outta be doin' the same."

"No," Maeldun said, "we shall go and have a look."

As the boat drew nearer, they could see that the tower rose right up in the midst of a small city perched on a low hill and surrounded by a high set of ramparts. The city boasted a snug, calm harbor protected by a breakwater, and the mariners rowed right straight into it without difficulty.

The little harbor held no other boats or ships, and the quay appeared deserted. They moored the craft and climbed up onto the wharf. The entirety of the little island, even the small city at its center, seemed shrouded in silence. The place appeared totally deserted.

Leaving Alim and three other men with the boat, the mariners set off to investigate. They walked the city's cobbled streets, finer than any streets any of them had ever seen. These men who were accustomed to living in simple, circular, stone raths had never experienced anything like it before. All of the city's great houses were as white as snow. And all of them were entirely empty. It was the largest building, which stood right at the center of the city, from which the tall chalk tower soared up above all else.

They entered this grandest of buildings, gawking at its massive stone pillars and intricate carvings. They climbed its broad, steep staircases, pausing at a high window to gaze downward. There, far off in the little harbor, was their curragh and the men they'd left with it.

"Can I shout out to them, Mael? Would that be okay?" Celtchar asked.

"No," Maeldun responded in little more than a whisper,

"do not do anything to shatter the silence of the city. I don't know what all this silence means. But I think we should respect it. So please, no one speak in more than a soft voice."

Eventually the party ascended all the way up to the highest room in the tower. It was surprisingly large, a spacious chamber with a dome-like ceiling and four high, large window openings that looked out in four different directions. The dome-like ceiling was supported by four massive columns, each with incised designs — lozenges, chevrons, double-x patterns, and the like, though the mariners would not have known the proper terms to describe them. In the very center of the room were four pure white marble pillars, each about four feet in height and flat on their tops.

Arranged about the walls of the chamber were couches and low chests upon which lay fine quilts and shining garments such as the mariners had never before experienced. Up on the chamber's side walls were three rows of stone shelves, each of them displaying objects of great value and wonderment. On the lowest one were brooches, armlets, and rings fashioned of silver and gold, and on each of these objects, in whorls and interlacing designs, strange beasts and birds seemed to frolic, creatures the like of which none of the mariners had ever seen.

The second shelf held golden neck-torques, some as huge as the hoop of a cask, and all of them ornamented with precious stones of red or green or purple. Displayed on the highest shelf were magnificent weapons — swords, shields, spears, golden daggers, and other weapons the like of which none of the mariners had ever seen.

Maeldun, noticing the glint of greed now shining in the eyes of several of his companions, hissed in a loud whisper, "No one touch anything! These objects do not belong to us. Whatever else we may be, we are not a pack of thieves. The food, though, which is surely laid out for guests such as we, I think we may eat." Maeldun was speaking of the food spread out on several low tables close to the four high windows. On the tables were sides of roast ox, flitches of bacon, cheeses and breads, and varieties of things to drink, including mead, wine, ale, and other beverages the mariners couldn't identify.

"Ferben, I want you and Ronan to bear some of this provender down to our fellow mariners in the harbor. The rest of us will stay here and eat, and we will also spend the night here. You stay with the boat and the six of you, in pairs, take turns guarding it tonight." Ronan did not look especially pleased with the duties Maeldun had assigned him, but he complied without voicing any complaint.

The ensuing night remained as quiet as the day had been. The silence was not even broken by the cries of a night bird. For a while the moon shone brightly through one of the large windows, causing the chamber to glow with an even eerier light than that which they had experienced in the daytime. But sleeping upon the soft low couches beneath coverlets of finely embroidered cloth brought the mariners the finest sleep they had yet had since leaving Rath Murtagh. All of them awoke in the dawning even more refreshed than they had been a few days earlier on the Fruitful Isle.

And then, as they were rousing themselves from their slumber, into the room on its tiny little paws walked a cat. The startled mariners stood frozen where they were and watched. The little cat was the first living creature they had seen since landing on the island.

Ignoring them entirely, the little cat leaped up on top of one the four white pillars in the center of the room. For a moment it just sat there, then raising one forepaw it began to lick it with its eyes shut tight. Satisfied with that one, the little cat began on the other. The mariners watched in silence.

Then the cat leaped — from the top of the pillar on which it sat to the top of a second pillar. Soon it was amusing itself by leaping from pillar to pillar, all the while never showing any interest in the men in the room who gazed upon it. At one point it stopped again to lick its paws, before once again beginning the pattern of pillar hopping. The little cat seemed totally oblivious of those who were watching it.

"We should go now," Maeldun whispered to the others. "Our companions will be worried about us."

Moving slowly, the men began to troop from the room. It was Maeldun's foster-brother March who exited the great chamber last of all. As the others began to descend the wide staircase, March halted, waited a moment, then began to retrace his steps.

Back inside the chamber, he ran his eyes about the chamber walls, scanning all of the glorious treasures displayed there. Then, stretching up as high as he could reach, he just managed to grab hold of one of the most beautiful neck-torques on the middle row of stone shelves. Holding it firmly, he brought it down and eyed it greedily. With a swift movement he snugged it securely beneath his thick woolen over-cloak.

"March!" came Conn's stern voice from the top of the staircase. The weapons master had not spoken in the soft tones used earlier by Maeldun. "March!" he shouted again. "You must come now. We must all leave here together!"

At the sound of Conn's harsh voice, the little cat suddenly looked as if it had just awoken from a trance. Looking about, it spotted March still standing in the room. In the blink of an eye, the little cat sprang from atop the pillar straight at the human intruder.

The little cat, like a flaming arrow, shot right through the body of the youth. March, completely stunned by the creature's sudden attack, remained standing there for just a split second, then descended to the floor in a heap of gray ashes. March's entire body had been completely incinerated.

The little cat, with total nonchalance, leaped back up onto one of the pillars. It paused for a moment to lick one paw, then it began to play its game again, leaping from pillar to pillar, just as it had before.

Now all of the mariners stood at the threshold to the chamber, their eyes moving back and forth from the little cat to the pile of gray ashes. None of them dared enter.

The one who finally did was Celtchar. As quietly as he could, the stolid youth stepped into the room, bent down, and began to sweep up all that remained of March's body. He gathered as much of the ash pile as he could, enfolding it into his uplifted cloak. When he emerged from the chamber and out onto the landing of the great stairs outside, all the mariners stared at Celtchar and the ashes he was carefully cradling before him.

"Come," Maeldun whispered. "We have overstayed our welcome."

On the quay, the other mariners who'd been waiting nervously since daybreak were relieved to see their companions finally return.

"But where is my brother?" Ronan inquired. He glanced down the wharf behind them but saw no one else still coming. "You haven't abandoned him, I hope — though I wouldn't put it past you."

"No, brother, we haven't abandoned him," Dris replied. "March is here with us now." He pointed toward Celtchar, who was holding up the bottom edge of his cloak with both hands, cradling what was left of March.

Ronan, completely confused, gazed at the gray ashes. "*March?*" he said, in hardly more than a whisper. "How can that be March?"

"Scatter the ashes gently upon the water of the harbor," Maeldun ordered. "Then we must leave. We shall defile this place with our presence no longer."

As Celtchar began to sprinkle the little heap of ashes out onto the water, all of the mariners bowed their heads in silence.

"Go, little brother," Dris said softly. "Go and take your place amongst our ancestors."

Ronan, still in a state of shock, stared down at his brother's ashes as they dispersed upon the calm waters of the harbor.

No one else spoke, though all of the mariners remained standing in silence for another long minute.

"Now we must leave," Maeldun said softly.

"Yes," Conn Iron-fist agreed, "it is time that we did."

CHAPTER 14
A Persistent Pursuit

As they set out again, the morning was brighter than on previous days, and with a gentle breeze helping to push them in the direction of Eire, the mood of the mariners took a cheerful turn. Maeldun, too, found himself strangely unmoved by March's sudden demise. Of the three brothers, the devious March was the one he'd liked the least, and he strongly suspected that March had done something up there in the chamber atop the high tower to bring destruction upon himself. Maeldun, glad that March hadn't brought destruction upon them all, soon shared in the lighthearted mood of the others.

Believing they had a real chance of reaching Eire by nightfall, the joyful mariners raised their voices in song — mostly bawdy ballads, exuberant songs of lustful longings and sexual bravado. Sometimes they all sang together, sometimes two or three sang, and a few times just a single mariner raised his solitary voice. It was remarkable how many ribald songs they knew, and it was Alim who knew more of them than anyone else. The most vulgar one, unexpectedly, was sung by young Taman the Harper, whose high tenor voice possessed a remarkable sweetness, in contrast to the coarse, gruff voices of most of the others.

"Lad," Diuran said when Taman had finished his shockingly explicit song, "did someone teach you that song? Or did you make it up yourself?" Taman, blushing, just pointed his finger at his own chest. "Well, Taman," Diuran went on, "I must say, you've quite a vivid imagination for someone I thought was just an innocent, naive youth." Taman blushed again.

It had been ten days since they'd left Rath Murtagh, and while the men had by no means forgotten the sole reason for their undertaking — wreaking bloody vengeance upon the Reavers of Roonah — by this point in their voyage other kinds of desires had begun to intrude themselves upon the thoughts of most of them.

"I was thinking about Fintan," Garluan said during a lull in the singing. "About how he'd nearly died from exhaustion, after being forced to have sex with all those women. I was wondering about how many of those fifty women he'd actually pleasured before he decided he'd had enough and headed for the hills."

"Lad," said Alim, "ya've had sex on the brain ever since we set out on this little adventure o' ours. I don't s'ppose I can blame ya too much, though. But when ya gets ta be my age, it's a bit less o' a problem than it were before. Still 'n' all, I have ta admit that some o' them feelings never do go completely away."

"And what about you, Conn?" Diuran said quietly to his old friend. "Are your old bones starting to feel just as lusty as those of the rest of these lads?"

"Me?" Conn replied, ". . . feeling lusty? . . . Perhaps a small twinge here and there. And how about you, Rhymer? If you tell me about your desires, I'll tell you about mine."

"In that case," Diuran said, "never mind."

"Rhymer, why do I suspect the two of us are feeling much

the same things the rest of these lads are feeling?"

"Mael," Garluan said, "remember that girl named Etain? The one with the big — "

"The big eyes?" Maeldun said. "Of course I do. And without meaning to brag or anything, I have to tell you, Gar, that I gave her a night she'll never forget for the rest of her life."

"You never did!"

"Now that I think of it, I believe it was more than just one night."

"It never was!"

"Why do you ask about her? Was she someone special to you? Frankly, I felt like I could pretty much take her or leave her."

"That's about how I felt about her too," said the grinning, toad-like Celtchar, joining in the discussion.

"You didn't!" Garluan said.

"That's kind of how I felt about her too," Ferben said.

"You did not!" Garluan said.

"Gar, laddy," Alim said. "I think them gobshites are havin' a bit o' fun with ya."

"Bunch of bastards is what they are," Garluan said. "All a bunch of bastards! Etain's way too good for the likes of any of them."

"Garluan," Maeldun said, "Etain certainly was good. I surely can't deny that."

"Maeldun MacEoin, I never realized what a bastard you truly are!" said Garluan.

"I never claimed to be perfect," Maeldun said, grinning at his friend.

"Lads!" Maeldun shouted out, "it seems we all have some pent up energy that needs to find an outlet. I'll tell you what. Let's use that pent up energy to get ourselves safely back to

Eire. Then if we have any of it left over, perhaps we can find what we're all in need of and put that energy to even better use." Maeldun's words were greeted with enthusiastic shouts of endorsement.

"So lift up your hearts and lift up your oars. In a few hours, we may find ourselves back within sight of our land."

Indeed, it was only a couple of hours later that a voice cried loudly from the back of the boat, "Is that land? I think it is. It really looks like Eire!"

"It does to me also," cried a second voice. "Whatta ya know about that, mates? I think we're finally back — thank the merciful Dagda!"

The rugged, rocky cliffs of the west coast of Eire now rose up to view not many miles to the east ahead of them. A few high mountain peaks could be seen as well; perhaps they were some of the great Bens of western Connachta.

Along with all the others, Conn Iron-fist felt his spirits soar. Perhaps now they could get this mission back on track. Indeed, perhaps at last they were nearing their true destination.

"Mariner," Maeldun said to Alim, "do you recognize this stretch of coast? Do you have any idea of just where we might be?"

"Aye, Mael, that I do, leastways in a general sort o' way. I make it that we be a bit farther to the north than we should be wantin' ta be, but not by no vast distance, neither. When we get closer in, I'll see if I can't get a clearer notion o' just where 'xactly we might be. But let's not be gettin' too close in, neither, 'cause this bit o' coast is 'mongst the most treacherous for sure."

The rowers rested on their oars as the current and western breezes moved them closer in toward the land. Among the entire crew only Conn and Alim had had any previous experience of this stretch of coastline. Now each of them scanned the terrain for identifying features.

"Maeldun!" Garluan suddenly shouted, "I see another boat. It's closer in to shore than we are and a good ways to the south of us. By the look of things, I think they've spotted us, too."

"It's not just one boat, Gar," Dris said, "it's more than one. Three of them, I think. And they've all just altered course. They weren't heading in our direction before, but now they are."

"Quickly, lads!" Alim shouted. "To the north! We must fly to the north! Step the masts. Then row like mad men. Row like your lives depended on it — for surely they do!"

"Who are they?" Diuran asked Conn. "Do you recognize them? Is it the Reavers of Roonah?"

"From this distance, who can say? I think we are a good bit north of where they have their main camp, but they've always roamed this whole coastline without hindrance. It may not be them, but whoever it is, they're clearly pursuing us. They may view us as possible enemies; or they may think we are someone on whom they can prey. I hate to run from them like cowardly cur-dogs; but since they have three boats to our one, that's the wisest course."

The curragh shot forth, moving with greater rapidity than at any time thus far in their voyage. But the pursuing boats began moving more quickly also. The chase was on, and for the next hour the distance separating the pursued and the pursuers remained fairly constant. But as the long, slow minutes dragged passed, the boats of the hunters showed no signs of giving up. They seemed firmly committed to a relentless pursuit. Their boats, the mariners could now see, were smaller, each of them carrying about a dozen in their crew. And as those boats appeared to be less heavily-laden, it was now evident that, ever-so-slowly, they were gaining ground on Maeldun's boat.

Far into the afternoon the chase continued, with the pursuers very gradually edging closer. It wasn't until the sun had dropped behind a thick cloud bank in the west that the daylight finally began to fade. "Keep a-goin', laddies, keep a-goin'!" Alim shouted. "Give us a couple more hours and we'll evade 'em in the dark! The moon won't be risin' up 'til late tonight, thank the Dagda."

His words provided fresh encouragement to all of them. Now Maeldun, Conn, Garluan, Celtchar, and Dris, all of whom were fully rested, took over for several of the exhausted oarsmen, and with their efforts, the boat burst forth at a greater speed.

"If we can just get ourselves free o' them," Alim declared, "I knows of a harbor where we can tuck ourselves safely away. Once it's dark, we'll hafta back track ta get past 'em. That'll be the tricky bit. But if we can manage ta dodge 'em, then we can tuck ourselves safe and secure inta the place I'm a-thinkin' of."

"Sounds like a reasonable plan, Mariner," Maeldun said. "So let's see if we can't make that happen. Do you concur, Weapons Master?"

"Frankly, I don't," Conn replied. "My advice would be to keep on heading north. If they see us or hear us as we're trying Alim's backtracking maneuver, we'll have served ourselves up on a platter. No, Alim's plan seems too risky to me. But it's your decision, Maeldun."

"Then we shall follow Alim's plan," Maeldun declared. "If we do blunder into their midst, then we shall *fight*. There can't be many more of them than there are of us, and in the darkness they won't have an easy time of it, especially if we run into them before they realize what's happening." Conn shrugged, acknowledging the possible truth of Maeldun's words.

Finally full darkness had descended. At last sighting their pursuers, though they'd gained a great deal on Maeldun's craft, were still several hundred yards behind. When Alim gave him his hand signal, Maeldun adjusted the steering oar. The craft veered sharply to the right, its nose now pointed straight toward the not-so-distant shore. For perhaps a hundred yards they moved eastward, then turned sharply once more to the right, placing them on a course that ran parallel to the coastline in a southerly direction. Not far off to their left the mariners could hear the sound of the surf crashing on the rocky shores of Eire — a sound much too loud for comfort.

Only four oarsmen, two on each side, now rowed. Everyone else was armed in preparation for a possible fight. Most of them clutched their short throwing spears, a few held swords, and Garluan, the mostly deadly slinger amongst the party, cradled his sling and a leathern pouch filled with perfectly round sling balls.

"No speaking," Maeldun ordered in a low voice. "Absolute silence." The two pairs of oarsmen slowly raised and dipped their oars in unison, doing all they could to minimize the sound.

In the thick darkness to the west of them Conn sensed movement. And then all of them could hear the plash of oars as the pursuers' boats moved past them with great swiftness. Alim signaled for the oarsmen to cease rowing altogether, and in a moment's time four oars were poised above the water like pairs of still wings.

For nearly a minute, the boat floated in silence. No one dared breathe. The harsh sound of the surf crashing on the shore just yards away thundered in their ears.

"They're past, lads," Alim said at last, in a near-normal

voice. "Now we gotta hurry and give ourselves a good bit more leeway. Don't like the sound o' that surf a-tall." So once more Maeldun shifted the steering oar, pointing the craft's prow back toward the west and away from Eire's rugged coast.

"Now row, lads," he ordered, and six men settled to the oars on each side. Working against wind and tide, they began moving the boat a safer distance away from the shore.

"Alim," Maeldun said, "it's time for you to get us to this safe haven of yours."

"Aye, lad, indeed it is. We need ta keep headin' toward the south." Before long, the dark outline of the west coast of Eire loomed off to their left once more.

For roughly an hour they moved southward along Eire's treacherous western shores. It was when they finally saw the black shape of a headland rising up before them that Alim began to cackle.

"Har, har. Well, lads, I still got the knack of it, don't I just. Now I s'ppose it's safe to admit that I weren't absolutely certain 'bout all this. But now I truly am. Oh yeh, lads, we really are right where I'd been a-hopin' we was.

"So, let's be gettin' ourselves 'round this here point, and then we can take 'er right straight on in. That lovely little cove in there, she's got a shallow, sandy bottom, she has. We can take 'er right on in and right on up onta the beach without doin' 'er no harm a-tall."

As they headed their craft in between the two long, surrounding arms of the headland, the darkness of the land soon enveloped them. Before them, all was pitch black. The sea sounds within the small cove were softer now, and the boat glided in easily upon the calmer water.

The men leapt out into a gentle thigh-high surf and propelled the craft up onto the soft sands of the beach. It was low tide and the sandy beach extended for quite a good distance. "Keep a-goin'," Alim ordered, "keep a-goin' 'til we reach where the sands do end."

When they brought the craft to a standstill, all of them paused for a long minute to catch their breaths. And all of them felt a palpable sense of relief. Here they were at last, safe and sound, back on the terra firma of Eire.

"Well done, Mariner," Maeldun said, "well done indeed. If there's ever been a man who's earned himself the right to a very stiff drink, it's you."

"Well, Mael, when this here little adventure o' ours is all over and done with, I'll surely be remindin' you o' those very words you just now spoke."

Suddenly from out of the darkness, only a few yards before them, came a high, clear voice.

"Hello, Alim," it said. "We'd been hoping you might come and visit us. And we're glad that you have. We'll be pleased to offer you and your companions our very finest hospitality. Yes, indeed we will."

"Ah, shite," Alim muttered, " . . . ah . . . shite."

CHAPTER 15
An Unwelcome Welcome

"By the gods, Alim!" Conn snarled. "What have you done!"

"Ah, shite," Alim muttered again. "Weren't what I intended, Conn, weren't a-tall. Sorry, lads. Sure didn't mean for this ta happen."

The men on the beach stared straight into the darkness before them. They could just make out the vague, shadowy forms of a large group of people.

"I believe I recognize the voice of Conn Iron-fist," said the same high voice from out of the darkness. "I wish to welcome you, Conn Iron-fist. And I wish to welcome you also, Maeldun MacEoin. As it happens, I once knew your father.

"Diuran the Rhymer, you are certainly welcome too. Perhaps you will amuse us with your tales and songs. Dris, I have to say that you are an unexpected guest. I wonder how it is it that you have come to be a member of this noble company?"

The high voice continued to speak, offering welcome to each member of the party, addressing every one of them by name. As the mariners listened to the voice, it slowly dawned on them that this high, strong voice was a woman's voice.

How she knew who they were, they hadn't a clue.

"Alim the Wanderer, you've brought a noble company with you, an impressive company indeed. No solitary wanderings for you this time, I see. I have heard of many of your companions, Alim, and there is one amongst them I have met before. Conn Iron-fist, do you not remember me? We have certainly met before. Ailill MacEoin, he of the Sharp Edge, and his brother Luga, and you, Conn — the three of you once paid me a memorable visit. Do you not remember? Was it so long ago that you have forgotten?"

"It was *very* long ago," Conn snarled. "Unfortunately, I have not forgotten. So, how are you, Eithne? Still up to your old tricks, it seems."

"My old tricks? Oh no, Conn, not at all. I abandoned my old tricks years ago. I've long since replaced those old tricks with a whole new set of tricks."

"I'm sure you have."

As the two of them exchanged their banter, three small boats glided silently across the little enclosed bay. A moment later, the mariners could hear the sounds of those boats being pulled up onto the beach alongside their own craft.

"Led you on a very merry chase, did they, Cliona?" Eithne called out to one of the leaders of those boat crews.

"Indeed, madam. Had they not entered the little harbor, it's quite likely they would have eluded us altogether." The reply came in the voice of another woman.

Maeldun's men were now able to see that all the people in the boats that had pursued them in the lengthy sea chase were women. They now stood in a long line on the beach behind the mariners, blocking any possible retreat to their curragh. Even in the darkness, it was apparent that all of them were tall and powerful of build. These were not ordinary women.

"Maeldun," said the woman named Eithne, "you and

your men must come with us now. Leave your possessions in your boat, including your weapons. They will be safe. You will not need them, for we shall provide for your every desire. Should a situation arise when arms are needed — always a possibility in this dangerous world — then we will supply you with everything you might wish.

"But Alim, it might be a good idea for you to bring your knife. Not your ordinary one, I mean that rather special one you have. The rest of you must leave all your weapons behind, including your knives. But Garluan, perhaps you might wish to bring your sling and sling balls. None of us possesses your level of skill. An able slinger might prove of value during certain events that may soon occur."

"Madam, how can you know about my sling and sling balls?" Garluan asked.

"I know much about each of you, Garluan. I wouldn't have decided to bring you all here if I didn't know who you are and what you are capable of. You see, it turns out that we have need of you."

"And when we have fulfilled that need, Eithne, then I imagine you will quickly dispose of us." The speaker of those bitter words was Conn Iron-fist.

"Conn Iron-fist, did you not hear me when I said I had abandoned my old tricks? I am not the person I used to be."

"I'll believe that when I see it," Conn muttered.

"As will I," came the sullen voice of Alim.

"Come," Eithne said, an order rather than an invitation.

The shadowy shapes before them began to move off in the darkness, and as they did, the women behind them began chivying the mariners off the beach in the direction of a path that ascended into the darkness. Reluctantly, the men, now unarmed, did as they were expected to do. They seemed to have no other choice.

The path they trod ascended a narrow defile. As the men proceeded up the steep trail, with large troops of women both before and behind them, they could hear below them the plashy sounds of a stream flowing down toward the sea. In the darkness they brushed against the leaves of large ferns growing on each side of the path; and when they'd progressed higher up the valley, the softer ferns gave way to thick clumps of gorse and heather. As they neared the top of the valley, a thin slice of moon was just appearing above the eastern horizon, providing only a small amount of illumination.

After trekking for perhaps another twenty minutes, they crested a final rise in the trail and looked down upon their destination — a group of round structures situated within the high walls of a wooden palisade. Entering through an open gateway, they moved along a smooth, wide path that threaded between various wooden buildings. Most of the structures were fairly small — perhaps the private dwellings of individuals or families — though there were also a few more sizeable ones. It was to one of those they were led. Still preceded as well as followed by many women, Maeldun and his men entered the large building.

"Maeldun, this is our Hall of Weapons," Eithne said, addressing the youth and thus indicating that she considered him to be their leader. The men stared about them, running their eyes over an impressive array of objects arranged upon the high wooden walls. "Tomorrow we will determine which of them will suit each of you best. Celtchar, perhaps that huge ax you've been staring at is one you might wish to wield against our enemies? You appear to be just the man to do that."

"What enemies are those, madam?" Maeldun asked.

"Ah, Maeldun, there's no nonsense about you, is there? You prefer to get straight to the point. You seem to be cut out of much the same cloth as your father. He was a man who liked to get right down to business — in more ways than one. What enemies are those, you ask? We will explain all of that to you soon enough, while you are enjoying a warm meal around a warm fire. You are surely worn and famished after your long day of rowing. Alim, I suspect you are greatly in need of a drink."

"Nah, I surely *ain't*," Alim snapped back at her. "Ya shaggin' piece o' crap," he muttered softly beneath his breath.

"I don't remember you as being so grumpy," she said. "Comes with old age, I suppose."

"I ain't old, neither," Alim declared.

"Of course you aren't. Perhaps later tonight Cliona will find out just how young and frisky you really are. Perhaps she will be able to put a smile back upon that sour face of yours."

"Don't need no woman," Alim said.

"No? Well, sir, I don't think you'll have any choice about that."

Indeed, while they were standing there, the vast array of weaponry wasn't the only thing in the room Maeldun's men had been eyeing, for they found themselves surrounded by women of remarkable pulchritude — tall, well-formed, athletic creatures, all of whom seemed to be about the same age. As for that, Eithne appeared to be no older than any of the others. With fiery red hair and eyes as green as a cat's, she was a striking woman who appeared to be in the full bloom of young womanhood. Maeldun wasn't sure how that could be, since she claimed to have known his father some years ago.

Cliona, who seemed to be Eithne's chief lieutenant, was equally striking. Even in the dim light Maeldun could see that her hair was the color of the mid-summer sun, her shoulders broad and trim, her arms long and sinewy. The others, though slightly less remarkable, were still among the loveliest creatures the mariners had ever set eyes upon.

"In the morning, we shall fit all of you out with swords, shields, helmets, spears, battle axes, weaponry as fine or better than anything you have ever possessed. It's quite likely that you will need them during a little adventure that lies ahead of you. But for now, come and eat and warm yourselves. Then you must rest. I believe we will be able to find comfortable beds for each of you — though maybe not for you, Alim." She smiled as she spoke about comfortable beds; and so did all the other women in the room. So, indeed, did most of the men, though Alim wasn't one of them. Nor was Conn Iron-fist.

As they dined on great, juicy slabs of roast mutton and imbibed a great many cups of a dark and potent ale, the men listened as Eithne gave them a brief description of "the little adventure" she hoped they might be willing to undertake for them at a ford not too far distant. She spoke as if they actually had some choice in the matter, as if she and the others would be extremely grateful for whatever help the men might give them against an enemy that now threatened them. Throughout her remarks, Alim and Conn remained grim-faced.

When Maeldun pressed her again about the enemy she'd said she wanted them to repulse tomorrow at the ford, she continued to be evasive. She revealed only that she and her friends possessed a particular something which these other people wished to take from them; and that for some unrevealed reason she and the other women were prohibited from fighting their own fight. The fight had to fought, she said, by what she called "outsiders."

"How do we know that you are the ones we should be fighting for?" Maeldun had asked. "How do we know that you are not the ones in the wrong?"

Eithne merely grinned. "How do you know? Because I give you my word on it." Maeldun heard Alim utter a disparaging remark beneath his breath.

All the while that Eithne spoke, Maeldun took careful note of the reactions to her words of the others in the room — the other women, Alim the Wanderer, and Conn Iron-fist, in particular. Mael's conclusion was that Eithne's hopeful words belied a harsher reality. He suspected that Conn and Alim's reactions were due to the fact that they'd had previous experience with one of Eithne's "little adventures."

Still, the plenteous food and the potent drink, not to mention the pleasing company of all those most desirable women, had quickly buoyed the spirits of most of Maeldun's companions.

When the meal was concluded, every man in Maeldun's company was sent off to find the comfort of a very warm bed. And that night, not a single man in Maeldun's company slept alone.

CHAPTER 16
The Fight at the Ford

The following morning the men were roused from their beds, fed once more in the large hall where they'd dined the previous evening, and then led out into a large open area in the center of the complex where Eithne and Cliona greeted them cheerfully. All in all, the men's morale seemed high, with the exception of Conn and Alim, whose demeanors had not brightened one bit.

In the light of morning the men were able to get a clearer sense of this place to which they'd been taken. It was a large compound comprising many individual dwellings and structures, most of them small round wooden structures topped by slanting thatched roofs, erected upon solid foundations of stone. The open assembly area in which they now stood seemed to be located at the very heart of the complex.

As they looked about them, they saw that many of the women were already engaged in their daily activities — re-thatching buildings, herding beasts off to nearby fields, and performing domestic chores of one kind or another. What they didn't see, however, were any other people. For in the entire compound there were no older women, no children, and no men.

"Eithne," Maeldun said, after taking all of this in, "the third of the three large buildings, the one just there, can you tell me what it is?"

"That is the Hall of Healing. I would show it to you now if we weren't quite so pressed for time. But it is essential that we attend to the matter of weapons for your men right away. For you and your men must get to the ford and take up your battle positions there well before sunset. For now, the Hall of Healing can wait. I've no doubt, though, that we will be visiting it in the morning. We will surely need to."

Maeldun gave Eithne a hard look. "We will need to?"

"Oh yes, there isn't much doubt about that," she replied, returning Maeldun's hard look.

Maeldun noticed Conn and Alim, who were within hearing of this conversation, exchange grim glances. He suspected they'd once made visits to the Hall of Healing.

"Mariner," Maeldun said to Alim when he had a chance to speak to him privately, "you seem rather disgruntled this morning."

"Nah, I ain't gruntled. What I am is mightily irked. With meself, Mael, with meself. There I was yesterday night, a-feelin' oh so proud o' meself, a-thinkin' I'd done somethin' just right, when all I done was mess up royally. Mael, I surely didn't want ta go and get nobody killed, I surely didn't."

"No one's been killed, Mariner."

"Nah, they ain't. Not just yet, leastways."

Following Eithne and Cliona, Maeldun's companions re-entered the House of Weapons. They gazed with awe upon the vast arsenal displayed on the walls, weaponry from which they were now invited to fully arm themselves. The mariners would need a good bit of time to do that, for choosing amongst all these remarkable objects was no simple matter. They took down a great many of them and took turns handling them, carefully gauging their heft and balance and weight. Each man had his own preferences; a weapon one might find suitable another might not.

Maeldun was surprised to notice that Conn Iron-fist, their Weapons Master and the most experienced warrior amongst them, seemed emotionally detached during the entire proceeding. Like everyone else, Conn did finally end up selecting a full set of weapons, though as Maeldun watched him, it seemed to him that Conn made his selections almost randomly, not much caring whether the weapons he came away with were well-matched to his skills or not.

"You don't seem especially overwhelmed by these weapons," Maeldun said to Conn.

"It isn't that the weapons are not to my liking," Conn replied. "This is a remarkable collection. And yet, in the end, I'm not so sure that the weapons we select will make much of a difference."

"Are we not about to fight a fierce battle against a terribly formidable foe?"

"Yes, apparently we are."

"Then why won't our choice of weapons make much difference?"

"When all is said and done, I will leave it to you to determine that for yourself." Then Conn shrugged his shoulders. "Perhaps I am wrong, Mael. Perhaps our weapons will be important. But I'll be quite surprised if they are."

"So what you are suggesting is that this battle we are about to engage in will turn out to be something other than what it seems?"

"Yes, Maeldun, that is precisely what I am suggesting."

"Conn, would you tell me something? When you and my father had your earlier experiences with Eithne, what was it, exactly, that happened to you?"

Conn reflected on Mael's question for several seconds before replying. "I think I would rather not say. At least not right now."

"The reason you do not want to say — is it because many of the men who were with you at that time ended up dying on account of these women?"

Again Conn hesitated before answering. Finally he said, "Just three of us survived, Mael, just three of us — your father, his brother Luga, and me. When we made our escape, we left behind the bodies of fourteen of our companions."

"Weapons Master, do you think history is about to repeat itself?"

"History always repeats itself," Conn replied grimly.

Eventually every single one of them — including Alim the Wanderer, Taman the Harper, and Diuran the Rhymer, the least likely warriors amongst them — had determined which weapons he believed would suit him best. For most of the mariners, the shields and swords they'd now chosen were far finer than any they'd ever imagined they might possess. Eithne had told them that in addition to swords they must each have a goodly supply of throwing spears, and thus each of them picked out several from amongst a wide array of spears that ranged from slender dart-like lances to much more hefty javelins.

Ronan, Maeldun's foster brother, who had selected a shining two-edged blade of middle length, now swirled it about him with childish delight. "Come on, you bastards," he cried out, "who amongst you is man enough to test your mettle against me now, eh? You, Garluan? You, Ferben? You, Maeldun MacEoin?"

"I ain't afraid o' you, ya feckin' pansy!" Celtchar roared

out, hefting a gigantic battle ax with both hands and swinging it in a tight circle above his head.

"Save it 'til later, lads," Maeldun snapped. "I suspect the mettle of all of us will be amply tested at the ford. I like your fighting spirit, Ronan; but I don't want you to be directing it at the wrong people."

"I'll direct it at whoever I want to direct it," Ronan replied. "Anyway, Maeldun MacEoin, who was it elected *you* king? All you are is a pathetic foundling, a motherless, fatherless foundling."

"Who elected Mael king?" Garluan declared. "I did, that's who."

"I did too!" Celtchar bellowed.

"As did I," Dris said. "And if you don't like it, little brother, I might have to beat the shite out of you."

"You're more than welcome to try it, Dris, any damn time you want," Ronan shot back. "Just because you used to beat up March and me when we were children doesn't mean you still can."

"Ronan, what in the name of the Dagda did I just say?" Maeldun roared at the rude lad. "Save it for later! Maybe then, if you still wish it, you and I can settle matters just between the two of us. For right now, damn it, I'm the one who's making the decisions."

Ronan said nothing further, though with his hand behind his back he made an obscene gesture.

In her instructions to them before they'd left the rath, Eithne had been quite explicit about what they should and should not do. She told them to wait until their foemen were entering the water before revealing themselves. Then they should loose their missiles and do all in their power to prevent the invaders from crossing the ford. Most particularly, she cautioned them against attempting to cross the ford themselves.

"You must avoid doing that at all costs," she insisted. For the most part, she advised them to adopt a defensive strategy: "Let the enemy bring the battle to you." Once the attackers had entered the water, if some of Maeldun's men wanted to engage with them in the river with their swords, that should be all right, just as long as they didn't allow the other fighters to drag them up onto the far bank. If they were taken over to the far bank, she said, it would seal their fate.

"Eithne, you still haven't told us anything about this enemy," Maeldun said. "Who are they and why do they wish to attack you? Why is it that you need us to fight them for you? You haven't explained why you and your women, capable warriors that you surely are, can't undertake this adventure on your own. Why must you enlist our aid?"

"For this encounter, Maeldun, it is you we need. Yes, we are capable warriors. But not against this particular foe. A powerful taboo has been placed upon us, a taboo that prevents us from taking up arms against this enemy. For you, though, there is no such taboo. That is all I wish to say about it for now."

"But what of them? What are they like? What can we expect from them?"

"You will see soon enough."

"I thought you'd given up your old tricks," Conn snapped at Eithne. "Doesn't sound like it to me."

"Hush, Conn Iron-fist, hush. Maeldun, if you do as I have told you, if you don't ignore my instructions, there is a good likelihood that all of you will survive this encounter."

"I seem to recall you saying something like that last time," Conn said.

*　　*　　*

The shallow ford crossing the River Bladmuir lay a few miles east of Eithne's rath. It was drawing toward late afternoon as Cliona led Maeldun and the eighteen men in his company along the trail to the place where they would take up their positions. The river flowed between two high banks, with narrow paths cutting through each of the banks and descending to entry points on each side.

Maeldun and his men were directed to position themselves behind an outcropping of rocks atop the bank on the near side of the river, rocks that would initially conceal them from the approaching force and then provide some protection once the fight commenced.

"Do you know what day this is?" Diuran the Rhymer remarked to his old friend Conn, as the two of them stood together gazing down at the ford.

"I believe it may be the fifth day of the week. Or perhaps it is the sixth. I am afraid I have lost track, Rhymer."

"That isn't what I meant. What I meant is, do you know what day of the year this is?" Conn looked blankly at his friend, then shrugged his shoulders.

"It's the Day of Turning," Diuran said. "I'm almost certain that it is, and I can't help wondering if that has any bearing on what we are doing here."

Now Conn looked more thoughtful.

"Conn," Diuran went on, "Eithne said they wouldn't try to cross the ford until just after the sun had set. Why do you think that is? Could that be important?"

"Rhymer," Conn said with a grin, "despite all appearances to the contrary, you are nobody's fool, are you?"

"Weapons Master, if I am not mistaken, you just paid me a compliment — in your inimitable fashion."

*　　*　　*

It was a few minutes before sunset when Maeldun's men began to hear the sounds of people approaching the ford over on the far side of the river. Through the narrow gap leading down to the river came a large, well-armed group that included both men and women. Most of them were on foot, though a few of their leaders were on horseback.

"Ready your javelins," Maeldun quietly ordered. "Do not throw until I tell you."

A group of maybe thirty people began assembling close to the water's edge on the far side of the ford. They were apparently awaiting their leader's order before crossing.

Eithne had said that Maeldun's men should launch a surprise attack upon this enemy, but that particular piece of advice offended the youth's sense of fair play. Celtic warriors, he believed, did not fight from ambush, the ploy of cowards. And so he called out to alert those people to his presence.

"You must stop now!" he shouted down to them. "If you do, no harm will come to you! Do not attempt to cross the ford! If you do, we shall defend it to the death!"

Sounds of laughter rose up from the group below. "You will defend it to the death all right," someone declared, "and that death shall be *yours!*"

"We have given you fair warning!" Maeldun shouted again. "Do not attempt to cross the ford."

"Has Eithne put you up to this, young sir?" boomed out the voice of one of the figures on horseback. "Has she enticed you into her service? Coerced you into her service, is more like. Well, young sir, more's the pity. We are coming across and there isn't a thing you can do to stop us. Warriors!" he shouted, "advance!" And the first line of figures began to move slowly into the shallow water of the ford.

Maeldun waited until they were perhaps a third of the way across before giving his men the signal to launch their javelins. "Now, throw!" he cried.

A great many spears flew through the air, and the aim of most of them was true. The advancing party, anticipating such a move, quickly lifted their shields and blocked most of the spears. The few that succeeded in striking chests or helmets glanced off harmlessly.

"Again!" Maeldun cried, but the result was little different. Now once more laughter rose up to the ears of Maeldun and his men.

"We must fight them in the water," Dris cried. "Let us go down to them now."

"Fourteen of you go. But Conn, Garluan, Diuran, and Taman, you remain here with me." The rest of the men rushed down the narrow path to the water's edge, their swords drawn.

As Maeldun and the remaining men watched from higher up, they could now see that the attackers were a motley group consisting of only a few younger men and a good many older men, with nearly half the group made up of women, many of them quite advanced in years.

Ronan was at the forefront of the charge, his magnificent shining sword raised high as he entered the fray. His powerful sword thrust found the body of an attacker, and yet the curved surface of the man's breastplate caused it to skitter harmlessly off to the side. His foeman quickly retreated, with Ronan in pursuit. The other people in the ford parted to let them through.

The river was no more than thirty yards wide, and it took only a few moments for Ronan to chase his foe nearly all the way to the far bank.

"Ronan!" shouted his brother Dris. "Stop! Don't touch the far shore!"

When he'd reached the farther bank, the man Ronan

chased swung about and waited as Ronan approached. As Ronan drew near, the man feinted at him, hoping to draw the zealous lad's thrust. His ploy succeeded. As Ronan lunged forward, his feet slipped on the mossy stones at the ford's edge, and he tumbled forward. His enemy reached out and grabbed at him. Ronan quickly rolled sideways to avoid his grasp. As he did, his sword arm brushed against the wet mud of the farther riverbank.

Dris, darting through the water, arrived at his brother's side. He grabbed Ronan's legs; using all his might, he jerked him back from the river's edge. But Ronan was already writhing in an agony of pain. His sword arm barely managed to maintain its grip on his weapon. In horror, Ronan watched as his powerful right arm began to shrivel into a dried-up stick.

From the motley group of attackers came squeals of laughter. They were amused by the ineffectiveness of Maeldun's men, to whom it was becoming clearer and clearer that despite the magnificence of their weapons, their strange, almost unearthly foes were completely impervious to them.

Garluan, standing beside Maeldun and watching from above, had readied his sling. He had yet to use it, but he remembered that Eithne had specifically asked him to bring it. Perhaps she knew it was one weapon that might have some efficacy against their attackers.

"Back! Everyone back!" Maeldun shouted down to his men. "Try to defend the ford from this side. Let them bring the fight to us!"

One of the last men to retreat was Alim, who was pursued by a man as ancient as he was. But his attacker was the swifter, and as he bore down upon Alim, the wily mariner suddenly spun about in a surprise move and buried his dagger in the old man's chest. Maeldun's company had claimed its first victim.

"I'll need ta have that back, ya shagger!" Alim yelled, carefully extracting his unique knife from his victim's chest.

On the far bank the leader, perched on horseback, shouted out to Maeldun, "Go now, and we will spare you all. We can protect you from Eithne. Go now, and you and your men will survive." The man who was speaking removed his large helmet and held it beneath one arm. Even from that distance Maeldun and Conn could see that his ancient face was as mottled and wrinkled as a withered apple.

It was at that moment that Garluan began twirling his weapon. And it was in the following moment that his sling ball was launched in deadly flight toward the ancient leader on the horse.

The sling ball hit its target squarely, splattering the man's head like a piece of fruit. As he toppled from his mount, a great wailing rose up from all of his followers.

Slowly, all the people who had been in the water began to slink back across to the far side. All those dark figures began moving back up the path toward the riderless horse. Their keening mounted to the skies. They raised the form of their slain leader and began to retreat back up the trail over which they had come.

Five minutes later, as Maeldun and Conn looked down upon the scene below them, it was as if nothing had even happened there.

With two exceptions. One was the dark form of the man whom Alim had killed with his ant's claw dagger. His body could still be seen lying in the shallow waters of the ford. The other was Ronan, who appeared to be completely in shock. Looking dazed and fearful, he held his withered arm cradled across his chest.

Dusk descended into darkness. The fight at the ford was over.

CHAPTER 17
All Good Things . . .

In the dimness, Maeldun and Conn discerned the figure of Cliona, who was standing only a short distance behind them. Had she been there the whole time, watching the entire encounter?

"They won't be coming back again tonight," she said calmly. "Indeed, they won't be coming back again before next Spring, if then.

"Maeldun, Conn, Garluan — you've performed brilliantly! You too, Alim, you old fuss-pot. Yes, Maeldun, you and your men have fulfilled our every hope. Come along with me now. We shall return to the rath for a night of feasting and celebration. Your wounds and injuries, such as they are, shall be treated in the morning by Airmed the Healer. She is the best of the best."

"I remember her," Conn said. "About the only fond memory I have of you, too."

"Perhaps before the night is over we can provide you with more fond memories," Cliona said, her words followed by a half-smile.

The men, at least for the most part, were quite happy to

follow Cliona's lead back to the rath. Dris walked beside his brother Ronan, his arm draped about Ronan's shoulders. Ronan no longer seemed to be in pain. He held his withered arm clutched against his chest. The shock of seeing what his powerful right arm had become remained upon his face.

As they entered the high, palisaded walls, the women of the rath rushed forth to greet them, many of them embracing the particular men with whom they'd shared their beds the previous night. Eithne bestowed her full embrace upon black-haired Maeldun.

"You are your father's son," she declared. "I was sure you would be. Ailill would be proud of you. Perhaps his spirit is watching you even as we speak. You've done magnificently, and we shall repay you handsomely. When you embark on your way tomorrow, we will send special gifts with you, gifts you may find useful when you wreak your vengeance upon the hated Reavers of Roonah."

"You continually astonish me, madam. How is it that you know these things? Are you a druidess? Are you perhaps one of those who possesses The Sight?"

Eithne's eyes glittered. She smiled and tilted her head a little to one side. "Maeldun, we are simple, humble women who are grateful for the service you've rendered us."

"Madam, you always evade my questions. You are no mere woman, Eithne, of that I am certain."

"Just like your father, Maeldun — always questioning, always seeking answers and explanations."

"I believe that you owe us some explanations."

"I could provide them, young Maeldun, though I doubt that even then you would fully understand."

"Try me."

"All right then, over dinner I shall do that. Let us dine and sing and dance and celebrate — and also let us talk. In the morning, we will see you off again upon your way, not so much the worse for wear. Indeed, I believe that when you embark tomorrow, you will find yourselves rather better off than when you arrived."

Cliona led Ronan, still accompanied by Dris, straight to the House of Healing. Since none of the other men's injuries were very serious, she said they should wait until morning before treating them.

So Maeldun and the others were led directly to the Hall of Feasting, where preparations for a grand celebration were now complete. The smells that greeted their noses were those of roast ox, broiled fish, and baked fowls of several kinds. Many loaves of fresh warm bread and large rounds of various cheeses, placed upon the trestle tables positioned about the room, contributed to the rich aromas already filling the spacious enclosure. Wine, mead, and dark foamy ale flowed in abundance.

Celtchar reached his huge hand into a large wooden bowl and procured a gigantic pickled onion. Plopping it into his large maw, he demolished it with gusto, its juices running down his massive, grinning chin. "Believe I'll just have me another one o' them whiles I be at it," he declared, reaching into the bowl once more. "Me ol' mam, she always did say they was good for keepin' off the agues."

The sounds of harps and pipes and timbrels began filling the room. Taman and Diuran went over and stood close to the women who were playing them, admiring their dexterity, among other things. Soon more instruments were brought for the use of the two men, who were happy to add their talents to the music-making. Inevitably, all the joyful tunes soon led to dancing. Ferben, who had the lightest and quickest feet amongst the men in Maeldun's company, was soon stepping and stamping, leaping and cavorting with the best of them.

As the festivities proceeded, it became clear that one of the biggest heroes in the eyes of these women was copper-haired Garluan, the man who had taken down the invaders' leader. The women competed with each other in flirting with him, treating themselves to soft little caresses of his limbs and slender torso, and even sneaking in a kiss or two. Garluan was beaming. He had never received so much feminine attention in his young life, and he was reveling in it.

"Hey, Mael," he shouted out at one point. "Did we ever decide what Fintan's record was? Think I could match it tonight? Whatever it was, I think I might just try to top it!"

Even Conn and Alim were laughing at the lad along with all the others. It finally seemed possible that the evening's activities might actually put a smile upon Alim's sour old face. He was still abstaining from drinking any of those hugely tempting beverages; but he seemed on the brink of intoxication nonetheless.

A few hours into the festivities, Ronan and Dris suddenly appeared on the scene. Dris was smiling, but it was Ronan who was exhilarated beyond belief. His withered arm was withered no more. He flexed it proudly, offering to arm wrestle with any man in the room, even Conn or Celtchar. One of the women came over to him and kissed his muscular biceps. Then she kissed him square on the lips.

"This is my kind of party!" shouted the exuberant lad. "So where's all this drink you've been hiding from me? You'd better not have drunk it all just yet, you worthless bastards! I have a thirst to match Alim's thirst after seven drink-less days at sea."

The feasting and celebrating went on late into the night, and as the evening wore on, couples began slowly disappearing, off to find other places where they could indulge their desires. Maeldun and Eithne remained behind, deep in conversation.

Though in the end, they too moved off to find some other place to continue their association.

In the morning, everyone seemed to be moving rather slowly. Eventually, though, the rath came to life and the mariners began to think about taking their leave.

The first matter to attend to was the return of their splendid armaments to the Hall of Weapons. When they entered, Cliona told them not to bother hanging the weapons back upon the walls but to set them down carefully in the center of the room. Others, she said, would clean them properly and return them to their places.

Many a man looked longing at his weapons before finally relinquishing them. Celtchar gave a final loving pat to the gigantic battle ax he'd so proudly borne into battle, then placed it down in the pile amongst all the other items. "Maybe when we gets back home I can get the smith ta make me one o' them," he said, talking to himself. "Sure did suit me. Sure will miss it."

Even though the borrowed weapons hadn't been especially efficacious during the fight at the ford, the men had become attached to them. The failure of the weapons, they felt certain, wasn't the fault of the weapons. There had been other factors at play, factors the men didn't quite understand.

Among the last to leave his weapons was Conn Iron-fist. But unlike the others, he returned his weapons with no sense of regret. He preferred the weapons he'd been forced to leave behind with the curragh, weapons he'd known and fought with since he'd been Maeldun's age.

Alim too, the last man in the line, didn't appear unhappy to dispose of his borrowed weapons. "Worthless shaggers," he muttered, as he left his weapons behind, "worthless pieces o' crap." As he said that, his hand reached down unconsciously and caressed the handle of the dagger he still wore by his side, a dagger he'd put to good use in the fight at the ford. He'd possessed it for a very long time. He expected to be buried with it.

When the men entered the Hall of Healing, they were struck by the immense heat filling the spacious room. The air was heavy with moisture though wonderfully fragrant. Many cauldrons of various sizes were sunk into the floor, and steam rose up from each of them. Apparently these baths were heated by natural springs beneath the floor. The floor itself was bestrewn with rushes and aromatic herbs which released their fragrance as the men walked upon them.

In the center of the room was a cauldron far larger than any of the others. It was filled to a foot below its rim with a darkish liquid from which steam was rising. All about its shining sides were individual panels depicting a wide range of figures and designs — of gods and goddesses; of strange beasts both real and imagined; of armed warriors engaged in combat; of ornate designs in swirling or interlacing patterns.

Female attendants led each man to one of the cauldrons. After stripping down, all of the men immersed themselves in the soothing waters. Those who'd suffered minor wounds in the fight at the ford were led to particular cauldrons, ones that apparently possessed certain medicinal properties. The others happily luxuriated in the warm, fragrant waters of their more ordinary baths.

Before they left the Hall of Healing, Maeldun and Conn walked slowly about the great central cauldron, trying to identify the figures depicted in the panels. Only a few of the scenes had them stumped. As they were puzzling over one in particular, Alim wandered over to join them. "Balor of the Baleful Eye," he said, pointing to a central figure, "the wicked shagger. But Lugh served 'im good, too."

"I believe you're right, Mariner," Conn said.

"Course I am," Alim said. "Ya never knowed me ta be wrong, have ya?"

"Not so very often," Maeldun said. "Only when it comes to finding us a safe haven. But that's about it."

"Now don't go rubbin' it in — ya shagger," his last two words muttered softly beneath his breath.

As Conn and Maeldun turned and began to walk away, Alim swiftly uncorked a small vial he'd held concealed in his left hand. Making sure no one was watching, he quickly dipped it into the vat, then swiftly re-corked it. Alim had just replenished his supply of special elixir. He knew it was so potent that he could dilute it many, many times, thus supplying his needs for years to come.

Clean and refreshed, the mariners prepared to depart. Many of the women of the rath were already about their daily activities, but several of them came to the central assembly area to say their goodbyes. Eithne hugged each man in turn, saving Maeldun until last.

"Fare thee well, young Maeldun MacEoin," she said. "Your visit to us had a happier ending than that of your father. Though I will always cherish his memory, as I will cherish yours. So fare thee well, young Maeldun MacEoin, Maeldun of the coal black hair. My spirit goes with you. We will pray for your success in your conflict with the Reavers of Roonah."

"Thank you, madam," was Maeldun's only reply. But he dipped his head in a final salute.

Once more it was Cliona who led the mariners through the compound and then up to the trail that would take them back to the little harbor. This time only a few of the women came along behind them.

When they reached the sheltered bay after a trek of half an hour, there on the sands lay their sturdy curragh. In their brief absence it had been tidied up and completely re-tarred. The oculi Alim had painted on its prow had also been re-touched, and now that pair of eyes seemed to gleam cheerfully at them as they approached.

"There ya do be, me lovelies," Alim said to them, and he patted the side of the craft close to one of the two bright eyes.

The men's possessions were safely stowed and the craft fully provisioned. This unexpected interruption in their larger adventure had now come to its end. At least, it almost had.

"Ronan," Cliona said sternly, "I'll need you to leave behind your sword. You were all told that the weapons you used were only on loan. I am sorry that you didn't leave it in the Hall of Weapons, but I shall take it now with no hard feelings."

"You shall *take it?*" Ronan responded angerly. Using his restored right arm, he reached down across his body to his left side and extracted the gleaming sword from where he'd hidden it beneath his long cloak. He brandished it before him. "You'll *take it?*" he said again. "I would like to see you try!"

"Ronan, what in the name of the Dagda do you think you're doing!" Maeldun shouted. "Give Cliona the sword!"

"I'll give her the sword," he screeched. "When she's taken it from me, that's when I'll give it to her." Ronan extended his sword arm in front of him, prepared to ward off any attack Cliona might make. "So take it!" he snarled.

In the blink of an eye the weapon that suddenly appeared in Cliona's hand slashed through the air. It landed high upon Ronan's sword arm, just beneath the shoulder.

Ronan was stunned. For a moment he just stood there as his severed limb, still clutching the sword, tumbled down upon the sand. Then a look of horror appeared on his face. He slumped down beside the arm and sword, blood gushing from the gaping wound. For a lengthy moment no one moved.

It was Dris who finally did. He rushed to his brother's side and knelt beside him, though he had no idea how he might comfort him. He raised his eyes to Cliona for guidance.

"*Help him*," he implored, "you must *help* him. We must carry him back to the House of Healing. We must make a platform on which to carry him. We must do that now!"

Cliona just stood there, her face showing not a shred of compassion. Finally she said, "It's too late for that. There's no hope for him now. I tried to warn him."

"You heartless bitch!" Dris cried out. "May the Dagda curse your soul forever!"

"Help me, brother," Ronan moaned, "help me. Dris, I'm dying. Do something. Help me!"

"There's no help for him now," Cliona said again, her face as cold and passionless as ever.

"Yes," Dris replied, "there is."

He reached out and picked up the sword from where it lay on the sand. He raised it high, then drove it deep into his brother's chest.

Tears flowed down Dris's stricken face. "May your spirit rest easy, my brother. May your spirit rest easy."

CHAPTER 18

The Island of The Hermit

The mariners rowed southward being careful to keep their craft well away from Eire's treacherous west coast. Conn Iron-fist, who knew this stretch of water, had a particular goal in mind. Alim, still smarting from having led them straight into the arms of Eithne, was keeping his own counsel. Maeldun commanded the steering oar, and the other mariners, sobered by Ronan's startling death, quietly went about the business of propelling the craft. Dris was lost in thoughts of his own.

The craft was as well fitted out as it had been at the beginning of their voyage, so at least one good thing had come from their recent adventures. Perhaps many of the men harbored memories of other good things as well, but now their thoughts turned toward the Reavers of Roonah, whom they expected to encounter in the near future, possibly within the next three or four days.

Diuran the Rhymer stood next to Conn Iron-fist in the curragh's prow. For several minutes neither man spoke, and Diuran knew that his good friend was studying many things — the landmarks along the coastline, the current, the wind direction, the look of the sky off to the west. Finally Diuran ventured a remark.

"It could have been worse," he said.

"It could have been *much* worse. Truthfully, I marvel at how well it all turned out. Last time, Ailill and I left fourteen men behind, this time just one, a marvel indeed."

"And looking on the bright side, that man was the one man we could most afford to lose," the Rhymer said hopefully. But it was the wrong thing to say, and it drew a fierce look from Conn.

"No, Rhymer, you are wrong. There's no such thing as a man you can afford to lose — not even if that man is as vile a man as Ronan was."

"I stand corrected, Weapons Master." Then the two of them remained silent for several more minutes.

"So now we are eighteen in number," Diuran finally said. "I wonder — "

"Hush, Rhymer, enough of your wondering! Why don't you go and compose a poem or a song or something and leave me alone. I'm tired of your nattering." Diuran the Rhymer looked stunned. He was used to Conn's moodiness, and he'd often experienced his barbs. But so rude a rebuke was something new. Seeing the shattered look on the poet's face, Conn quickly softened.

"Diuran, my friend, I have much on my mind. Forgive me." He reached out and placed his hand atop the Rhymer's shoulder, an apologetic expression on his face. Diuran sighed.

"I will leave you to your thoughts, Weapons Master. I am just glad you are capable of having some. I wasn't sure that you were." Conn merely laughed at his old friend's sarcastic remark.

"Since it so rarely happens," he replied, "it's best I take advantage of it when it does."

*   *   *

173

By late morning they'd come within sight of the small, inconsequential island that Conn had in mind. It lay several miles off the coast, its only inhabitants being sea birds and a small colony of seals. Conn believed it would provide them a secret and secure place where they could set up their temporary camp, a place from which they could scout out the enemy they were now so close to finding.

They rowed around the island and landed on the farther side, the side not visible from Eire's coast. It was a rough and shingly shore, so they carried the curragh well up above the tideline. They laid it down carefully among low dunes overgrown with scrub, a place where it would not be visible to sea travelers.

As the men began busying themselves with establishing their camp, Garluan remarked, "I thought you said no one lived on this island, Weapons Master."

The men all paused in what they were doing and looked where Garluan was pointing. Sure enough, just a few hundred yards farther up the slope toward the island's highest point they could see the curving stone roof of a small structure. It was the roof of a beehive hut, partially concealed amongst a copse of stunted trees.

"Those worthless shaggers!" Alim spit out.

"What is it, Alim?" Maeldun asked.

"It be the dwellin' o' one o' them feckin' hermits, no doubt about it. One o' them feckin' Christian lunatics. By the Dagda, if it be all right with you, Mael, I'll just go up there 'n' cut the shagger's throat!"

"No, you won't, Alim!" Conn snapped. "If he's a Christian hermit, he shall come to no harm from us. We must show him and his god every respect. We must show his god all the reverence we would show our own gods."

"Yes," Maeldun agreed, "Conn's quite right. Though I

think I will walk on up and have a few words with him to assure him of that fact. You all go ahead with setting up camp."

"Worthless shagger," Alim muttered. "Oughta have his feckin' throat cut, he should."

"You seem to've gotten rather blood-thirsty of late, Mariner," Garluan said with a grin. "Maybe it wasn't such a good thing that those women got your juices flowing again." Alim gave the lad a squinty glare.

As Maeldun began making his way up the gentle slope, he could see a thin wisp of smoke rising close beside the beehive hut. He picked his way slowly and carefully through scrub and bracken until he was about thirty yards from the hut, then paused to take a good look. Beside the hut he could see an old blackened pot hanging from a branch above a small cooking fire. Crouched on his knees stirring the pot was a small man in a coarse gray robe. Maeldun could see that his face was full-bearded but that his large round head was totally bald.

"Hello!" Maeldun called out. The man, not appearing startled at all, slowly raised his head and looked toward Maeldun. Then he gestured with his hand, signaling for Maeldun to approach.

The little man stood up and watched as Maeldun moved toward him. He motioned Maeldun toward a large rock close to the fire, a rock that apparently served as a seat.

"Thank you," Maeldun said, perching himself on the rock. "I am Maeldun MacEoin. Those are my friends down there. We plan to stay here on the island for a few days, so I wanted to assure you that we'll try not to bother you."

The small man reached down for an old clay jar half buried in the sand. He raised it to his lips and took a large drink. Then he made several throat-clearing sounds.

"I am Finian," he said at last, his hoarse voice barely able

175

to croak out the words. "You are the first person I have spoken to in some years — though, I confess, I do sometimes sing to the seals." Then his lips parted into a broad grin, his large white teeth visible through his thick gray beard. "You might not care for my singing. The seals, bless them, are not too critical."

"Do you sing to your god?" Maeldun asked.

"Only inside my head. No, about the only sounds ever heard here on this island are the sounds of God's own Creation. There is no more beautiful music than that."

"So you are a Christian?"

"You know of us?"

"Only a little. I know that you no longer believe in the old gods that I believe in. That you have found just one new god that you now worship."

"I didn't find Him, Maeldun, He found me. And He isn't a new god, He is the God of all Creation."

Maeldun sat quietly for a long minute. "Your god has my respect," he finally said. "I believe it is best to respect all gods. Well, I suppose I should be going now and leave you to your cooking. But before I do, would you mind if I asked a question?" The little hermit made a gesture of acquiescence.

"Do other people ever come to this island?"

The hermit thought about that before responding. "Almost never," he said. "Boats go past every now and again, but there is nothing here that anyone would want. Nothing but blessed solitude, which is why I came. I have been alone here for the last five years."

"Well, Finian, I have interrupted your solitude long enough. I won't bother you any further."

"No bother, Maeldun. Kind of nice to see a human face. Would you like to stay a bit longer and share a bowl of nettle soup?" The hermit glanced at the blackened pot he'd been tending. "I'm afraid I've nothing else to offer."

"No. Thank you, though. But Finian, now that I think of it, I do have one more question to ask you. I guess when you first came here you must've come in a boat."

"Aye, that I did."

"That boat, do you still have it? Is it still useable?"

"It's not much of a boat, but I do use it every now and again. Sometimes, I confess, I get a yen to do just a bit of sea fishing. Helps to vary my simple diet."

"Might we borrow it for a few days? We would repay you."

"It be down there near the seal beach," he said, pointing off to the right. "No, it's not so much of a boat, but you do be welcome to use it, if you think it might help you out — help you out with whatever it is you have come here to do." He paused and looked at Maeldun for a moment with raised eyebrows. "I won't be asking you what that might be. None of my business. Still, I do hope it won't be anything offensive to my God."

"I hope not too," Maeldun replied. "I hope that very sincerely."

"I hope it won't be offensive to your gods, also."

"As do I. I'm fairly certain, in the case of my gods, that it won't be offensive. Indeed, if we didn't do what we've come to do, that would surely be offensive to them."

"Perhaps your gods are not as gentle and forgiving as my God is."

"Perhaps they are not. Well, Finian, I'd best be getting back." As Maeldun rose to leave, he turned and looked one last time at the little hermit. With a smile he said, "If we hear someone singing to the seals, Finian, we will know who it is."

By the time Maeldun returned, their simple camp among

the dunes had taken shape, and now men were gathering firewood and beginning to make preparations for their evening meal. Maeldun told Conn and Alim about the hermit's boat, and Alim and Celtchar set off to find it and bring it to where their own boat now lay. If it really was useable, it might prove more suitable for the reconnoitering they'd soon be doing, since it was less likely to attract the notice their own larger boat surely would.

As the other men continued their activities, Maeldun and Dris walked off alone along the shoreline of the bleak little island, an island whose landscape seemed well suited to Dris's dreary mood. The two of them walked together for some distance before Dris finally broke their silence.

"Why were we so foolish as to try and follow you, Mael?" he said with a sigh. "If we'd only stayed home, March and Ronan would still be alive. I hated it at the time, but now I'll readily admit you were right from the start when you decided to exclude us."

"Perhaps we were," Maeldun replied, "though I am glad you're here now. I feel certain that before this adventure is over, your being with us will make a great deal of difference."

"If it's all the same to you, Mael, I think I'd rather just set off by myself now and try to make my way home on my own."

"No, it isn't all the same to me. I want you here, Dris. We are getting quite close to our final confrontation with the Reavers, and I very much want to have you here with us when we do. After Conn, it is you, my brother, who is our finest warrior."

The two young men walked on for a few hundred yards without either of them speaking any further. They had reached a point in their ambling where they could look across a wide expanse of water and see the far-distant shore of Eire.

"Conn says the Reavers' main rath is off over there," Maeldun said, pointing slightly to the right, "no more than ten or so miles from here."

"I suppose our plan will involve some kind of surprise attack?" Dris said, finally showing some interest in the adventure that lay ahead.

"A night attack is what Conn wants. What we may do is try to find another place much closer to their stronghold where we can lay up in secret and wait for bad weather."

"Bad weather? So that all of them will be inside and not be expecting that anyone else would be out braving the elements?"

"Yes, I believe that's what Conn thinks might be best. According to his plan, we would wait until very late at night in hopes that most of them would be drunk; then we would crash upon them like an angry wave smashing the shore." Maeldun smacked his right fist into the palm of his left hand.

"Doesn't seem terribly noble, somehow, does it?"

"Vengeance isn't always so noble, I suppose. Anyway, considering how outnumbered we're likely to be, perhaps that will help to make it noble enough."

"Yes, perhaps it will."

After their evening meal, the mariners were able to lie back and relax, something that hadn't been possible for the last several days, days that had been filled with a variety of vigorous activities.

Taman began playing soft chords on his harp, and before long Diuran was singing along with the harper, moving his voice in and out and around the harmonious chords, the two blending together to create a strangely beautiful sound.

"Those sounds," Diuran said, when he had stopped

singing, "they are the sounds that fell on Bran's ear the day he first heard the music." The mariners knew that Diuran was referring to the mysterious voyage Bran and his followers had taken to the islands of the western seas in an old, old tale.

"Bran was walking that day outside their stronghold," Diuran went on, "when he first heard the singing. It was before him and behind him, but when he looked all about he saw no one. That night when he went to his bed, the music was still there. It possessed such a sweetness that he didn't wish to sleep, though he finally did.

"When he awoke, there beside him he saw a beautiful silver branch covered with white blossoms. He carried it with him when he went into the royal house. And suddenly, there before all of them, appeared a woman who was dressed in strange raiment. She came over and stood in front of Bran and began to sing. The music he had been hearing had come from her. And now the entire host could hear her as she sang the fifty quatrains to Bran:

"*A branch from the apple tree of Emne*
I bring, one unlike those you know.
Twigs of silver lie upon it,
A crystal bough with blossoms.

There is a distant isle
Around which sea-horses frolic;
A beauteous race-course upon the white-foaming sea;
Four pillars uphold it.

Splendors of every color glisten there;
Through the gentle-voiced plains,
Joy is known to all, sweet music
Without harshness falls upon the ear."

"As she sang the fifty quatrains, all were entranced. And as she was finishing her song, she entreated Bran not to 'fall upon a bed of sloth' but to begin a voyage across the clear sea in order to come to the Land of Women.

"So on the morrow Bran set out with his men. On his way he encountered Mananna MacLir, who sang thirty quatrains to him containing much sound advice. After that Bran and his men had many adventures, visiting many different islands.

"Eventually they arrived at the Land of Women, where Bran was greeted by the woman who had sung to them back at their rath. 'Come hither on land, Oh Bran son of Febal, welcome is thy coming!' she cried out. Bran wasn't so sure he and his men should go ashore there, but she threw a great ball of thread out to him, and when he caught it in his hands, it stuck to them, and she drew their boat straight in to shore.

"There they went to a house where there was a bed for each one of them with a woman from that land. And there they found plentiful food served in silver dishes that never became empty. Nothing one could ever wish for was absent from them there. And so they remained there in great happiness for what they believed was perhaps a year.

"But eventually some of the men became homesick. A great desire came upon them to return to Erin. When Bran told the woman of their wish to leave, she said that their going 'would make them rue.' But when they still insisted upon leaving, she offered a final caution. She told them they could go, but she said that when they reached Erin they should not set foot upon the land. She said that if they did, it 'would make them rue.'

"Finally they made the long sea-journey and reached the shores of Erin. They were delighted to see the homeland they had so greatly missed. Bran reminded them not to touch the land, but one man, so transported by the sight of Erin, couldn't help himself. He leapt out and waded ashore. As soon as he touched the solid land, he collapsed into a heap of ashes.

" 'Who are you?' shouted some fishermen who had been watching them.

" 'I am Bran son of Febal!' Bran shouted back to them.

" 'We do not know who you are,' they shouted back. 'But we have an ancient story, a tale about a man named Bran. He led his men off to sea in search of the Land of Women and was never seen again. That happened many hundreds of years ago.' "

"Thereupon Bran sang the fifty quatrains to those men on the shore. He told them their whole story, and he told them to write it down in ogham letters.

"Then, sadly, Bran and his men began to row their craft once more back out to sea. Before long, the men on the shore had lost sight of them. After that, Bran and his men were never seen again."

"That ain't a-gonna happen to us, will it, Rhymer?" Celtchar asked, when Diuran had finished the old tale.

"You come along with me, lad," Alim said to Celtchar, "and when this here little adventure of ours be over and done with, you 'n' me, laddy, we'll go a-wanderin' off in search o' all them far isles and be findin' that Land o' Women all for ourselves."

"Have ya been there before, Wanderer?" Celtchar asked.

"Why, o' course I have, laddy, o' course I have." And then he slipped Diuran a big wink.

CHAPTER 19
The Rath of Roonah

When the fog finally lifted, Maeldun stared out at the black expanse of sea ahead of them. A thin trickle of moonlight slated the rippled surface of the sea. The curragh, with its eighteen men, began to move upon the sea. At last they were on their way — on their way to their destined and inevitable collision with the hated Reavers of Roonah.

Early that morning, Conn and Ferben had gone off in the hermit's little coracle, just the two of them making the arduous sea-journey to the shores of Eire. By mid-afternoon they had returned from their scouting expedition, pleased with what they'd discovered. For Conn believed they had located just what they'd been looking for, a place where Maeldun's men could tuck themselves away while awaiting their chance to launch their fateful attack.

So now, in the dark of night, they were on the move once more in their large curragh. If all went well, in a few more hours they would have secreted themselves within a little glen only a few miles from the Reavers' main stronghold. During the day they planned to rest up and ready their weapons. Then, if the weather proved advantageous and the moment seemed propitious, they would launch their raid late that night — or more accurately, very early the following morning.

The night crossing went precisely as they'd hoped it would. The early moon, shrouded in sky mist, shone but hazily about them as they moved swiftly across the dark expanse of water. The ocean was fairly calm, with only a gentle sea breeze at their backs to help speed their craft along its way.

Only a night bird cried out a greeting to them as they landed at the entrance to a small creek. Wading waist deep in creek water, they guided the boat well upstream to a place where they could leave it amidst a thick cluster of tall rushes in a dank and boggy marsh. Carrying all of their possessions, they proceeded on foot farther up the rocky valley to the higher, dryer spot that Conn had found earlier. They stopped when they reached a place where the creek was filled with mossy rocks, the creek banks darkly shaded beneath massive trees of vast age. Such a secluded place, they hoped, would prove to be one where no one would have any reason to go.

The light of morning, when it came, barely penetrated the heavy tree limbs above them. They breakfasted on dried meat, fish, cheese, and bread — all provided by Eithne and her women — and then many of the men lay their heads on their packs and dozed. Maeldun posted sentries both above and below along the creek bank, on the off chance of having unexpected visitors — though it proved an unnecessary precaution.

Along toward late morning, however, they began to hear noises. It sounded as though someone was shouting, someone who seemed both excited and angry. Now fully alert, the men sat up quickly and listened. All they could make out was a single high voice. As it grew nearer, they also began to make out other noises. They were the noises of animals — the noises of sheep.

"Gar," Maeldun said softly, "go and have a look."

Garluan nodded, and then he was on his way, creeping quietly up the hill through the dark woods in the direction from which the noises were coming. As the quickest and most light-footed member of the entire party, he was the logical one to send, though for a moment Maeldun wondered if he shouldn't have given that honor to Dris. But no, Garluan was the right one to send.

In under half an hour the slender lad was back. No one had even heard him coming until he suddenly materialized in their midst. He stood before them with a twinkle in his eyes, pleased at his remarkable skills.

"It's only a lad herding sheep," he said, speaking just below a normal tone of voice. "Just the one boy. There's no one else with him. He's a slave-boy, by the look of him. From where I was hiding, I could hear him talking to the sheep, but I could hardly make out what he was saying. At first I thought he was merely speaking gibberish. I believe he may be a Welsh boy. Either that or he's a half-wit — though being Welsh and being a half-wit are pretty much one and the same." Garluan smiled at his own joke.

"You saw no one else?" Maeldun asked.

"No. I even explored the surrounding area just to be sure. The boy is all alone. Not far from where he now is there is a small hovel, probably where he sleeps at night or where he goes to retreat from rough weather. I suspect he stays out with the sheep for days at a time, much as our herders at Rath Murtagh do. These sheep, I'm guessing, belong to the Reavers. As does the lad. Perhaps they kidnapped him from Wales, though knowing them, they probably just stole him from some other clan."

"He can help us," Conn said, joining the conversation. "We can use him as our guide. He will know much about their stronghold that will be useful to us. Do you agree?"

"Yeh, but only if we could understand what the feckin' Welsh ejit is a-sayin'!" Alim chimed in.

"Hush, Alim. I will be able to understand him well enough."

"As will I," said Diuran. "I once made a study of the Welsh poems and am reasonably familiar with that barbarous tongue."

"We're agreed, then," Maeldun said. "You and Ferben go and get the lad. Gag him and blindfold him, just for good measure. Don't let him make any sounds of alarm." Garluan nodded his understanding.

"What about his sheep?" Diuran said.

"His sheep can go shag themselves," Alim said with a grin.

"The Dagda will look after his sheep," Maeldun said, frowning at Alim.

The Welsh lad, they discovered — once they'd managed to decipher his speech — knew little about the comings and goings of the Reavers. He'd been in the fields with his sheep for the last week, having seen no other person. He was a slave-boy, stolen by the Reavers from a clan in the southeast of Eire, a clan who'd raided in Wales last year and enslaved many Welsh boys, including most of his friends. Now he had no friends. He was familiar enough with the layout of the Reavers' rath to lead them there. But if he did, he said, they would surely kill him and kill all of Maeldun's men, too. The Reavers, he said, had at least three times as many men as Maeldun.

"Yes, they may kill us," Maeldun said, "that's as may be. But if the Dagda is with us, then it may not be. Anyway, we plan to take our chances. If we survive the experience, and if you do, we will free you from your thralldom." The lad had no idea what Maeldun was talking about. But he was happy enough to accept a large piece of cheese and a hunk of dry bread.

A late afternoon rainstorm blew in off the sea, and the men sheltered as best they could beneath the canopy of tree branches. It was an uncomfortable evening, and before the night was over, they reckoned, it was likely to become far more uncomfortable.

The wind was blowing in heavy gusts as the men, led by the Welsh boy, began the trek to the Reavers' stronghold. The rain, fortunately, had now passed on. But it was a cold night, and only their vigorous physical exertions helped provide them some warmth. They followed the lad for the better part of an hour before they made their final approach to the rath.

Maeldun sent Dris and Conn on ahead at that point in order to deal with the gatekeepers. To their astonishment, there were none. The only challenge they received came from a lone dog who, scenting the strangers, launched into a high-pitched yowling. Someone yelled at him to quiet down, and he did, for about five seconds. Then he was at it again.

Maeldun's entire troop slipped quietly inside the main gateway of the imposing stone fortress. While the bulk of them stationed themselves just inside the opening, Conn, Dris, Garluan, and Ferben began moving stealthily, fanning out within the complex to get a clearer reading of the general situation. Most of the inhabitants of the stronghold seemed to be asleep. As he listened intently, Maeldun couldn't even hear the sounds of drunken revelry, as one might expect at such an hour on such an ugly night.

"The only lights and sounds are in their main hall," Conn said when he returned. "We may be in luck. Most of them may have fallen into a drunken stupor by now. Let us hope so."

"Lead us there," Maeldun said.

When they reached the large building with its high timbered roof, Maeldun left four men outside on guard and then motioned for the others to follow him in cautiously.

It was a cavernous structure, with a large central fire pit and several smaller braziers positioned about the room. There were people there, but not many. An old woman beside one of the braziers was weaving at her loom. A mangy-looking old dog that was lying by her feet raised his snout and offered a soft growl. Yes, there were people there, but not a single warrior.

"Where are the men?" Conn said sternly to the old woman.

She seemed surprisingly calm. "Gone," she said. "Three days now. Though they may return tonight. You might still have time to get away before they do. If you don't . . . "

"Why is the fort so unguarded? Are the Reavers so foolish as to take no precautions when they are off raiding?"

The old woman just laughed. "Why should they take precautions? Who would be foolish enough to walk right into the stronghold of the Reavers of Roonah? Anyone who did such a thing would not live long — nor would their wives or children or kinfolk. And nor will you."

"As for us, old mother, we are not killers of women, so you may go on about your work without fear," Maeldun said to her. "We do not mean to harm you."

"Perhaps not," she said, "though doing harm is why you have come."

"Doing harm to those who have done harm to us."

"Yes, that is the way of you men. I have seen the deaths of two husbands and five sons, just because that is the way of you men."

"You are wise, old mother," Conn said harshly, "but right

now you'd best be quiet. Or I might be tempted to pack your spirit off to join those of your kinfolk."

The old woman just nodded. "Yes," she said, "I don't doubt that you might do that. That is the way of you men."

"Weapons Master," came Garluan's excited voice. "Come here. Come and take a look at this."

What Garluan was staring at were rows and rows of heads, all neatly positioned in niches in the wall. Human heads — the heads of warriors the Reavers of Roonah had taken over many long years.

Conn stood there beside Garluan, running his eyes over the grisly sight. For the Reavers, it wasn't a grisly sight but a glorious one, for it was a record of their many triumphs in battle. For Conn, it only harkened back to the saddest day of his life, a day when he had stood on a lonely hillside beholding the headless bodies of his closest friends. He had promised those friends when he'd buried them that one day he would retrieve their heads, or he would die trying. Now, perhaps, he could make good on that promise.

Indeed, after only a few minutes he had identified the heads of his friends, for he found the eight of them positioned in a small niche separated from the others. As he looked at them, Conn couldn't help recognizing Ailill's familiar amulet, as well as Luga's, both of which had been draped about their heads on slender silver chains. Conn remained standing there for several moments with very mixed emotions. In the end he turned away, tears still in his eyes. Maeldun came over to Conn and pulled him to him in a powerful hug. Maeldun had tears in his eyes also.

It was Garluan who searched out a lidded wicker hamper. He looked about further until he'd found a woolen blanket to nestle inside the hamper. When Conn realized what Garlaun was about to do, he nodded his approval. But he didn't watch as Garluan gathered the heads. Conn Iron-fist turned away and walked out of the great building to be by himself.

The old woman, her eyes taking in all that was occurring, said nothing. She reached down and patted the old dog at her feet. He no longer growled softly. He was asleep.

"We must leave," Maeldun said. "We could lie in wait here for the Reavers' return, but there is no telling when that will be. I have no doubt that once they realize we have been here, they will be coming for us soon enough. We will still have our vengeance, I promise you that. By the Dagda, we will still have our vengeance! But it won't be this night."

No one disagreed, though Maeldun suspected that Conn would have, had he not been so distraught by the arresting sight of the decapitated heads of his closest friends.

Taking the Welsh lad with them, Maeldun and his men began the trek back to the creek where they had left their boat. The dawning was upon them before they reached it.

CHAPTER 20
Maeldun's Plan

The mariners returned to the hermit's island. There they would rest up and formulate a plan. The previous day had been long and emotionally draining. Even though many of them had not expected to survive the fight with the Reavers, still they were disappointed that they hadn't been able to bring about their much-desired vengeance.

"Now the shaggers'll know we be after 'em," Alim said grumpily. "That sure does eliminate the possibility of takin' 'em by surprise, now don't it."

"The gods want us to take our revenge, Alim," Maeldun averred. "They sent us on this mission to do that. They will not abandon us now. And we will not abandon our intentions to do their will."

Alim muttered something indistinct beneath his breath. When it came to the will of the gods, he apparently had his own ideas.

Later in the day, when Conn and Diuran had a chance to be off by themselves, Conn revealed his private concerns to Diuran. "Rhymer, I greatly fear that the gods are still angry with us. Our gods and the Christian god, also. We are still too many, and now with the Welsh lad we have added yet another."

"We couldn't very well abandon him, after using him the way we did."

"No, we couldn't. Maybe we could leave him here with the hermit."

"I don't know how pleased the hermit would be with that!"

Conn remained quiet for a while before speaking again. "Maeldun remains convinced that he should still seek out his mother. I believe it was that desire which caused us grief to begin with. The god of the Christians wishes her to be left alone. We have done enough harm to that woman. We should leave her be."

"How is it that you are such a great expert on what the god of the Christians wants? Might it not be just the opposite? Might not all of our troubles stem from the fact that we didn't go and see her as Maeldun wanted? Perhaps the Christian god is angry at us for neglecting him?"

"Did anyone ever tell you, Rhymer, that you can be a terrible pain in the arse?" Conn said, looking mightily irritated.

"Weapons Master, did anyone ever tell *you* that?"

"Regardless," Conn said with a sigh, "we have too many men. We will never succeed until we are seventeen, and seventeen only."

"I would volunteer myself," Diuran said, "if I thought it might help."

"No, you will not. We must have a Rhymer, a lad like a toad, a lad with coal-black hair, a lad with red-gold hair, and a warrior who is not of us. So you and I, Rhymer, are in it for the duration."

"Yes, I was afraid you might say something like."

*   *   *

The exhausted mariners enjoyed a warm and sunny early fall day, mostly just dozing in the sunshine. Maeldun, too, slept for several hours, and as he slept, he dreamed of his mother, a vivid dream in which the two of them finally came face to face. He had feared that she might deny him, refuse to speak to him, turn her back on him. But she hadn't. She'd smiled warmly and welcomed him. She told him she thought of him often — of Maeldun, the little boy who was flesh of her flesh.

When he awoke he felt much refreshed; and now he knew what they should do next. His dream convinced him it was imperative to seek the little island with the nunnery and find his mother. Indeed, he greatly wished they had done it sooner.

As the men began preparing their evening meal, Maeldun set off once more to say his farewells to the hermit Finian, to let him know they would be leaving the island for good in the morning, and to thank him for the loan of his coracle. And also because he found the gentle little man's company a welcome change from that of his rough-and-tumble companions.

When he reached the beehive hut, the hermit was nowhere to be seen. Maeldun glanced about and then he decided he could wait for a few minutes. He seated himself on the large rock by the fire pit, his face turned toward the late afternoon sun. It was going to be a glorious sunset. Maeldun was just about to leave when he heard someone approaching from the direction of the seal cove.

"Ah, Maeldun," the hermit said in his hoarse voice. "I am glad to see that you are still in one piece. I was afraid that you and your friends might have done something yesterday to place yourselves in jeopardy."

"We did do that, Finian, though things turned out a bit different from what we'd expected."

"I was afraid that you might've been involved in some sort of a raid, that you might've been involved in the horrid business of the taking of lives and the losing of them."

"We took no lives, Finian, nor did we lose any. Perhaps we even saved one, for we rescued a young Welsh lad from captivity."

"Captivity is a terrible thing. You must take good care of that lad and find a good home for him."

"Were you just now with the seals?" Maeldun asked. "Perhaps you were regaling them with song?"

"No, I wasn't singing to them, just visiting with them. They make rather perfect companions, you know. Not much for conversation, those seals, which is only one of their virtues. They have very distinctive personalities when you get to know them. Some are quite serious, some are comical, some are grumpy, and some are very affectionate."

"Perhaps they are actually humans who, for one reason or another, were transformed into seals. There are many old tales about such things."

"Or perhaps you and I are really seals who, for one reason or another, have been transformed into being humans." The hermit had a twinkle in his eye.

Maeldun couldn't help laughing. "My closest friend among the men, Finian, is a lad named Garluan. Like you he has a lively sense of humor. That's one of the reasons I like him so much. You would like him also."

"I believe that the Lord of All Things wishes us to be joyful, Maeldun, and humor is one of the things that creates joy. I am glad your friend has a lively sense of humor. Life would be very dull without it."

The two men visited for a little longer before Maeldun rose to be on his way. "Finian, I am glad to have met you. I hope we haven't intruded upon your solitude too much."

194

"Just the right amount," the hermit said. "But Maeldun, perhaps you will give some thought to the Lord of All Creation. He is a God whom you might come to love."

"I certainly do love his creation," Maeldun replied. "Even his seals."

"The Lord's blessing upon you, my son. And also on your friends."

"Thank you, Finian. And his blessing upon you as well."

The men had lazed and relaxed for most of the day, sleeping a lot and eating very little, so by evening they were more than ready for some hearty fare. Taman and Diuran were the cooks that night, and they'd prepared a thick and savory meat stew made mostly from food stuffs provided by Eithne and Cliona.

As the pot steamed and came to a boil, Alim strolled over to take a sniff. When he saw that no one was paying him any attention, he added just a very few drops of his secret elixir. "That'll give 'er a special tang," he said to himself. "That'll give 'er just what the doctor ordered."

As the men ate, Maeldun began outlining his new plan. In the morning, he told them, they would set off again, now having two particular goals in mind. Most importantly, they would return to the grassy hillside they'd visited early in their voyage, the one with the great cairn. There they would reunite the heads and bodies of his father and Conn's slain friends. On the way there, they would make a brief stop at the island of the nuns, where Maeldun hoped he might be able to find his mother. According to Conn and Alim, Maeldun told the men, the nuns' island was perhaps a journey of two days, with the grassy hillside with the cairn being another two days beyond that.

As for the Reavers of Roonah, Maeldun said he felt

confident that they would no longer have to seek them out. "We won't need to be finding them," Maeldun said, "for it seems certain that they will be finding us. And we must be prepared for that at all times. So you need not doubt that an opportunity to take our vengeance upon the Reavers will come. It will come."

The young Welsh lad, whose name was Davi, was devouring the stew with the best of them. He was grinning ear to ear, his face covered in stew juice, for it had been a very long time since he had enjoyed such a scrumptious meal. Although few of them could understand anything he said, he was already becoming a favorite among them.

Early in the day some of them had seen Davi fiddling with a strange object. What they'd assumed was only his walking stick, or perhaps his shepherd's crook, turned out to be something quite different. Indeed, what the lad possessed was a strange weapon, a weapon none of them were familiar with.

"What in the name of the Dagda is that thing of yours?" Garluan asked him, pointing to it.

Enjoying the attention, Davi put on a quick demonstration. Bending one end of it toward the other, he quickly attached a sturdy piece of twine to each of them.

"This is my bow," he said in Welsh, which of course only Conn and Diuran could understand. "It shoots arrows." He held up a small, pointed shaft and fitted it onto the string of the bow. He pulled it back taut, then launched the small missile a full fifty yards.

The mariners who'd been observing this little demonstration cheered and clapped. Most of them still assumed that what Davi had shown them was merely a clever toy. But a few minutes later when the lad proceeded to shoot a rabbit, some minds were quickly changed. What they had on their hands, they believed, was nothing but a young genius — which just went to show that not every Welshman was actually a feckin' ejit, as Alim continued to insist.

"Teach me how it works," Garluan said, speaking in gestures as much as in words. And for the remainder of the evening, the two of them experimented with Davi's ingenious device. Davi, it appeared, had long since mastered the use of it. Garluan, to begin with, was all thumbs. But he was determined to keep at it, for Davi's weapon, he felt sure, was something quite worth knowing how to use. Indeed, when he got the chance, Garluan planned to make a larger one for himself.

The next morning they made an early start, hoping to cover at least half the distance to the nuns' island that day. As the mariners rowed vigorously, they kept a sharp eye out for other sea craft. It was possible the Reavers were already pursuing them; it was possible, too, that they might encounter them by chance as the Reavers were returning to their stronghold from wherever they had been raiding. They needed to be ready.

But as Maeldun's curragh moved swiftly down the western shores of Eire, no other vessels came into view. Constantly buffeted by chill winds on the gray, uninviting day, they still managed to move quite a distance before finally pointing the boat's prow toward a small cove tucked neatly between a pair of sheer cliff faces. It was a place where both Alim and Conn had sought safe harborage before. They crept in cautiously, wanting to be sure that no one else had decided to do the very same thing. But the cove was deserted.

They augmented their meal that night with the pair of hares that Davi had brought back within half an hour of their coming ashore. The young lad was quickly becoming their good luck charm, and rather than feeling like they'd been saddled with an extra burden, the men delighted in his company and his boyish exuberance, and they were awed by his bow skills. The lad's simple presence helped raise their spirits, just as his bow skill helped fill the stew pot. Only Conn remained dubious about having the young Welsh boy with them. He alone among them seemed to be doing a lot of fretting; but only Diuran and Maeldun took much notice of it.

"Tonight," Diuran announced as they were finishing up their meal, "I will tell you a Welsh tale that I was taught long ago — with apologies to Davi for my pitiful pronunciation. It is a tale about a game of chess and at the same time, a tale about a battle between a troop of men and a troop of ravens."

As Diuran told the tale, he spoke first in Welsh and then in Irish so that all could understand what he was saying. The boy, who was not familiar with this story, was completely enthralled. And toward the end of it, when the troop of ravens suddenly turned upon the men who had been attacking them and began to rip them to bloody shreds, the boy hooped and hollered with delight.

"Suddenly the ravens came swooping down upon them, in joy and in anger," Diuran recounted, "inflicting terrible wounds and injuries upon them. Some carried off heads, some eyes, some arms, some ears. As they rose into the air, their cawing created a great and triumphant din."

The boy was leaping up and down and waving his arms with delight at the ravens' victory over the men. The mariners were more amused by the boy's joyful reactions than by the tale itself.

When they finally settled down to sleep an hour or so later, Maeldun noticed that it was close beside Garluan that the boy had chosen to lay himself down.

CHAPTER 21
Nuns' Island

The mariners were exhausted from an arduous day of battling rough seas. It was already dark when they landed the curragh on the warm and welcoming sands of the small island. As they carried the craft up among the dunes and began to establish their temporary camp, Conn's mind was filled with memories of this place.

If Conn's mind was filled with memories, Maeldun's was filled with anxieties. Already he was having doubts about the wisdom of coming here. The possibility of his mother rejecting him loomed ever larger in his thoughts. For him it would be a sleepless night. It would be for Conn as well.

Late in the night Maeldun sat up. Across the dunes from a short distance away came the sound of voices singing. Although Maeldun didn't know what it was, it was the voices of the nuns who were singing the service of Matins, the first of the eight divine services they sang at three-hour intervals throughout the day and night. Their voices sounded lovely to his hearing, so very different from the rough songs of the mariners or even the more gentle tunes that Taman or Diuran might sing. Sometimes back at Rath Murtagh women had sung, but nothing like this. The singing of the nuns seemed to Maeldun to have an unearthly quality.

The singing went on for half an hour, the voices of the nuns singing their simple chants completely in unison. The Irish singers that Maeldun had always known blended their voices together to create complex harmonies; they always took great pride in being able to embellish their music with many interwoven subtleties. But this music was nothing like that. Unaccompanied by instruments, it offered a simplicity and a purity the like of which Maeldun had never heard.

Maeldun wasn't the only one who was listening. For Conn, the singing of the nuns, like so much else, brought back stark remembrances of events that occurred here long ago — of the fateful night on which Maeldun was begotten; of Conn's later visit to the island and the old nun who had requested his help with Maeldun's mother, an event which had done much to shape Conn's future; and of his old friend Derga, who in the end had chosen to stay here and assist the nuns rather than follow the more challenging path that Conn knew he himself must follow.

Thinking of Derga again made Conn smile. He'd always suspected that Derga, after his innocent fashion, had fallen in love with the nuns. When Derga had chosen the nuns over him, Conn had not been offended. He knew it was probably a very wise choice for Derga, a choice that offered him a real possibility of achieving happiness. Conn wondered if he might see his old friend tomorrow. He hoped that he would. How many years had it been since he had last seen him? At least sixteen or seventeen, he guessed.

In the morning the men breakfasted on cold rations. Maeldun, unsure how he should begin to go about things, seemed in no hurry to do anything. His second thoughts had not dissipated. Indeed, he felt sorely tempted just to tell the men they should pack up and head off again.

"Come on, lad," Conn said to him firmly. "If we are going to do this, then let's do it."

Maeldun sighed. "*Are* we going to do this?" he said.

"You're the one who insisted upon coming here. It wasn't my choice. So either we do it, or we don't. It's entirely up to you."

"Go and find your mother, Mael," Garluan said. "If she were my mother, I wouldn't hesitate for a single moment. I would rush to her and embrace her like she'd never been embraced before."

"Then maybe you had better go in my stead," Maeldun said, smiling at his friend.

"Go, Mael. You will not regret it. If you don't go, you will regret it terribly."

Maeldun sighed yet again. "Conn," he said, "I am ready to go."

The two men climbed the dunes and stood there together, their eyes turned toward the small stone building surrounded by the low stone wall. Conn remembered the sight vividly. It had hardly changed at all, though now to one side of the small building there was a churchyard containing half a dozen gravestones. The graves were marked by simple crosses. One of them was slightly larger than the others, and Conn wondered if it might mark the grave of the old woman whom he had helped.

Beyond the church was a garden that had not been there before, and out beyond that there were several small buildings. It appeared that a little community might be forming in the environs of the abbey.

As they stood there watching, they saw a man come out of one of the small buildings that lay out beyond the church. He was carrying gardening tools, and trailing along behind him were two children, a boy and a girl. As Conn studied him, it suddenly dawned on him that the man was his old friend Derga. Were the boy and the girl his children? It seemed very likely. Derga's red hair was now mixed with gray, and he'd put on weight. Derga looked middle-aged, but it was surely he.

It was right at that moment that Derga glanced over and saw the two men standing upon the high dune. He did a double take and nearly dropped his tools. He just stood there, his mouth agape.

Conn raised his hand in greeting. For a moment, Derga remained standing there as if he'd been turned to stone. Then he, too, slowly raised his hand in greeting. It was too great a distance for either of them to exchange spoken greetings, and Conn was not about to violate the peaceful scene by shouting. So the two men just stared at each other, Conn grinning at his old friend and Derga still looking wonder-struck.

A young nun exited the abbey and began tolling the bell by the lich gate. And a few moments later, a procession of nuns exited the abbey and began crossing the churchyard in a long single line. There were about a dozen of them in all, each one garbed in a simple gray robe, their ages varying from quite young to fairly elderly. The one who walked last in the procession looked to be in early middle age. She could only be distinguished from the others by a plain, wooden pectoral cross that hung from her neck by a thickly corded rope. Conn knew who she was.

It was a slow and stately procession. Apparently there was some particular observance the nuns were about to make.

The nun who came last in the procession glanced over at the figure of Derga, who was still standing stock still, frozen in the spot from which he'd first spotted Conn and Maeldun. Seeing the look on his face, she swiveled her head and looked to see what it was that Derga was staring at.

On the high dune not far from the church she saw the two tall men. She stopped and turned toward them. Now both of them had their eyes glued to her face. It seemed to her that both of them were looking at her hopefully, perhaps wishing that she would offer them some sign of recognition or of friendly welcome. As she looked at them, she realized that she knew one of them. The other one she did not know.

The nun remained there staring at the two tall men. The younger man, with his great shock of coal-black hair, was handsome indeed. Of course he was, she thought, suddenly realizing whose son he must be. She found herself thinking back to that time so many years ago, that time when she had hoped so much that a certain man who had professed his love to her would come back and claim her. But that man had never come.

Now, though, it was his son — and her son — who had at last come back. The thought of seeing her son standing there, her beautiful son, a man who had come back to see her, brought warmth to her heart and a tear to her eye.

Slowly, she raised her arm in greeting.

The older man didn't return her greeting. Instead, he placed his hand atop the shoulder of the younger man who stood beside him. It was the younger man who slowly raised his arm in greeting.

The nun and the young man both held their arms raised like that for a full minute, as the eyes of each of them held the eyes of the other.

Finally, working up his courage, Maeldun began to slowly advance toward the woman.

The woman stepped away from the procession of nuns and walked a short distance toward the young man.

Now the two of them stood just a few yards apart, staring at each other wordlessly.

It was Maeldun who finally spoke. "I wanted to see you, Mother," he said softly.

The woman stood there, smiling upon the tall and handsome young man.

"I'm glad you did," she said. "I have thought of you often."

Maeldun walked slowly across the last few feet that separated them. He stopped and stood in front of his mother, who was nearly a foot shorter than he was. He looked into her very blue eyes, eyes that were even bluer than his own eyes.

Slowly, the woman reached out and placed her arm upon his. Maeldun felt her gentle touch. Then he too reached out and placed his hand softly upon the woman's shoulder. The two of them remained standing there like that, just barely touching each other, neither of them speaking.

Finally Maeldun said, "I should go now. My men are waiting."

The woman nodded. "Yes, I should also. But you and your men would be welcome to stay."

"No, we should go. There are important things we need to do."

Again the woman nodded. "I am glad you came, Maeldun," she said, "so very, very glad."

"You know my name?"

"I *gave* you your name."

"Mother," Maeldun said, "perhaps you have given me even more than that."

The nun watched as the two men retreated back across the dunes. She wondered if she would ever see them again. She had her doubts. But she rejoiced in that fact that she had seen them. She rejoiced in the fact that in the end, a man she greatly loved had returned to find her.

CHAPTER 22
Storm

As the curragh sped southward, Maeldun remained quiet and pensive, harboring a deep sense of personal satisfaction. He had seen his mother and made himself known to her. She had not rejected him, as he'd feared she might; indeed, he now felt quite certain that she held a deep affection for him. That was enough. That was all he'd hoped for. He would never intrude upon her life again. But he would always cherish the memory of their very brief meeting.

The mariners had made an early start, and for most of the day the weather had been perfect — calm seas, gentle breezes, a bright sky flecked with quickly scudding white clouds. Manannan, the great sea god, seemed to be with them.

Now they moved along a familiar shoreline, one with sights they had seen earlier in their voyage. Fintan's Cave came and went, and they knew that they were no more than a full day's journey from their destination, the grassy hillside with the great cairn.

Conn was slowly coming around to Diuran's way of thinking. At least to the point where it crossed his mind that the Christians' god might be on their side after all. In any case, he certainly felt a strong sense of relief about how things had gone at the nuns' island. It still bothered him that they had two too many men in their company; but he'd begun to wonder if that was going to matter after all.

Dris seemed largely recovered from the terrible shock Ronan's death had given him. He had genuinely mourned his brother and rued the role he'd played in his brother's final moments. But at the same time, he knew it had been necessary to alleviate Ronan's suffering.

Now, though, he'd begun to turn his thoughts toward the future — toward the major part he hoped to play in the impending battle with the Reavers; and toward finally returning back to his home, back to Rath Murtagh. He knew it would be Maeldun who would receive the hero's welcome when they finally got there. But to his surprise, he realized that he wasn't unhappy about that. Maeldun had won his respect. Maeldun, he believed, had helped him to change. He'd come to believe he was a better man now than he'd been before; and if that was so, it was Maeldun who deserved the credit.

Garluan was teaching Davi to speak Irish. As they worked away at it, they soon realized that the two languages weren't really so very different. They had a great many words in common. The biggest differences seemed to be in pronunciations. Davi was a bright and inquisitive lad. He had an innately cheerful nature, though it was also apparent that he harbored a great loathing for the Reavers of Roonah. Although he didn't speak of it, Garluan knew they must've treated the lad most cruelly. Whenever the mariners referred to the fight they soon expected to have, the boy unconsciously ran his hand up and down the smooth, well-tended wood of his bow, a smile of anticipation flickering at the corners of his lips.

*   *   *

Alim stood in the prow of the curragh, continually alert to everything concerning his beloved craft — the movements of the sea, their distance from the shore, the appearance of the sky off to the west. It was the latter that began to cause him consternation, for far off on the western horizon he'd noticed a long, thin line of dark clouds that had suddenly appeared. To Alim's experienced eye, what he saw did not bode well for the mariners.

"There's a storm a-buildin', lads," he declared in a loud voice. "It be a-buildin' fast, too."

"Should we make a run for shore?" Maeldun asked. "Do you know of any place where it might be possible to make a safe landing?"

"This ain't no welcoming shore, Mael, nothin' here 'bouts but rocks and cliffs. Was we ta try it, we could get ourselves busted up mighty bad. I'd say we might best weather this blow far out ta sea." Even as they were having this exchange, the dark clouds to the west were taking on an even more ominous look, billowing higher and clearly moving toward them with great rapidity. Now, too, the seas were growing choppier.

"You take the steering oar, Mariner. We shall trust your judgment."

Larger swells began rising and billowing all about the craft. Moment by moment the skies grew darker. A huge storm was brewing, racing in from the west, racing toward Maeldun and his men. There would be no escaping it.

"We need more sea room!" Alim cried out to the rowers. "Pull, lads, pull! Keep her nose headed inta the blow." The broad-beamed, flat-bottomed craft lifted and fell upon the ever-growing swells.

The air about them was filled with cold spray. The flying seawater entered their eyes and noses. Soon they were entirely drenched. The sky was now so dark they could hardly see any distance beyond the boat.

"Toss in the sea anchors, the killicks!" Alim shouted. "Then hold on for dear life, lads! Pray to the Dadga, pray to Manannan! They ain't nothin' else left ta do! Hold on, lads. I'll try ta keep her pointed into the storm." No one heard Alim's last words, for they were completely drowned out by the howling winds and crashing waves.

If the craft turned sideways, it would founder for sure. But Alim had a steady, strong hand. And the well-built curragh — light, sturdy, and flat-bottomed like a seabird — battled the fierce elements bravely. Alim muttered a steady stream of endearments to his much-beloved boat, coaxing her, cajoling her, encouraging her. And she was responding nobly.

But the cresting waves now reached towering heights about them, some as high as thirty feet or more. The mariners clung to the thwarts, clung to each other, clung to their most prized possessions.

Water sloshed all about them as the engulfed curragh slowly took on more and more water from the fierce foaming seas.

Suddenly a massive wave lifted the prow high up upon its towering crest. The boat tilted straight upward, reaching a point of near verticality. The wave was going to flip the craft over, dropping it back down again, bottom-side up. But it didn't. Miraculously, the huge wave pushed on beneath the noble craft, bringing it crashing down and burying the prow deep into the trough between the successive waves.

It was the boat's sudden downward plunge that brought about disaster. Nearly half of the crew found themselves violently tossed out into the dark and chilly water — it was as if they'd been thrown from the back of a wild bucking beast. Garluan, one arm clutching the wicker hamper, the other clutching a thwart, was not among them. But loosing his hold on the thwart, he groped with his free hand in the hope of feeling the body of the Welsh lad who'd been crouching safely close beside him. The lad wasn't there. As Garluan's hand scrabbled back and forth in the area where the boy had been, all he found was the lad's bow, which had somehow wedged itself securely between the thwart and one of the curragh's ribs.

For a few moments an odd calm came over the sea. It gave the men still in the boat a chance to collect their wits and a chance to scan the seas for their companions. The air about them was not as dark as it had been, and they could make out several heads bobbing in the water at various distances from the boat.

Dris tossed a rope toward one of them, and a hand reached up and grabbed it. Dris quickly reeled the man in. Garluan prayed to the Dagda the hand would belong to young Davi. Garluan's prayer wasn't answered. The hand belonged to Taman the Harper.

Three or four men swam to the safety of the craft on their own and others were reeled in by rope — Ferben and Celtchar among them. As Garluan glanced about him, he could see that Maeldun and Conn and Diuran were all still safely in the boat, none of them having been pitched into the raging sea.

The seas were beginning to get wild again and their little moment of calm was ending. And yet the dark head of another man now popped up above the surface of the sea. Perhaps as much as thirty yards distant, this man began stroking his way swiftly through the roiling water.

This person, who was by far the lightest member of the crew, had been flung the greatest distance. But now, looking like the Great Selkie himself, he knifed his way through the sea with quick, deft strokes. As he neared, Garluan snatched up the lad's bow and held it out over the side of the curragh. His slender hand reached up and grasped it. With the deftness and grace of a fine young athlete, young Davi vaulted in over the side, straight into Garluan's warm, if wet, embrace.

The storm continued for the better part of an hour, with the exhausted mariners bailing desperately; but it was finally on the wane. Eventually the skies lightened, the fierce waves subsided, and with the increased visibility, the mariners could see that they still maintained a margin of safety from the treacherous shore, a slim margin of safety, but a margin nonetheless.

As Maeldun and Conn quickly tallied up the mariners, they realized that two men remained unaccounted for. They were two of the older warriors the king had agreed to send with them. Now the mariners scanned the seas in search of them. They rowed slowly in ever-widening circles for most of an hour.

"We'll be losing our light, Mael," Alim finally said. "We'd best find ourselves shelter. It's not impossible that they can make it to shore on their own. But there ain't much we can do for 'em now. We'd best look to our own needs." Maeldun glanced over at Conn, who just nodded his head to indicate his agreement with Alim.

"May Manannan protect you," Maeldun said, bowing his head for a moment. All the other men bowed their heads as well. Then Maeldun motioned to Alim, signaling that he should direct the craft where he would.

They moved on southward for a short distance, then turned sharply toward shore. Alim had a place in mind, a narrow inlet at the foot of one of the great bens of western Connachta. He wouldn't have risked going there in the midst of the storm, but now with the softer seas, he felt sure he could get them in there safe and sound. And he proved to be right.

Wet, shaken, exhausted, famished, the men set up their camp near where a small stream flowed into the sea. It was a gravelly spot but not inhospitable. They had lost most of their packs and scrips, and also their large bag of spears, though not their great cooking pot. And so crabs and shellfish, spiced with worts and herbs from a nearby meadow, were soon simmering in fresh water drawn from the stream.

Maeldun sent several men back along the shore to search for their missing fellows. The men were gone for nearly two hours and didn't return until well after dark. They bore the body of one of the men. Of the other they'd seen no trace. They'd also found some of their lost possessions, including two of their oars and several of their packs.

The storm had been a harrowing experience and a tragic one. Two of their men had been lost, the only casualties thus far from their original party. Their meal that night, though savory and nourishing, was a sober one. It was not leavened by song or tale. Indeed, Taman the Harper was mourning the loss of his much-cherished harp, his most prized possession.

At one point in the meal Diuran looked over and caught the eye of Conn Iron-fist. He didn't have to say what he'd been thinking. When Conn's eye met Diuran's, he just nodded his head. He knew the thought that was in the Rhymer's mind. For as both of them had looked about them at the men, they'd both realized that now — for the first time since Maeldun had rescued his foster-brothers — they were back to having seventeen men in their company.

And it was only because of the presence of Dris and the young Welsh lad that the total came up to that number. At long last, they were seventeen mariners once again.

CHAPTER 23
A Game of Chess

In the morning the mariners, still feeling battered and bruised, slowly began busying themselves with all that had to be done.

Again Maeldun dispatched a small party of men to scour the shoreline. Alim, meanwhile, began inspecting his beloved curragh. After a cursory inspection, it appeared to have come through the sea-tempest in remarkably good shape; but Alim intended to spend the day giving it the most careful scrutiny, checking every seam, every rib, every individual skin.

With the two oars the men brought back last night, they possessed a total of eight, though not a single one of their small wooden paddles. So a couple of the men were put to work shaping paddles and oars to replace the ones they'd lost.

All of the men, fortunately, still possessed their swords. But their entire cache of spears had been washed away. They would need to be replaced. So under the direction of Celtchar, several of them set off to a nearby grove of holly in search of just the right saplings and young trees they would need.

Davi's bow had survived but only two of his arrows. Nevertheless, he and Garluan set off to hunt game armed with bow, arrows, and sling. Davi's two arrows would suffice for now, and Garluan's pouch of lethal sling-balls remained full as ever. And so as the two young friends wandered off, they both felt certain they wouldn't be returning empty-handed. Later in the day, perhaps, they would have time to fashion a fresh supply of arrows for the Welsh lad.

The body of their dead companion rested silently nearby, covered by his cloak. At day's end they would have a small service to mourn him properly, before raising a small cairn over him. If the body of the other missing man were found today, the spirits of the two of them would be sent on their way together.

A little past mid-day Garluan and Davi returned. Garluan was grinning from ear to ear, for draped about his neck was a fat roebuck. If Davi's grin wasn't quite so large, what he carried was every bit as welcome — a brace of pheasants, a rabbit, and half a dozen wood pigeons. The men would eat well tonight; indeed, they would eat well for several days to come.

Garluan immediately set about brittling the deer, carefully instructing Davi every step of the way. Taman and Diuran took charge of the rest of the game and began the tedious process of plucking and skinning.

Not long after Davi and Garluan's return, the search party returned as well. They'd gone several miles along the coastline in each direction, finding no sign of their missing man. But their efforts hadn't been entirely in vain for they'd found a number of items washed from the craft during the storm — two more of their oars and several of their paddles; a couple more of the men's personal knapsacks; and most wondrous of all, Taman's harp still safe and secure within its snuggly fitting skin covering.

Maeldun deeply regretted the loss of their friend. He'd

known since they'd set off from Rath Murtagh that many of the men stood a good chance of not surviving their expedition. But he'd found the loss of March and Ronan, and now the loss of two more of his men, bitter pills to swallow. He suspected that the deaths of friends was something one never became inured to, no matter have often one experienced it.

It was around the middle of the afternoon that a small boat appeared making its way up the inlet. Four men were in it. One of them held the upraised signs of a herald — a peeled hazel wand in his left hand, an unsheathed sword in his right — indicating that theirs was a peaceful mission. They beached their craft close beside the curragh and greeted Maeldun and Conn.

"I am Froech MacRoss of the Clan Conaille. Ours is the territory you are now in. Ours are the beasts you are now preparing. But if your intentions are peaceful, you are welcome to them. We are happy to welcome visitors who come in peace."

"Thank you. We appreciate your warm greeting and your hospitality. I am Maeldun MacEoin and this is my friend Conn Iron-fist."

"Ah, so that's who you are. I've long known the reputation of Conn Iron-fist, Maeldun, and lately there have been rumors about you and your band, too. You have managed to stir up the Reavers, never a good thing. The word we now hear is that they are in search of you. Nadcrandel swears he will soon have the head of each of you perched on a pole outside his rath."

"Nadcrandel?"

"The fierce and venerable leader of the Reavers of Roonah. Do you not know of him?"

"Perhaps we will have *his* head on a pole," Conn interjected.

"That would take some doing, Conn Iron-fist. But if you were able to accomplish it, you would hear shouts of rejoicing from one end of Eire to the other."

"Do you know where the Reavers are now?"

"No, I do not. But they are looking for you, you can be certain of that."

"Well, Froech MacRoss, since we will be feasting on the beasts of your clan tonight, would you stay and join us?"

"No, I must decline your offer. However . . . " — and he paused to take from his pack a game board and a set of game pieces — "I would love to challenge your finest player to a game of fidchell before I go. Is there anyone here who believes he might compete with me? I enjoy nothing in the world more than a spirited match. The truth is, I seldom find anyone who can beat me. Whenever I meet strangers, I always ask them for a game. Is there perhaps one among you who might wish to play?"

Dris stepped forward. "And what stake might you wish to play for?" he said.

"You are the guest in our clan's territory, so you should choose the stake."

"Your cloak for my brooch," Dris replied.

"Yes, let us do that."

Froech quickly set the pieces out upon the board, with the red pieces clustered in the center, the black pieces arranged upon the spaces around the outer edge of the board. As all of the men knew full well, the object of the game was for the red king, now perched on the very center square of the board, to make his way safely to the outer edge; or, conversely, for the black pieces to hem him in and capture him before he could do that. If the red king managed to reach the outer edge, then red won. If he were trapped and couldn't move, then black won.

215

"You may be red or black," Froech said.

"I'll choose red," Dris replied.

The game took half an hour to complete, with Maeldun's men (aside from the lookout) and Froech's three companions all watching intently. The skills of the two players seemed well matched, though Dris's subtle maneuvering won out in the end, to the glee of Maeldun's men. Now they would play again, with Dris playing the black pieces and Froech the red.

"What shall we play for this time?" Dris asked. "I had my choice, now it is yours."

"Would you mind playing for the same stake? I would very much hate to lose my cloak. If you win, you can add my brooch to the cloak you've already won." Dris nodded his agreement.

This time the game went to Froech, whose men were just as gleeful at its conclusion as Maeldun's had been after the first game. They would now play a third and final match to declare the winner.

"Choose your pieces," Froech said.

"I will play black again. Black has yet to win, and I would like to prove that I can do it."

"And will you allow me the choice of the stake? So far neither of us has gained anything over the other. Third time pays for all, as they say. Let's see, what shall we play for?"

"I suggest," Garluan sang out, "that if Froech wins, we give him the most beautiful girl in Rath Murtagh. If Dris wins, he gets the most beautiful girl in Rath Conaille." All the men cheered at Gar's proposal, and the two players both smiled. But then it was down to business again.

"The choice of the stake in this final game shall be yours," Dris said. "What shall it be?"

"If I win," Froech replied, "what I would like to have is your sword."

Dris blanched at that request. And Maeldun's men stood there in shocked silence. Froech's request was a wholly inappropriate request. One never sought to take away another man's most prized possession, his sword. It was both a terrible breach of decorum and a terrible insult. A warrior without his sword was a man unmanned.

"You may choose whatever you wish, in the event that you win," Froech said. "But the stake I seek is your sword."

Dris remained sitting there in silence. He was on the horns of a dilemma. It would be cowardly and discourteous to deny Froech's request, however inappropriate it was. But did he really want to risk his sword? It was his pride and joy and far and away the finest sword possessed by any man in Maeldun's company.

Finally Dris spoke. "Yes," he said, "I will agree to that. What I want in return, should I win, is this entire set of game pieces and the game board as well."

Now it was Froech's turn to blanch. Although Dris's request did not involve a personal insult, it too put at jeopardy the man's most cherished possession. Now it was Froech who had to swallow his pride and agree. Slowly, reluctantly, he nodded his head.

This time the game proceeded very slowly, each player considering at great length his every move. Much more was at stake now than just a cloak or a brooch. Froech was employing a wedge strategy, amassing his pieces in front of the red king and slowly moving them forward as a unit before him, forcing the black pieces back. It seemed to be working well. But one by one Dris was picking them off, removing them from the board, and Froech's line of protecting pieces was thinning.

But Froech had a secret plan. Indeed, he was drawing Dris straight into his trap. Dris was apparently unaware of what Froech had in store for him. As he put his fingers on a piece

217

and was about to move it, he snuck a quick peek at Froech's face, hoping to see his opponent's reaction to what he was about to do. Instead, he saw something else.

Right behind Froech stood Alim the Wanderer, his eyes bright. He'd been closely following every move and nuance of the game. As Dris fingered the piece and glanced toward Froech's face, his eyes also took in Alim's face. And as they did, he noticed Alim make an almost imperceptible shake of his head.

Dris dropped his eyes back down to the board for a moment, looking at the piece in his fingers, buying himself just a little more time. Then he slowly raised his eyes again, this time to just above Froech's head. Once more he saw Alim make the tiniest shake of his head. Was Dris about to make a crucial blunder?

Yes. And now, as he continued studying the board, he saw what it was. The move he'd been about to make, a move that had seemed the most obvious one to make in the situation, would actually have cost him the game. And then Dris spotted the right move, the one that would win him the game. He shifted his fingers to a different piece. But before making that move, he shot a quick glance at Froech's eyes. And Froech flinched. Now Dris knew for sure that if he made that particular move, all was lost for Froech. Dris fingered the piece, lifted it into the air, and made the move. Froech looked down at the board. Then he reached out and toppled his king. He conceded the game.

Standing behind Froech, Alim's face bore a look of total innocence. Eventually, he too took his turn along with all the others in congratulating the victor. Neither of them exchanged a word.

Before he and his men departed, the disconsolate Froech asked hopefully, "Could we play again tomorrow before you set off? You are a most worthy opponent."

Dris clapped the crestfallen man on the shoulder and promised him they would play again sometime in coming years. "I was lucky to beat you, Froech, and you shall definitely have your rematch. In the meantime, I shall care for your pieces and board as lovingly as you have done. One day you shall have your chance to win them back."

When the men from Clan Conaille were gone, Maeldun and his men conducted their sad little ceremony over the body of their fallen friend. When they were finished, they raised a cairn over him. They sang a hymn of farewell to his departing soul. Then they remained standing in a circle of silence for a good many minutes about the cairn.

"The nerve o' the bastard to play for Dris's sword," Alim declared, as they were eating their evening meal. "The worthless piece o' shite. Served 'im right ta lose his board 'n' pieces. Playin' for a man's sword! Who's ever heard o' such a insultin' thing!"

"It was kind of an unfair match, though," Maeldun said, "one man having to play against two."

"Huh?" said Celtchar. "One against two?"

Most of the men shared Celtchar's puzzlement. "Whatta you mean, one versus two?" Ferben asked. "It were just Dris versus Froech, weren't it?"

"I really have nothing more to say about it," Maeldun said with a grin.

One of the ones who did seem to know what Mael was talking about was the young Welsh boy, whose sharp eyes rarely missed a thing. Finally, making a brave attempt at speaking Irish, he said to Dris, "I would like to play you also. Would you teach me? Or maybe it is the Wanderer who should teach me." He looked over and smiled at Alim when he said that.

"I ain't so much at playin' games, laddy," Alim replied.

"Oh yes," the lad replied, "I think you are very much at playing games."

The mariners laughed at the boy's remark, though few of them understood the full meaning of what he was hinting at.

CHAPTER 24
Conn's Contemplations

As they pushed on southward, finishing up the last stage of their journey back to the high grassy hill, the mariners felt a fresh sense of confidence. They'd recovered the heads of Conn's friends, and if all went well, they would soon be reuniting them with their bodies at the cairn. They'd replaced the spears they lost in the storm and readied their other weapons for the approaching showdown with the Reavers. And they found the optimism and good humor of the young Welsh lad so infectious that it raised the spirits of all of them. When the battle came, the lad would be a rallying point. He had become their pet, the "beloved little calf of their hearts," as Alim put it. Every one of them would fight to the death to protect him. And now, too, many of them had begun to turn their thoughts toward going home to Rath Murtagh. If they survived the final battle, that's all most of them wanted to do.

Davi, with Garluan's help, had a new set of arrows, fletched with pheasant feathers. As the boat continued on its way, the lad further sharpened them and practiced fitting them to his bow, enlarging their notches if there was a need for it. Garluan had replaced his bowstring with a strand of heavy twine, and coated it with bee's wax. He'd fashioned a special pouch from the roebuck's hide for the lad to carry his arrows, a pouch that could hang from his shoulder. Now Davi wouldn't have to tuck his arrows, three or four at a time, beneath his belt, as had been his practice.

At one point Diuran made his way over to visit with the lad. When Diuran began speaking in Welsh, the lad shook his head and said in Irish, "What foreign gibberish is that? You must speak in a civilized tongue, one I can understand."

The mariners who overheard his remark all laughed, none louder than Alim. "Foreign gibberish," he muttered with a grin. "Ya lovely piece o' crap." The lad had quickly become one of them. He had embraced them and their ways as swiftly as they had embraced him.

"You are a marvelous swimmer," Diuran went on, now speaking in Irish. "When you saved yourself during the storm, you were swimming like a pup seal. Oh, how I wish I could swim as gracefully as you. Do you know the tale of Dylan? I was thinking that perhaps we shouldn't be calling you Davi, we should be calling you Dylan."

The lad nodded. "I know the tale of Dylan. And maybe I swim almost as well as he. I was raised in a small village close by the sea. I've swum in the sea as long as I have walked on the land. But still, Rhymer, I do not think you can call me Dylan. For Dylan was a tow-headed boy while I am a dark-headed one."

"It seems that you know the tale even better than I. I'd forgotten that Dylan was light-haired. So I guess we'd best stick with calling you Davi."

"I believe so too. Let Dylan be Dylan and Davi be Davi."

"Davi, you are wise beyond your years."

*   *   *

It was an uneventful day. A couple of times, when they spotted boats off in the distance, they feared they might be the boats of the Reavers. But they were only fishermen who quickly shied away from Maeldun's large, swift curragh.

They beached their craft that evening on a peaceful shore only a short distance away from their destination. Although they could have finished their journey, Conn said he preferred not to. He didn't want to spend this night camped out so close to where the bodies of his friends lay beneath the great cairn. He didn't explain why he didn't, but the mariners respected his wishes.

As their evening meal was simmering in the great pot, Conn walked off by himself, eschewing the company of either Diuran or Maeldun, his usual companions. He was gone for a long time. Perhaps he was communing with the spirits of his long-dead friends. Since the mariners had retrieved the heads from the Reavers' rath, Conn had become a quieter, more contemplative man. There was no doubt that the events of the coming days held great significance to him. For the last seventeen years, returning the heads to the cairn was one of the two things he most desired to achieve.

Taman, his harp tuned and oiled and shining as of old, played and played and played. There was little conversation. The Welsh boy came and sat by Taman and watched and listened. At one point he began to sing along wordlessly with the harper, his voice far higher in pitch than that of any of the men, even Taman's high tenor. The mariners listened, captivated by sounds the like of which they had never heard.

As Taman played and Davi sang, Maeldun glanced over at Conn. The Weapons Master — Maeldun's long-time teacher and mentor, a man who'd been his father's closest friend, and the bravest man Maeldun had ever known — had tear-filled eyes. Maeldun felt sure it wasn't just the unearthly music that was causing the Weapons Master's tears.

Since they'd retrieved the heads from the Reaver's rath, Garluan had been their self-appointed guardian. He'd kept them safe and secure within the wicker hamper where he'd first placed them. Since then they had always been at his side, except for the few hours when he'd gone off hunting with Davi, when Maeldun had taken charge of them.

Now, as the fire burned low and the darkness thickened around them, Maeldun noticed that Conn Iron-fist had moved over close to where Garluan had placed the hamper. Conn seated himself beside it. He was preparing himself for a long night's vigil.

The high hill rose before them, as green or greener than any hill in Eire. As the sunshine glistened upon the morning dew, the grassy hillside sparkled like a jewel. Two-thirds of the way up the steep hillside was the great stone cairn, the same cairn the men had visited early in their voyage. But while the hill gave every appearance of being a place of great calm and serenity, Conn Iron-fist harbored very different memories of it. For Conn, it was a place where a horrific event had occurred — the most horrific event of his life.

There was a level spot at the bottom of the hill suitable for landing boats, and Alim navigated the craft toward it with consummate skill. The decision made long ago to ask the Wanderer to come along as their master seaman was one no man among them regretted, despite the Mariner's occasional foul moods. By that point in their adventures, each man considered it a badge of honor, not an insult, when Alim referred to him as a "worthless piece o' crap."

With the better part of the day still before them, they busied themselves establishing their camp at the foot of the hill. Maeldun assigned several of them to make the long trek on up the hill to the fresh water springs in order to re-fill their water pouches. Later in the day they would begin the arduous task of re-opening the cairn. It was likely to be tomorrow morning that they would hold their ceremony, a ceremony in which they would reunite the heads in Garluan's wicker hamper with the bodies in the cairn. Among those eight bodies, of course, was that of Maeldun's father, Ailill of the Hard Edge.

Once more Conn walked off alone, keeping himself a good distance away from the high hill. More things seemed to be weighing on his mind than just the ceremony they would be performing in the morning. For the night before, Conn had had a sobering dream. In his dream Ailill had come to him, along with Luga and the others who had died here. They welcomed him with warm and loving words. They told him how much they'd missed him, and how glad they were that they would finally be reunited with him. They thanked him for making it possible for their spirits to be released. They were pleased that his spirit would be going along with them on their final journey.

It was only a dream, Conn told himself. But it was a dream he did not intend to reveal to anyone else, not even to Diuran. He had never feared death. But his dream, he believed, was more than an idle dream. It seemed to him a presentiment, a premonition of things to come. But perhaps it was merely the result of all his pent up anxieties about so many things — tomorrow's great ceremony; the final confrontation with the Reavers; and about what the future would hold for him when their voyage was finally over.

Conn had given little thought to the future. His life, for so many years, had been dedicated to just two things, retrieving the heads of his friends and taking vengeance on the Reavers.

When those two things had been accomplished, what was there left for him to do? Now he realized that his future beyond the next few days held no shape, no certainty. It was a blank. For once in his life, Conn Iron-fist had no plan. All he knew was that he would accept whatever it was that the fates had in store for him.

In the afternoon, a group of the men began opening up the cairn, working from the side highest on the hill. They removed the heavy stones one by one, gradually forming another pile off to one side. They planned to leave most of the lower portion of the cairn intact, but in order to accomplish their goal of fully uncovering the bodies of Conn's beloved friends, they would need to displace more than half of the stones.

Conn did not help them. Instead, he made another long trek, this time on up the hill to the fresh-water springs. It was the same trek he'd made on the day his friends died, the same trek he made once more with Derga, when they'd first returned to construct the original cairn. He had no particular reason for going to the spring. It was just something to do. The mariners realized that their Weapons Master was lost in his own thoughts. They knew that all they should do was to go on about their tasks and leave the man alone.

Conn didn't return until late afternoon. By then the men had completed their work on the cairn and gone back down the hill to their camp. Now several of their cloaks were draped across the back half of the exposed cairn. Conn came to the cairn and sat down upon the grass. He didn't lift the cloaks. He sat on the hillside looking out at the great expanse of the sea. As the late afternoon sun slanted across the hillside, Conn Iron-fist remained alone beside the cairn.

Even as the smell of the men's evening meal wafted up the hillside, Conn remained where he was. As the soft sounds of

Taman's harping floated up to his ears, he remained where he was. When the mariners finally settled down to their sleep, Conn Iron-fist was still up on the hill beside the cairn, alone with his thoughts.

CHAPTER 25
A Fated Fight

Conn had fallen asleep on the hillside. When he awoke, he felt certain that he'd had soothing, gentle dreams, though he couldn't quite remember what they had been. Whatever they had been, his anxieties were no longer so great as they'd been before. He stood up and stretched to get the stiffness out. He looked down at the camp on the landing area by the curragh and saw the men beginning to bestir themselves. He realized he was hungry. He would go down and have a hearty breakfast.

Maeldun waved his greeting to Conn as the Weapons Master approached. Conn smiled at the handsome young man, a young man who had come to remind him so much of his friend Ailill. For more than seventeen years, Conn had adjusted his life to fit the life of this young man whom he had trained and formed. Conn was proud of the man Maeldun had become. He felt certain that Ailill would have been proud of him also. Together, he and Maeldun, they would finally achieve justice for the cruel slaying of Maeldun's father.

"Come and eat," Maeldun said. "You must be famished."

"That is true," Conn replied. "Every one of us must eat. Today we will need all of our energies."

"Today?"

"Yes, I feel certain that today is the day."

Most of the other men overheard this little exchange. Some looked down at their food, some glanced nervously toward the sea, some felt a churning in their stomachs. They'd been eager for their long-awaited, long-delayed, conflict with the Reavers to arrive; nonetheless, now that it seemed to be upon them, they couldn't help the feelings of fear and dread that crept silently upon them.

Given Conn's certainty that today was the day, they hid the curragh behind a thick screen of alders. Then when the men trooped up the high hill for the great funeral ceremony, every one of them brought with them their entire arsenal of weaponry. There was no knowing when the enemy might come upon them, but the readiness was all.

Participating in this funereal observance was a sacred obligation powerfully felt by each one of the men. Nevertheless, two of them were positioned where they could scan the sea approaches at all times.

Throughout the solemn service, their cloaks remained draped over the bodies of Conn's friends. In his hands, Conn held the pair of amulets they had found with the heads of Ailill and Luga in the Reavers' rath. When the time came toward the end of the service, he would place them beside the heads and the bodies of his two closest friends.

For several minutes, Taman played soft and sorrowful tunes on his harp. They had a dirge-like quality suitable to the occasion. Although most of these men did not think of themselves as being particularly religious, their beliefs assured them that the spirits of these men would be finally released. For years they had been thwarted, but now they could go free. Now they could take whatever final journey the fates had in store for them. Even though these men didn't know it, in regard to the spirit's final journey, their beliefs and those of the Christians who now threatened to replace the old religion, were not so very different.

As Taman played, it was the young Welsh lad who first began to hum along softly with him. It produced a moving sound, and soon several of the men found themselves joining in. Before long they were all doing it, even Conn. Singing together created a strong sense of communion, with each other and with the spirits of the men lying before them.

Finally Diuran began to speak the words of the Ceremony of the Dead. They were familiar words. Indeed, Diuran had spoken them only a few days before over the small cairn of the man who had died in the storm. But here on this hillside, before this great cairn, before the bodies of the eight slain heroes, they seemed to possess an unusual poignancy and dignity. As Diuran spoke, most of the men wept. There was no shame in that. It bespoke the great love they had for Conn and Maeldun, and the great love Conn and Maeldun had for Ailill of the Hard Edge, for his brother Luga, and for their six companions.

The mariners remained upon the hillside for over an hour. At last the time had come for the final re-uniting of the heads with the bodies. Garluan stepped forward and placed the wicker hamper he'd been guarding close beside the cloaks draped over the bodies. Then, just as he stooped to pull back the cloaks, one of the watchers suddenly cried out.

"They are coming!" he declared fiercely. "The Reavers are coming!"

Garluan did not pull back the cloaks. He quickly raised himself back up to his feet and then he, like everyone else, looked out toward the north, focusing on a narrow strip of sea along the western coast of Eire. There they could see four boats moving quickly over the water. These boats were each somewhat smaller than the mariners' great curragh, and so they surely held fewer men. And yet — there were four of them.

Four boats. Each boat, perhaps, bearing ten fighting men. That would make long odds for Maeldun, Conn, and the other mariners.

At Maeldun's direction, Conn quickly assembled the entire company on the hillside just below the cairn. For this fight, he would be their battle leader.

"All right, lads, this is what we've been waiting for, what we've been wanting." His words produced nods and murmurs of agreement. "There are many advantages to fighting them here. We'll have the high ground and they will have to come to us. As they climb the hill, we can rain missiles down upon them, our light spears and our sling balls, whereas they won't be able to do anything to us until they get quite close. Save your heavy spears until they do.

"I suspect they will come at us in a massed force, since they have far greater numbers than we have. They will try to overwhelm us, I think, and I hope they do try. The thing I fear the most is that they might spread out and try to encircle us. We must not let any of them get behind us.

"Once they reach us, it will become sword versus sword and ax versus ax. That's where all our days and long hours of training will pay off. It better had — or our heads will be deposited in those gruesome niches you all saw back at Rath Roonah. Lads — in order to win today, each of us will have to take out at least two or three of them. Can you do it, lads? Are you up to it?"

As one, the mariners proclaimed that they could, that they were.

*   *   *

The Reavers beached their four boats where the mariners had landed earlier. As their warriors disembarked, Maeldun and Conn could see that they had close to forty men. They could also see that each man possessed a large, rectangular shield. Although they couldn't make out the details from that distance, they knew that those stout shields would be made of oak covered with thick hides and possibly edged with iron — they were the shields commonly borne by Celtic fighting men.

"They will have good protection against our spears and stones," Maeldun said.

"Yes, but also a greater weight to bear as they climb the hill. Their shields will protect them, but at a price, for they will also encumber them. We are better off without having them. We will be more mobile." Maeldun nodded his agreement, though he wasn't really certain about that.

The Reavers took their time sorting themselves out and getting their equipment organized. But in the end they finally formed two rather ragged lines of about twenty men each. It appeared that they intended to march up the hill in a double battle line, with one line ten or fifteen yards behind the other. But that remained to be seen.

It was at that point that a group of four men separated themselves from the others and began to climb the hill slowly. One of them bore in his two hands the symbols of a herald, the peeled hazel rod and the upraised sword. Apparently the leaders of the Reavers wished to have a parley.

"We should go down and see what they want," Conn said. "Let's hope it isn't a ploy. I do not trust the bastards."

"Garluan, you and Dris come with us," Maeldun said. "Ferben, stay here with the men, but be ready in case the Reavers play some devious trick."

But as it turned out, that was giving the Reavers too

much credit. The only ploy their leader had in mind was intimidation.

The two sets of men halted about ten yards apart. They stopped and stood there staring at each other. The Reavers' herald was a mere youth; he looked even younger than Maeldun and Garluan. The other three, though, were grizzled veterans. One of them stood half a foot taller than the others. Conn iron-fist was a tall man, but this man was three or four inches taller than Conn. His shoulders and chest were broad and large, too, though his body seemed to taper down to long but rather spindly legs. A grim smile flitted across Conn's lips as he imagined striking a sideways blow and cutting this man off at the knees.

"Conn Iron-fist," the tall man said in a voice as deep as Celtchar's. "I am Nadcrandel. Though I expect you already know that."

"Nad *what*? Nad *who*?" Conn replied. "Nad*crandel*? No, I have never heard of you, Nadcrandel."

"Hah! Before today is over you will wish you hadn't. Well, you lying piece of scum, if you have never heard of me — which is the biggest lie I have heard so far today — I have certainly heard of you. And what I have heard about you is not so favorable. I have heard that here in this spot, on a day many years ago, when your companions were fighting valiantly for their lives, you, Conn Iron-fist, ran off and hid in the bushes. While your companions were dying and losing their heads, you were nowhere to be found. That is what I have heard of you."

"It was fortunate for you, Nadcrandel, that I wasn't with them. Had I been, you would not be standing here today. Your bones would have been gnawed and chewed and devoured by crows and ravens along with those of the dozen men you lost that day. A dozen men, Nadcrandel! You had nearly as many men that day as you have today, and yet eight men took out a dozen of you before you and your thirty companions could defeat them. That does not speak well for you, Nadcrandel. If you wish to fight us today, I hope you have brought better men with you than you had on that day."

Conn's insulting words brought scowls to the faces of the two older men who stood next to Nadcrandel. One of them gripped his sword and was starting to extract it when Nadcrandel reached out and stopped him. Dris, who'd been watching the man's movements, dropped his hand to his sword also.

"There are just three of us left, Conn, my two friends and I, who were here that day. The rest of my men are too young. I suspect yours are too young also."

"These are not my men," Conn said. "They are Maeldun's men." He placed his hand on Maeldun's shoulder.

"*You* are in charge? Hah. So it appears that the men we will be fighting today may not be made of the same stuff as those we fought before. And yet my men," and Nadcrandel made a gesture back in the direction of the warriors waiting at the bottom of the hill, "are far abler than the ones old Illan had with him then. Well, young Maeldun, for your sake I hope I am wrong about the kind of stuff you are made of."

"We shall soon see," Maeldun replied. "But Nadcrandel, why are we standing here talking? What is the purpose of this parley? Have you, perhaps, come to surrender? I don't understand what we are doing here."

"Hah, come to surrender. No, young Maeldun, not to surrender. Curiosity. I wanted to see who and what you are. When the battle begins, we will see no more of Conn Iron-fist. He will be hiding somewhere off in the bushes. But you, perhaps, may actually stand and fight. I wanted to take your measure. I confess that I like what I see. For many years to come, young Maeldun, I will be seeing your head. But I always like to see a man as a man before I take his head."

"You had better take a good look, because I feel quite certain you will not be seeing my head for many years to come. Nor will I be seeing yours. Because yours will be left here on the field for the ravens and crows. We have no interest in you, or your head, or those of your two old friends. Today, all three of you will pay a price for your crimes of seventeen years ago. You and your friends are murderers, Nadcrandel, and the price for murder is the man-price. Today you will pay the man-price — a life for a life. As for the rest of your men, they are free to leave. They committed no crime here. But you three must stay. And stay you will — permanently."

"Hah. You speak a good game, young Maeldun. Now we shall see how well you can back up your words with deeds."

"Indeed we shall."

Both sets of men turned about and strode back to their troops.

Conn moved their troop of seventeen men partway down the hill, deploying them in a crescent-shaped formation, the men at the two ends of the line standing slightly lower on the hill than those at the center. They were widely spaced, about five yards between each of them. Beside each man, their points stabbing the earth, were their two sets of spears, their lighter throwing spears and their heavier stabbing spears. Most of them also had slings and pouches heavy with sling balls and round stones. Although Garluan was easily the best slinger amongst them, several of the others were quite adept also, especially Maeldun and Dris.

Maeldun and Dris stood at the center of the line. Maeldun was flanked on the other side by Ferben, Dris by Celtchar, the four of them creating a solid central core. Garluan anchored the line at the far left, Conn at the far right. Beside Conn stood Diuran the Rhymer, his close friend but also the least experienced warrior among them.

Davi, the young Welsh boy, squatted low on his haunches beside Garluan. His left hand continually slid up and down his smooth bow in nervous anticipation of what was soon to come. His bow was strung and his new arrow pouch fully loaded. Davi's bright eyes never wavered from the men down by the boat landing. Several of them he recognized. They were men against whom he felt a terrible grudge; they had stolen him and abused him and forced him into a life of servitude. Davi felt those injustices deeply. And he also felt certain that in the hour now approaching, he would settle many a score.

The Reavers were on the move at last. A line of about twenty men began marching up the lower slope of the high hillside. Only about a yard separated each man from the next. Each of them held his long, rectangular shield before him, his left arm looped through a pair of leather straps on the back. The shields were held across their chests, their top edges reaching nearly to the men's necks, the bottom edge to about mid-thigh. Most of the shields were flat, though a few were curved. Each of the warriors wore a long sword on his left hip and carried a stout piercing spear in his right hand. Some wore iron helmets, others wore heavy caps of thick animal hides.

Ten yards behind the first line came the second, walking directly behind them. In between the two lines walked Nadcrandel and the two grizzled veterans. From that position it was easy for them to bark out their orders to both lines of men. Thus far the Reavers showed no sign of doing what Conn had feared most, sending small groups of men skirting the two sides of the hill and attempting to work their way around behind Maeldun's small force. By the look of things, their intentions were simple — march straight up the hill en mass and smash the small force of their enemy.

When the first battle line of the Reavers had reached a point where they were still about fifty yards downhill from Maeldun's men, Maeldun gave the order to ready their throwing lances. The men understood the particular strategy they were to follow, one Maeldun had outlined to them earlier.

"Throw!" Maeldun shouted. And eight men launched their light throwing spears. They arced gracefully through the air, and the men's aim proved true. Each man in the first line of the Reavers, seeing the spears coming, dropped quickly to one knee and raised his shield above his head to block the spears. The spears that hit their targets bounced harmlessly away, though one of them remained embedded in an oaken shield. Several of the Reavers could be heard laughing.

But as they stood up and lowered their shields, they found themselves targeted by an unanticipated second volley. These spears had not been sent into flight by a verbal command; by design, the second group of Maeldun's men had waited just five seconds after the first flight before launching their own light lances. The stratagem succeeded well, as two of those spears proved lethal weapons. In their fight against the Reavers, Maeldun's men had claimed their first two victims.

The Reavers, though stunned by this surprise maneuver, quickly closed ranks and began moving again. Now they found themselves bombarded by sling stones. Some missed, some glanced harmlessly off their hard helmets, some rattled off their shields; but a few of them succeeded in hitting exposed portions of the warriors' bodies. One man felt a sudden pain against the side of his head, and while he wasn't yet aware of it, he no longer had a right ear.

Some of the marching men now began to hear little

whizzing, whining sounds closer to the ground. Suddenly, one man experienced a searing pain in his left calf. When he reached down, he felt a slender object embedded deeply in his flesh — it was one of Davi's arrows. A second man was stabbed in his thigh. This man bravely snapped the arrow off and kept right on walking. A third man wasn't so lucky. When Davi's arrow took him in his unprotected throat, he died a moment later as his life's blood gushed out upon his breast.

But the Reavers kept coming, and now the distance between them and their foemen had dwindled to only twenty yards. Soon they would plunge into their foemen's midst and ravage them.

Then Conn shouted the order to retreat. The mariners had been expecting it, indeed, some of them had begun to fear Conn had left it too late. Turning their backs on the Reavers, they scurried higher up the hill to a point just below the great stone cairn.

The Reavers heaped verbal abuse upon the fleeing cowards. But Nadcrandel shouted at them to shut their mouths, save their breath, and continue their pursuit. Doggedly, they did. But Conn's plan — to exhaust them as much as possible before attacking them — seemed to be working. A few of the Reavers, tired of bearing their heavy shields, tossed them aside to make climbing the steep hillside easier.

The last of the mariners' throwing spears rattled about them, again a few of them finding vulnerable targets. Again sling stones poured down upon them. One put out an eye, another smashed a man's kneecap. One of Davi's arrows crippled a warrior, another ripped through the right biceps of a man, rendering his sword arm useless.

As the exhausted Reavers again came within fifteen or so yards of the mariners, Maeldun's men suddenly rushed down upon them. Screaming like banshees and wielding their piercing spears, they bowled over many of the men in the first line, and then began hacking away like enraged beasts against those in the second. The Reavers scattered in all directions. Each of the mariners picked out a particular man to pursue.

Celtchar's ax dropped a man with his first swing. When he dropped another man with his second, the Reavers fled from him in a panic. When one of the Reavers thought he had Alim trapped by backing him up against the cairn, he lunged at him with what he hoped would be a fatal sword thrust. Alim, sucking in his mid-section and mostly avoiding the blade, slipped past the man's extended arm and buried his special knife deep in the man's neck.

Dris had singled out one of the grizzled veterans. He was the same man who'd angered Dris at the parley when he'd reached for his sword at hearing Conn's insulting words. Dris had wanted to take this man out then, and he wanted to take him out now. But it was no sure thing. Although Dris was one of the finest young swordsmen at Rath Murtagh, his foe was a veteran of many mortal battles. And Dris's foe was as eager to get at the lad as Dris was to get at him.

The other rugged veteran was squared off with Conn Iron-fist. This man had been part of the unfair attack that had killed Conn's friends; perhaps he had even taken the life of one or two of them. Those thoughts were in Conn's mind as he attacked the man viciously, forcing him to give ground. Throughout their encounter, Conn maintained the higher position on the hillside, keeping his opponent on the upslope and on the defensive. This man, as good as he might be, had no chance, for Conn Iron-fist's battle fury had fully come upon him. He slashed viciously and repeatedly at the man, knocking away his weapon and inflicting many deep and unforgiving wounds. Though still on his feet, the man had become a seething mass of blood and gore. But Conn, so intent upon his vengeance, hadn't noticed the pair of figures who loomed behind him, figures with heavy spears poised high above their heads, poised for the stabbing.

All the while, Maeldun pursued just one man—Nadcrandel, the huge leader of the Reavers, a man who'd played a part in the murder of Maeldun's father. Now Nadcrandel must pay the man-price. But the tall, broad, powerful man had anticipated Maeldun's attack. The two of them squared off by themselves in a small area free of other fighters, both of them ignoring all the chaos reigning about them. They knew this would be a fight to the death. They refused to be distracted by anything else.

They faced each other, swords uplifted.

"I remember a man," Nadcrandel said, his harsh, deep voice grating on Mealdun's ears, "who looked a lot like you. He gave me this scar on my forearm. I remember his vicious sword thrust, which caused him to slip on the wet grass. I remember piercing him with my sword – this very sword – in his lower back before he could get up. I remember his scream of pain. With my dagger, I stabbed him again, this time in the throat. That ended his scream of pain. I remember cutting off his head. Those are things I will never forget."

Maeldun didn't reply. He made a quick feint with his sword, causing Nadcrandel to move his weapon to parry the blow. With lightning quickness, Maeldun slipped his blade beneath that of Nadcrandel and stabbed him in the shoulder. The huge man winced as Maeldun extracted his sword; and yet somehow, Nadcrandel still held on to his own weapon. Blood began welling from the deep wound.

When Maeldun thrust his sword again, this time it was Nadcrandel who parried the blow and drew blood with his sudden riposte, carving a deep gash in Maeldun's left side. The lad took a quick step backward, trying to steady himself in the face of the excruciating pain.

Seeing his chance, the leader of the Reavers decided to use his great bulk. Without hesitating, he went straight for Maeldun, smashing his massive upper body into the smaller man. His great weight and the momentum of his charge sent them both to the ground, Nadcrandel on top.

Suddenly the huge man's body shuddered and made a final spasm. Maeldun managed to roll the heavy body off of him. Nadcrandel lay on his back, staring at the sky. A weapon protruded from his entrails, hilt first. Nadcrandel had impaled himself upon Maeldun's sword.

Maeldun wasted no time in leaping to his feet and extracting his sword. With one swift blow he severed the huge man's head from his body. Holding his weapon aloft, with the severed head upon it, Maeldun screamed out as loudly as he could, "Nadcrandel is dead! Nadcrandel is dead! The man-price has been paid! Nadcrandel is dead!"

There was a sudden calm and cessation in the fighting. And then the remaining Reavers, knowing all was now lost, began slinking back down the hill, first in ones and twos, and finally all of them, perhaps sixteen or eighteen in all. Many of them were limping and leaving trails of blood. Some of them wouldn't live to see tomorrow's sunrise.

"Let them go!" Maeldun screamed again. "The man-price has been paid. The man-price has been paid!"

CHAPTER 26
Grief & Sorrow

The surviving Reavers dragged themselves back down to the boat landing. Including their wounded and their dying, they barely totaled enough warriors to man two of their four boats. From high on the hillside, Maeldun and his mariners watched as those boats slowly limped away to sea. The Reavers' other two boats remained at the landing.

Their enemies gone, Maeldun's men turned to assessing the harm and damage the Reavers had done to them. Every man among them, they soon realized, had wounds of one kind or another, some of them quite serious. Attending to them was a matter of the first importance. Later, they could attend to the men who hadn't survived.

Although none of them had escaped injury, only a few of their wounds threatened to be mortal. The person least harmed was young Davi. His knees and elbows bore many deep gashes, but they were self-inflicted, sustained as Davi had dashed and darted about during the affray, trying to settle scores with every man who'd tormented him. Alim, too, bore only a few wounds, the major one being a bloody scrape across his belly caused by his now-dead opponent, whose blade had missed skewering Alim by the smallest of margins.

Instead of assisting the others, the Master Mariner had chosen to wander off by himself. Maeldun saw him down on the lower reaches of the hillside, examining the bodies of the remaining Reavers. As Maeldun watched, he saw Alim whip out his special dagger and plunge it into a man's chest. Maeldun didn't like what Alim seemed to be doing. Yet at the moment he was too exhausted and too concerned about his own men to rebuke the man. Perhaps, he told himself, Alim was bent on alleviating the suffering of men who would die anyway — though he didn't really believe that.

Only a few of Maeldun's men still lay upon the hillside. One of them was Celtchar. Another of them was Conn Iron-fist. Celtchar was alive, though just barely. Conn Iron-fist was not.

Maeldun and Garluan stood together, looking down at the body of their Weapons Master. They could see that he'd been attacked from behind by two men wielding stabbing spears. Those two craven cowards now lay there also, their hands still grasping the shafts of their murderous weapons. An arrow had pierced the neck of one; the other's head had been chopped clean off, likely the work of Celtchar's battle ax.

Sprawled on the earth not far from Conn was the body of the man he'd been fighting. The corpse was terribly mangled, but Maeldun recognized the man as one of the two older Reavers who'd come to the parley along with Nadcrandel.

Garluan knelt down over Conn, hoping to find some signs of life. It was a vain hope. Finally he removed the two great lances from Conn's body and rolled the man over onto his back. He reached down and closed Conn's eyes, then he draped a cloak over the Weapons Master's body.

Maeldun turned his head to one side, tucking it down against his shoulder. He brought his clenched fist up and held it against his mouth and trembling chin. Overwhelmed by the moment, Maeldun turned and walked off a good distance by himself. He needed to be alone with his grief.

As Maeldun took some time to mourn his friend, Dris and Garluan continued doing all the things that needed doing. They placed a warm cloak over Celtchar, too, and heard what they believed were the man's dying coughs. Clearly, the lad didn't have long to live. He'd been lying on his back, holding his entrails in with his own hands. As Garluan draped the cloak over him, Celtchar's eyes flickered open for just a moment. "Rest easy, dear friend," Garluan whispered to him.

As Dris and Garluan moved off to attend to others, it was Alim, now having concluded his grisly activities among the fallen Reavers, who approached the dying man.

"Ah shite, laddy, ah shite! What did the shaggers do ta ya?"

The old mariner stared down at Celtchar through tear-filled eyes. When he reached out and placed his hand gently on the lad's shoulders, Celtchar's eyes flickered open once more. "Water?" he managed to groan.

Alim opened his water flask and was about to bring it to the younger man's mouth when a thought struck him. He reached into the secret pouch where he kept his vial of elixir, then poured a few drops of it into the flask. Placing one hand gently behind Celtchar's head, he raised it up and poured some of the liquid into the lad's mouth.

Celtchar's eyes opened again. "Thanks, Wanderer," he said in a hoarse whisper. "That helps a lot."

"Ah, laddy," Alim lamented, "ya can't be leavin' me now. No, laddy, ya can't be a-doin' that."

Steeling himself, Alim looked down at where Celtchar was holding his lower abdomen. The lad's strong hands were all that were keeping his insides from gushing forth. "Laddy,

I'm goin' ta have a look at ya. See if there's aught I can do," he said. But when he gently spread the fingers of Celtchar's hands, what he saw beneath them was horrifying.

"Shite," Alim said within his own head. "Shite. No remedy a-tall."

Nevertheless, once more Alim pulled out his vial of elixir from the secret place where he kept it. He uncorked the vial and peered into it. It was nearly full. He'd used very little since re-filling it at Eithne's House of Healing.

This time Alim didn't use just a few drops. Tipping the vial very, very slowly, he gradually emptied out its entire, undiluted contents down onto Celtchar's wounds. What Alim was doing was something he'd never done before. He had no idea what the effect might be. In that undiluted state, it might well fry the lad's innards. But Alim didn't care. It was the only thing left to do and he knew he had to do it. Slowly, the elixir seeped down between Celtchar's fingers and into the lad's horribly torn and shredded abdomen.

"It's all I got, laddy, it's all I got. But I know we gotta give 'er a try. Laddy," Alim said, bending down close over Celtchar's face, "I just want ta tell you, laddy, that you are one in a million." Celtchar, his eyes still open, managed a small grin. But he didn't speak.

Alim settled the cloak back over the body of his young friend. Then he gave him a parting nod. "You'd best have yourself some sleep now, lad," he said. "A good little sleep'll do you a power of good." Though not a sentimental man, Alim couldn't help wiping away a tear.

Alim moved off down the hill to take a look at the two boats the Reavers had left behind. He needed something else to occupy his mind. Maeldun was nowhere to be seen. Dris and Garluan and Ferben were attending to men's wounds, and

Dris had assigned a few of the more physically able men the unpleasant task of moving all the bodies of the slain Reavers to a space off to one side of the hill. In Maeldun's absence, Dris seemed very much in charge of things.

Diuran the Rhymer came and sat down beside the covered corpse of Conn Iron-Fist. Hugging his upraised knees to his chest, his eyes closed, the Rhymer began rocking back and forth and softly keening a haunting little melody of his own invention. As he was doing that, the young Welsh lad came over and stood nearby. When Diuran realized he was there, he motioned for the lad to come and sit.

Davi stepped lightly to the other side of Conn's body and sat himself down. After he'd listened to Diuran's melody for a few minutes, he began to hum along also, but only very softly. He didn't want to intrude upon the Rhymer's own farewell to his much-loved friend.

It was two hours later that Maeldun returned. As he stood there on the hillside, he saw that a great deal had been accomplished during his absence. Dris and Garluan had moved things along extremely well. Maeldun marveled at how much Dris had changed in these few short weeks. He'd become a man with whom Maeldun might actually be able to develop a true friendship. Maeldun had never imagined that such a thing could occur.

Now, Maeldun knew, they must proceed with a service for the dead. The partially opened cairn above them would now become the resting place for Conn Iron-fist also. It was fitting, Maeldun thought, for Conn to be laid to rest with his eight close friends, men who had died on this hillside. Now Conn had died here too, and the nine of them could rest together beneath the great cairn.

As Maeldun was thinking those thoughts, he saw Alim

ascending the hill, coming back from the boat landing. Dris and Garluan were now returning as well from the area where they'd overseen the depositing of the Reavers' corpses. Diuran and Davi were still sitting beside the body of Conn. When they noticed Maeldun, they raised their hands in greeting.

Maeldun summoned his entire company, and they'd soon gathered about him. As the mariners waited for him to address them, they were startled to hear another loud voice.

"Where am I?" it blurted out. They turned their eyes to see a thick, squat figure who'd been lying on the ground covered by a cloak now sitting up. It was Celtchar. When he saw all the men standing there he declared, "Ya didn't go and have the battle without me, did ya?"

"What in the name of the Dagda?" Garluan said.

"Why, ya lovely piece o' crap!" Alim shouted out. "Whatta ya doin' a-sittin' up like that?"

"I just had me the strangest dream, Wanderer," Celtchar said, now getting up to his feet. "It had Eithne and Cliona in it and they were . . . ." Then the lad began to blush. "Guess I better not say what they were . . . Hey, ya didn't go and fight the battle without me, did ya?"

"No, Cel," Maeldun said, "we certainly didn't fight the battle without you. You were the biggest hero amongst us."

"I was? By the Dagda, I don't remember a single thing about it. You sure I was? You're not just a-sayin' that?"

"I'm certain," Maeldun replied. "You removed many a man's head with that great battle ax of yours."

"I did? Well, that's good . . . , I guess. Did we win?"

"Look around you, ya lovely piece o' crap," Alim shouted. "You don't see no shaggin' Reavers, does ya?" Celtchar actually did look around him.

"I guess that means we won?"

"Ah, ya lovely, lovely piece o' shite," Alim kept saying,

grinning at the toad-like lad, "ya lovely piece o' shite." His hand slipped into the secret place where he kept his vial of elixir. It was empty, but Alim had not thrown it away. Who knew? Maybe someday he'd get another chance to refill it.

CHAPTER 27
Many Partings

After the final ceremony for the dead, the mariners worked together to rebuild the great cairn on the hillside. Now Conn Iron-fist lay there too, alongside Ailill of the Hard Edge and his brother Luga. The amulets of all three men lay with them as well.

When they uncovered the remains of the eight men who'd been there for the last seventeen years and then re-united those men with their heads, Maeldun stood there looking down at the men's bodies.

He soon realized which one of them was his father's. As he stood there staring at the man's remains, he noticed a leaf-shaped silver brooch lying upon it. It looked familiar. He reached down and picked it up, then held it in his hand. From his own cloak Maeldun removed his own brooch. It was a small silver dragon with a red gemstone for its eye. He placed it down upon the body of his father. Then he took the brooch he'd picked up and attached it to his cloak.

Maeldun didn't know that the brooch he'd picked up had been left there long ago by Conn Iron-fist, though he knew it looked familiar. He didn't know that the brooch he now wore carried with it both his father's spirit and the spirit of the man who, for all of Maeldun's life, had been his virtual father.

It was Diuran the Rhymer who left his personal amulet, a small silver piece of intricately carved Celtic knot work, down upon the body of Conn Iron-fist. Conn had long been his closest friend at Rath Murtagh. Diuran would greatly miss him.

The mariners, carrying all of their possessions, moved back down to the boat landing. They would camp there tonight. Tomorrow, they would finally depart for home. Their mission was now completed. And it had been completed more successfully than any of them had imagined it would be. Conn Iron-fist had had a lot to do with that. But so had Maeldun, Alim, Garluan, and even Dris. Indeed, every one of them, including one very brave Welsh boy, had played an important part.

Many of the men remained in a good bit of pain from their wounds. All of them were worn and spent. They needed a hot meal, and they needed something potent to drink. And to their delight, the two remaining boats of the Reavers provided them with the something potent to drink.

They ate and drank and listened to both Taman and Diuran play and sing. It was a huge relief to just about every man in their company to know that within only two or three more days, they would be back home at Rath Murtagh.

In the morning the mariners, despite all their physical woes, were in a cheerful mood. They wasted no time in breaking camp and stowing their possessions in their stalwart sea-craft.

They were ready to go.

It was Alim who surprised them by slinging his few belongings into one of the Reavers' boats.

"Mael, laddy," he said, "this be where we part company. I won't be goin' no further with you. You'll all be fine without me. You've all become real good expert seamen, and from here on, the way be mighty simple. Shite, even Celtchar could find his way home from here."

"He could," Celtchar said, "but that ain't what he'll be a-doin'. That worthless piece o' shite named Celtchar, he's a-plannin' to keep on a-wanderin' — a-wanderin' with you, Mariner, if you can put up with the worthless piece o' shite."

Alim was grinning ear to ear. "Ya mean I hafta keep ya with me? Well, ya useless shagger, come on, then. I s'ppose I can manage ta stomach ya for a bit longer."

"Ya think we could find ourselves that island o' women, Wanderer? I sure would like ta do that."

"The island of women?" Garluan said. "By the Dagda, in that case maybe I should be coming along with you!"

"Nah, laddy, it'll be just me 'n' old Celtchar this time. But if we do get ta the land o' the women, maybe we'll send for you."

"Or maybe not," Celtchar said with a grin.

At that point Maeldun finally spoke up. "Dris," he said, "from now on you are the one who will be in charge."

"I don't understand, Mael. Me in charge? Why?"

"Because I won't be coming either. Rath Murtagh is no longer my home. I have another home, the home of my father. I don't know what I will find there, but that's where I'll be going."

"As will I," Garluan said. "Mael and me, a pair of worthless foundlings, sticking together, as worthless foundlings are wont to do." Maeldun smiled at Garluan. The two of them had hatched this plan long ago, in the event that they actually survived the fight with the Reavers.

"So I guess that means just twelve of us will be returning

251

to Rath Murtagh."

"No, eleven." The speaker was young Davi.

"And where will you be going, Davi?" Dris asked.

"With those two," he said, "pointing to Garluan and Maeldun. It will be three foundlings traveling together, not two."

"Har, har," came Alim's laughter. "Ya lovely little piece o' shite."

"We'll be taking the Reavers' other boat," Maeldun said. "It appears to be quite seaworthy.

"It sure ain't great," Alim said, "though it'll do for a short trip, I s'ppose. But by the Dagda, I may not miss any o' the rest o' you fellers, but I sure will miss my curragh. Dris, ya shagger, ya'd better take damn good care of her. Or you'll be havin' me ta deal with."

"I promise you, Wanderer, I certainly will. But Wanderer, don't you want to have a parting drink? If there's any man here who's earned himself a good stiff drink, it's you."

Alim looked thoughtful. "You're right about earnin' that drink. But Dris, thank ya anyways. I done all right on this journey without it. And I think, maybe, I'll just stick with that."

Diuran the Rhymer spoke up for the first time. "So it's fare thee well, then, is it, Maeldun? I do wish you were coming back with us. Anyway, perhaps we shall see you again before too long. But there's one thing I certainly do know. On this voyage we've shared, you men have given me everything I need to spin a tale that shall long be remembered. I think I shall have to call it The Voyage of Maeldun."

"I hope it won't contain too many lies," Garluan said.

"*Lies?*" Diuran replied, smiling. "Perhaps just a few."

Before the men departed, Alim walked over to the curragh to say his farewell. He stood near the front and patted the boat gently, close to where he'd painted the eyes. "Be safe and be swift, my lovely." He said. "You're the best I ever did have."

Maeldun, Garluan, and Davi, and also Alim and Celtchar, remained on the landing as the other men departed in the curragh. When Dris's party was well out from shore, the men in the boat all gave a final wave of farewell and then made three great shouts. The men on the shore returned both.

"Well, Mael," Alim said with a grin, "didn't really wanna share this with ya, but just for luck I will." He began rummaging in his personal knapsack.

In his hands Alim held five beautiful red-green apples.

"One for you, Gar, one for you, Mael, one for you, Cel, one for you, Davi, and one for me."

"Gifts from the Lady of the Fruitful Isle?" Maeldun said.

"Just for luck, Mael, just for luck. Always a good thing to have the Lady with ya, doncha know."

The time had come for the men and the boy to exchange their final, parting hugs. Then Alim and Celtchar climbed into their boat, pushed off from the shore, and set off in the direction opposite to that taken by the larger curragh.

"Say hello to all the women in the land of women!" Garluan shouted after them.

"Har, har!" came Alim's voice, floating over the waves.

"Are we ready, then?" Maeldun said to Davi and Garluan. Davi nodded, and Garluan was already pushing the craft out into the water.

"Say, Mael," Garluan asked, after they had rowed in silence for an hour or so, "do you suppose at this place we're going they might have a fair number of good-looking women?"

"They damn well better have," Maeldun replied.